THE NIGHT MAYOR

THE NIGHT MAYOR

KIM NEWMAN

TITAN BOOKS

THE NIGHT MAYOR
Print edition ISBN: 9781781165669
E-book edition ISBN: 9781781165676

Published by Titan Books
A division of Titan Publishing Group Ltd
144 Southwark Street, London SE1 0UP

First Titan Books edition: April 2015

2 4 6 8 10 9 7 5 3 1

Did you enjoy this book? We love to hear from our readers.
Please email us at readerfeedback@titanemail.com or write to us at
Reader Feedback at the above address.

To receive advance information, news, competitions, and exclusive offers online,
please sign up for the Titan newsletter on our website: www.titanbooks.com

For Fiona Ferguson, Saskia Baron and Amanda Lipman,
Hellcat Film Editors

And above all, shadow upon shadow upon shadow... Lee Garmes, Tony Gaudio, Lucien Ballard, Sol Polito, Ernest Haller, James Wong Howe, John F. Seitz and the other great cameramen of the era pitched every shot in glistening low-key, so that rain always glittered across windows and windscreens like quicksilver, furs shone with a faint halo, faces were barred deeply with those shadows that faintly symbolised some imprisonment of body or soul. The visual mode was intensely romantic, and its precise matching to the stories of fatal women and desperate men – straight out of *The Romantic Agony* – gave Forties *film noir* its completeness as a *genre*. A world was created, as sealed off from reality as the world of musicals and of Paramount sophisticated comedies, yet in its way more delectable than either.

CHARLES HIGHAM AND JOEL GREENBERG,
Hollywood in the Forties

PART I

GET RICHIE QUICK

1

It was two thirty in the morning, and raining. In the City, it was always two thirty in the morning and raining.

Streets away, in the Kit Kat Klub, Nat King Cole was singing. I heard him under the permanent hiss of the rain and the sizzle of water on neon. In the distance, someone was shouting. There were three gunshots in swift succession, and the someone wasn't shouting any more. A siren wailed, cutting into Nat's plaintive purr, fading out as he hit the final verse. There was more gunfire, indiscriminate this time, and a car careered down the road, throwing up a splash of gutter water that fell just short of my shoes. I couldn't see who was driving, but there was an interesting pattern of bullet dents in the vehicle's rear, and the back window was white sugar, holed and dissolving. A police car, screeching like Mario Lanza trying for a note just out of his reach, came by in pursuit. The cars, bound together by a story I could only guess at, disappeared around a corner. Soon, even their noise was gone.

There are eight million stories in the City. The trick is to keep to your own, and not be distracted. All the others twine their plot lines around you like strangler's spaghetti.

Back in the world, they had warned me about going crazy. I had almost laughed at them. It wasn't so funny now it was my head in the mangle.

All of a sudden, hunched against a wall, I felt very old, very tired. Mine is a cold, wet, late-at-night profession, but just now life was colder, wetter and later than even I normally care for. Nat had finished his set now, and Judy Garland was on, singing 'Over the Rainbow' as if there were another world beyond the City limits where troubles melt like lemon drops. In the alley behind me, hunched down among the garbage cans, something shifted and laughed. I turned my back on it, more exhausted than brave.

I looked down at the gutter. An attenuated ghost rippled darkly in the stream. I recognised myself, but only just. There was a haunted quality about my eyes that I didn't want to acknowledge. I was wearing my dark-grey fedora, rain-silver trench coat, powder-grey suit, white shirt, black knit tie, black patent-leather shoes and dark-grey socks with light-grey clocks. I was sheltering under the elevated railway, sucking on a soggy cigarette, waiting for the lead that was supposed to bust my case wide open.

The lead was several reels overdue.

Already, I had sleepwalked through a montage of fruitless searching. Blinking white signs, each with one letter missing: Cocacaba a Cabin, Mild ed's, The Blue Pa rot, Grea y Joe's Diner. Unhelpful extras expressively turning away from silent questions. My feet pounding the shimmering sidewalk, soaked trouser cuffs whipping chilled ankles. Cruising taxicabs, waving windscreen wipers, and the abstract shapes of rain on glass. Bit players lying, denying all knowledge of the man I was after. Through it all the orchestral swell of my music, a purposeful yet melancholy jazz. And, in the end, nothing to show for it.

All I had was a name. A name that closed doors and emptied bars. A name that, spoken aloud, invoked sewn-shut lips, pulled-down shades, drink-up-and-get-out looks, hastily remembered appointments and muttered warnings. Just a name.

Truro Daine.

Back in the world, the name of Truro Daine had plenty of associations. Murderer, arsonist, dope peddler, pornographer, blackmailer, flamboyant thief and a lot of other things, all unhealthy. Now, he was the last of the escaped convicts. My clients wanted him found, and dragged back to his prison of permanent steel and perishable flesh.

Sounds simple, huh?

There was a catch. The prince of catches. It would floor Dempsey in the first round, keep John Wayne off the beaches of Iwo Jima. The City belonged to Daine. Not just the Mayor and the cops and the courts... the City. Every rainwashed alley, Art Nouveau penthouse, backstreet gin joint and deserted warehouse was his personal property.

Out there in formless dark, where the sidewalk ends, Truro Daine was waiting, a coal-eyed panther in the asphalt jungle. I cupped a palm around the dying end of my smoke, snatching the warmth while it was there. I couldn't taste tobacco any more. Taste was just one of the senses that had started to let me down.

Earlier, the rain had been heavy, a constant sheet that soaked through my hat and coat, trickling down the back of my neck. Now, it was a fine drizzle, almost invisible, pricking my exposed hand. For some stupid reason, I didn't have gloves. My hand looked white and dead in the lamplight, smudged only from constant smoking, and felt like a shrivelled skin glove on my aching fingerbones.

A newspaper, folded headline out, slid past in the gutter. It was the *Inquirer*. G-MEN BUST AXIS SPY RING: VEIDT, SANDERS, ZUCCO INDICTED. Untrustworthy faces peered out from mug shots. Yesterday's news.

A train shrieked overhead, lights raking the street. It was on schedule, spotlighting rickety fire escapes. In one of the apartments, Edward G. Robinson was strangling a girl. The passing train pixelated the murder. The girl was obviously a cheap floozy. Joan Bennett? She bent backwards out of the window, unable to do more than kick and gurgle. Edward G. was twisting a string of pearls into her throat. The girl lashed out with the last of her strength, knocking over a lamp. A bare wall whitened behind struggling silhouettes.

The train clickiticlicked on, empty as always.

The string broke, and pearls showered past the El, shining like freshly pulled teeth. Edward G. scrambled over the corpse and squeezed onto the fire escape. Rain streamed over his horror-struck, flabby face. His music swelled, faintly audible from the street. He crawled into the clattering cobweb of iron ladders and landings, descending with monkey-like agility.

Dropping the last ten feet, he landed across the alley from me. He was without an overcoat and hat, and his disarrayed suit instantly two-toned with the cascade that fell from the shaking fire escape. He looked at me, panic shivering his jowls. I looked at him. My cigarette went out, and I threw it dead into the water. Edward G. turned and vanished into the night. Two flights up, the rain was falling into the open eyes of the dead girl.

Death. It's never pretty. Except for Greta Garbo, luminous with consumption.

But this wasn't my case. The cops could handle it. It wouldn't be difficult. Either a merciless investigator would badger the apparently harmless Robinson into a confession, harping endlessly on alibis and clues and motives. Or the murderer would be tormented by a nightmare tangle of memories and break down just as they were ready to file the killing under 'unsolved'. Either way, Eddie G. was already on the last mile. Some things were predictable.

I waited, still wondering where my lead was.

After an age, a limousine slid out of the night, its surfaces rain-blobbed ebony mirrors. I saw myself broken into a million wobbling pieces and had the uncomfortable impression that might be a prophetic image. The headlights flashed as the car turned, dazzling as the naked sun. The giant was impatient, confined to a labyrinth of narrow streets, a raging beast tethered to a steady ten miles an hour. It stopped dead beside me, and growled. The windows were a flat black, the interior as dark as the devil's heart, except for the rat-like eyes of the man-shape looking out from the back seat.

The front passenger door opened, and Mike Mazurki got out. With his gorilla shoulders crammed into a double-breasted jacket, he looked ready to go fifteen rounds with an enraged moose. His fingers were a bunch of fat white bananas. I had to look twice before noticing the automatic stuck like a child's toy in his giant fist. He didn't have any dialogue, but the gun said 'get into the car' in fifteen different languages. The back door swung open, and the rat eyes leaned forward into the light. I recognised Dan Duryea. He flashed a smile as full of teeth as a piranha's.

Mazurki prodded me from behind, and I wound up in the back seat, wedged between the two hoodlums. The gun was still talking, holding a close-up, intimate conversation with my ribcage. I could get to dislike that.

Marc Lawrence was driving. We took the scenic route. Thunder Road, 711 Ocean Drive, 99 River Street, Nightmare Alley, Scarlet Street, the Street of Chance, the House on Telegraph Hill, Flamingo Road….

When we went under streetlamps, Duryea's slicked-back hair shone. He fancied himself as a sharpie, and wore a thin-striped suit. He was pleased with himself, but everyone in the car knew he had made a wrong decision buying cologne.

'Where are we going?' I asked. 'Will we be long? I promised to take my kid sister to the Philharmonic.'

'You ask a lot of questions, shamus,' said Duryea.

I don't like being called 'shamus'. It sounds stupid. I also don't like being called 'gumshoe', 'flatfoot', 'dick', 'tec', 'snooper', 'peeper', 'cheapie', 'the perpetrator', 'dead meat' or 'Elihu J. Stemwaller' for related reasons.

'I have an enquiring mind. A handy thing in my line of work.'

'Yeah?'

'Yeah.'

'Mr Daine don't like questions so much.'

I refrained from commenting on his grammar. 'Why not? Doesn't he have any answers?'

Mazurki held my shoulder. 'You a wise guy?'

My shoulder hurt. 'I wasn't always a detective. I started as a gag writer for Bob Hope. Now I can't kick the habit.'

'Funny, huh?'

'No, not particularly. That's why I got into this business. The pay's lousy, the hours stink, you get beaten up every day of the week with an "a" in it, but at least there's no pressure on you to make jokes all the time.'

'Wise guy.'

Mazurki disgustedly took his hand away, and my shoulder hurt some more. Duryea giggled, like ice cubes cracking in blood. Maybe Daine had him mixed up with the young Richard Widmark. It's an easy mistake.

I was tired. That's the way I tend to feel at half past two in the morning if I've been out in the rain for hours and get abducted.

And in the City it was two thirty a.m. for ever. That was late, no matter how I looked at it. I felt like a hungover zombie.

The situation demanded Bogart, but the best I could manage was Boris Karloff. Stretched out on a slab. A few bolts of lightning and I'd be okay, but right now the torch-carrying villagers would have nothing to worry about. I practiced curling my upper lip back in a Bogartian sneer, but couldn't carry it off.

I looked out the window. Cagney was dying in a gutter, holding his insides in. Glenda Farrell was kneeling by him, explaining to a caped cop with a smoking tommy gun. I couldn't hear the words, but I recited her dialogue along with her. 'He used to be a big shot.' Kiss tomorrow goodbye, Jimmy.

Shit, I thought. But I couldn't say anything stronger than 'hell'. The City was getting to me. The Hays Code was invading my mind. I shut my eyes. Sleep was tempting, but I had the feeling the Body Snatchers were in the neighbourhood. My guess was that if 1 were to sleep, I'd wake up changed.

Of course, unless I got to Daine soon, I'd be changed anyway. I had figured that out for myself, without any help from the governor of Princetown. After a few more spins with this crazy croupier, I'd bet away my independence. I'd be a permanent resident. It didn't appeal as an afterlife: a possible eternity as a private eye in the City. Slugged with blackjacks, kicking in doors, finding icepick-stuck corpses, betrayed by black-lipped blondes. Being beat up, locked up, busted, mistrusted, got at, shot at, framed, maimed, frayed, mislaid and underpaid.

An important lesson: just because it isn't real doesn't mean it can't kill you.

Or worse.

'You been taking an undue interest in Mr Daine's affairs, shamus,' said Duryea. 'He will be most displeased.'

'Shamus, shamus, what's with this "shamus"?' I snapped back. 'How would you feel if I kept calling you "torpedo", "mobster", "thug", "gnat-brains", "gunsel" or "chiseller"?'

'I wouldn't like it.'

'Well, just imagine how I feel.'

'Ah, but there's a difference between us.'

'Which is?'

'I'm not sitting next to a 200-pound professional wrestler with an automatic held to my kidneys.'

'You know, Danny, that makes a lot of sense.'

The limousine faded out along Main Street. A fade-out is like hyperspace. It's supposed to cut out the journey, but really it just rips off a few hours of your life and gives you a skull-cracker of a headache. Me, I'd rather ride the streetcar, but I don't make the rules.

During the fade, it wasn't just night outside the car, it was the total darkness of the blind, an endless absence of anything. The sound cut out, but I still had vision. Duryea and Mazurki grinned at each other. Their mouths opened too wide, and their faces distorted like scary clowns. I told myself it wasn't real. But even if it wasn't, it felt as if it was. The city demanded you take it seriously, play by the house rules. Otherwise, you could be due for an extended vacation in the Snake Pit. I concentrated on the back of Lawrence's head, and tried to ignore the deep space beyond the still-waving wipers. The dandruff on the driver's collar wasn't very interesting, but at least it wasn't a threat.

Lawrence took his hands off the wheel and reached behind him, to scratch the back of his head with both hands. His thinning hair parted under his fingers, and a diseased eye winked at me from his scalp.

Cheap trick, I tried to say. But there was no sound.

The limo faded in. The engine and the rain were momentarily deafening.

'...ick!' came out of me. Lawrence looked round, sad-eyed, a waxed failure of a moustache clinging to his upper lip, hands back on the wheel. A cigarette dripped from the corner of his mouth.

'Keep ya eyes on the road, weasel,' snarled Duryea, and Lawrence turned back. He didn't have an eye in the back of his head. Not now.

We had faded in on Poverty Row. I had been in town long enough to know the place. It was the worst slum in the City, far from the swish Metro and Paramount districts. Jerry-built tenements cramped together, as convincing as cardboard flats. Every hotel room had an irritating sign flashing outside the window. Every alley had a mangy black cat set to cringe in a flashlight beam. When a door got slammed, the walls shook. There weren't many people on the streets at any time of the day. Extras cost money. This was the world of peeling paint, tap-dancing cockroaches and the constant shadow of the boom mike. On Poverty Row, life had a low budget and a short running time.

'Get out of the car,' said Duryea. I thought of two or three wisecrack answers, but kept them to myself. I even got out of the car.

Back in the rain, I found my shoulder still hurt. Plus my ribs hurt, my calves hurt, my head hurt. I could go on, but you've got the general idea.

Duryea and Mazurki joined me on the sidewalk. The car crept away. I noticed a human hand protruding from the trunk.

'Lawrence has another delivery to make, shamus,' said Duryea, overdoing it. 'To the East River.'

'Anyone I know?'

'No, but I hope you get a chance to get acquainted real soon.'

We were in front of a cheesy office block, the Monogram. Duryea kicked the aged front door in. The sky shook unconvincingly. The lobby was empty, except for a derelict curled up in a spill of garbage between an overstuffed chair and the reception desk.

'Lookit the bum!' Duryea prodded him with the toe of his black-and-white shoe. The old man turned over. His throat was a mess of black blood. Outside, something bayed at the painted moon. Mazurki crossed himself, and muttered darkly in Ukrainian.

This wasn't part of my plot. Poverty Row was a catch-all place, an open sewer of clichés feeding into the elephants' graveyard of ideas. Mazurki reached into his pants pocket and produced two silver coins stamped with Walter Huston's head. He put them on the corpse's eyes and stood back.

'That'll keep him down.'

'Yeah, yeah,' crowed Duryea, impatient with this time out. 'But where's the night man? He's supposed to keep this stuff out of the foyer.'

Duryea hitched his shoulders, a hand-me-down Cagneyism that looked bad on him, and jammed his palm down on a bell on the desk. A door behind opened, and a stooped figure shuffled on stage. The night man had large, watery eyes behind Coke-bottle glasses, quivering lips and a sparse moustache. It was a familiar face, but I couldn't have put a name to it without the

Scrabble prop on the desk that spelled it out. Byron Foulger.

Duryea reached out and grabbed Foulger's striped tie.

'Where wuz ya, worm? Scared of the big bad wolf?'

Foulger whined and dithered, and Duryea dropped him.

'Mr Daine is gonna be displeased, Byron. Ya better start combing the situations vacant in the *Inquirer*. I'm sure someone somewhere wants a squealing rat. Now, call up the boss and tell him his guest is here.'

The night man rattled an antique telephone and talked quietly into it. I was close enough to him to hear the nothing at the other end. It wasn't even connected to the wall socket.

'He's expecting you,' said Foulger, spitefully.

Mazurki jerked me towards the elevator. We did a minor fade instead of riding up.

The penthouse was surprisingly plush. A panoramic window laid the rain-distorted city out like a corpse. The place was decorated in Early Modern Uncomfortable, with coffee tables shaped like swimming pools and chairs like big black marshmallows. Monochrome etchings hung conspicuously, looking more like sketches than finished work. Daine was a collector.

Duryea poured bourbon. Thick liquid gurgled. An unseen gramophone oozed over-orchestration. 'Charmaine'. Strings sawed at the brass, the melody drowned.

I took the glass offered me, and drank it down. The hell of it – is that in the City you don't taste anything. You get drunk, but it might as well be sugared water. Then, I didn't even want to get drunk.

I handed the glass back to Duryea, and felt the whisky grab my brain. Mazurki hit me in the stomach.

'Chew on that, wise guy!'

I doubled up, and collapsed onto a grey bombazine couch. It felt like fabric stretched over a concrete lump. I'd have vomited, but no one throws up in the City.

The pain got worse. While I was trying to rearrange my insides into their original configuration, someone came in. A smooth, tall, slightly plump man in a quilted smoking jacket. I didn't need to match him to the description.

It was Truro Daine.

2

Susan Bishopric entered the White Room. A violent black-red shape marred the glaspex sheen of the walls. It was her own reflection. She couldn't Dream with a distract like that. She twisted her chameleon cameo, and the kimono dragons pinked and passed. Susan scanned the tanned backs of her hands. Ideally she would have had a skinpale too, but now she couldn't spare the time or expense. Besides, she only had an update scheduled, not a full Dream.

She couched and swung the slab over her lap. She intapped a polite ID and inslotted the *Vanessa Vail* master. A dreamflower bloomed in the bowl; she plucked it. Hooking a stray tress behind her ear, she pressed the flower to her temple. The subcutaneous terminal pricked in with a slight tickle. She blinked, and melshed with the machine.

Susan did not intend a complete surrender to *Vanessa Vail*. Just a mnemonic skim to check the externals. Volume up, vision up, sens up. She was inside:

Vanessa Vail: deadly, glamorous, capable, highly-sexed international adventuress.

For a moment, she was overwhelmed, feeling the unfamiliar

strength of the similie's limbs, the ease of her pleasures. Was it only five years since she had Dreamed *Vanessa Vail*? Had her body really changed that much? Or had she idealised her former self more than she had thought? In realising the fantasy of lithe Vanessa, Susan had built a heroine out of herself. Vanessa Vail had a mind like a stiletto. For a moment Susan was uncomfortable inside it.

Here's to you, Dr Frankenstein. Just you wait, Henry Higgins. Susan knew what it was like to be outstripped by her creation. Children always turn out to be bastards.

But Vanessa Vail was comfortably doomed by the concept. No need to waste good envy on her. Susan pulled out and dipped into:

Vanessa's three lovers: Ray Chance, taciturn CIA agent. Nikolai Kropotkin, fiery Soviet commissar. Lord Roger Marshaller, suave English aristocrat.

And sometimes into:

The air, as a detached, invisible presence in the *Vanessa Vail* sub-universe. Swooping over a firesabre duel in the Finnish wastes. Peeping åt troilist romance on a blazing Cuban beach. Observing intrigue in a Jesuit opium den within the walls of Vatican City. Vanessa demolishing a troop of Liechtensteinian police andrews with balletic *baritsu* kicks.

The D-9000 had concepted *Vanessa Vail*, tailoring it precisely to audience requirements. But Susan Bishopric had Dreamed it, depthing out the internals, filling in the externals. As a professional, she knew she had to take the commissions that came up on the slab. At the time, she had been pathetically grateful to Tony for chancing on her for such a solid product. She had even got a few good crix on it. And the sales had been good. Not in the John Yeovil slot, but enough to establish her name. Even she was prepared to admit that her solo stuff hadn't then been up to much. Typical juvie nonsense, most of it. *Vanessa Vail* was far less embarrassing to her now than, say, *The Light of the Bright World Dies*, with its fuzzy emotional politics, or *Deaf and Blind,* which must surely count as the archest Dream of its season.

But that was then. Now she was at a different career stage. Since *Vanessa Vail*, the nature of the collaboration had changed. With each Dream, Susan had wrestled more control and with *The Parking Lottery* – due, Yggdrasil willing, to scoop the Rodneys this autumn – she had almost edged the cranky computer out. Soon she would be popular enough to declare her independence. Then she could concept her own Dreams. And now, she hoped, she was strong enough to think on her own, to create something of lasting merit.

Meanwhile, she resented being yanked back five years to hackery. But needs must…

She quickskimmed to the finish, and sunk into:

Nurse Ted Crozier, attending Vanessa in her terminal tank. Starched linen, hospital smells, the buzzes and bleeps of life support. Nikolai, Ray and Lord Roger, enemies united in grief, crowding around the bed of the dauntless heroine. The dracula from the transplant league outside in the corridor, waiting for the usable organs to be liberated, pacing up and down to frighten the non-terminals in the nearby suites.

The nurse was a clever authorial touch. He provided a necessary break from the Vanessa Vail POV. Thanks to brave little smiles, hair rainbowed on the pillow, choked-back tears and an emotional confrontation with the fey little girl due to receive Vanessa's surplus heart, it was possible to make dying of cancer look all right. But by no stretch of subjectivism could it be made to feel pretty. There was a market for pain, but the

D-9000 did not cater to it. Ted Crozier could naturally have medical externals vital to the concept flit across his mind during the dreamer's tenure. Also, Susan knew her lady dreamers liked a good handsome nurse.

The subliminal infilling of background external from a minor character's memory was a typical Susan Bishopric touch, she knew. When she was free of the D-9000 she wanted to experiment with more complex uses of the device: conflicting recollections, false impressions, mental delusions. Dreams were at about the same stage as the flatties in 1912 or ice sculpture ten years ago. The medium was waiting for its Griffith, its Eisenstein, its Chillmeister Freaze…

Susan in:

Ted Crozier watches with heartfelt admiration as the still-beautiful Vanessa Vail lifts herself up to bid her lovers goodbye. His manly tears give the scene a misty, soft-focus effect.

Quickskim:

Nikolai weeping, Ray getting drunk, Lord Roger planning suicide.
    'Darling. Darlings. Before I zed out for the last time, I… There's one thing I want you all to know. Something important…'

Susan pulled out. The D-9000 had dialogued *Vanessa Vail*. She had not been qualified to handle that. She rewound.

She tapnoted the obvious external changes. In the next edition Vanessa would wear her hair orientally, a black fringe and pigtails instead of the outmoded red beehive. Fashions in clothing, food and sex updated easily.

The politicals were only a shade more difficult. Since the War Between the States, the CIA was the OSS again, but Ray Chance could still booze and womanise for them. The fall of Premier Romanova meant a few alterations to the Moscow sequence. The

D-9000 liked to include real-life characters, and had had Nikolai briefed for his mission to Lapland by Romanova herself. The scene would have to be re-Dreamed for Sobienkin.

Susan thought that, in the light of his treatment of his immediate predecessor, the ascetic new premier would be unamused to learn that his complete change of the Kremlin did not warrant any radical re-Dreaming. In *Vanessa Vail* the premier was just a face and a voice, plus a few cartoon mannerisms. Romanova's dialogue would do just as well for Sobienkin. The decor in the office would have to change: Susan would have to make it more like a provincial skimmer waiting room, less like an eighteenth-century bordello. And, of course, the sex was out, unless… No, another brush with the International Libel people was not what she wanted. The Dreamer would stay inside Nikolai anyway. IL excluded Susan from the minds of real people.

A shame: she could think of a few intriguing uses of that trick. One of the pirates had recently offered a bootleg of the King having sex with a goat. The Dreamer had been into the heads of the King *and* the goat. The pirate had been remaindered, and his tape run wiped clean. A shame, the goat had been an interesting characterisation. She hated to see raw talent go to waste.

The *Vanessa Vail* headache was cancer. It had been preventable five years ago; now things were worse, it was reversible, even in the formerly terminal phase. Vanessa Vail, condemned to a beautiful death by the unconscious wish of the dreamership, needed a new disease. Or something.

The D-9000 would do the bulk of the research, but selecting the appropriate lingering malady would still be a drearo business. Susan mourned the great romantic disorders: leukaemia, consumption, sickle-cell anaemia, AIDS, chemical warfare. Cancer had been the last hope of the morbid love story. Now the ogre of generations past was extinct. And whatever substitute she found – mutant measles, perhaps, or foot-and-mouth disease – was bound to be pestered out of existence by the next edition.

She toyed with the idea of making something up. A real-sounding, exotic wasting disease. No one could find a cure for that. Perhaps, during her stopover in the jungles of Ecuador, Vanessa Vail could be dosed with a rare native poison. It was the sort of thing that was always happening to her.

Tony would fight it: 'There are doctors dreaming out there, Sue-love, and they'll know. With something as loony as *Vanessa Vail* it's bloody vital to get the externals right.'

Susan dropped the dreamflower into its glass of purple. She saved her tapnotes into the slab.

She considered a few internal changes, unnecessary but interesting. *Vanessa Vail* could do with a complete re-dialogue. Susan cringed at practically every line the D-9000 had stuck her with. But Tony would only allow her to tamper with any obsolete slang; substituting 'squitch' for 'kink', 'bove' for 'zooper', stupid stuff like that. *Vanessa Vail* sold by the million, and was practically sacred in publishing terms.

Rats! Susan spitefully thought of giving Vanessa Vail a sobering dose of realism. 'Sorry, gang, I can't fight any cybernetic squid today. I'm menstruating.' Serve her right, the unreal bitch.

No. She would just polish up the externals and field the whole thing back to Tony. This little Dream wouldn't hurt. She would save the good stuff for the next Susan Dream, the Great English Dream the crix were expecting from her.

Susan exed the White Room. In contrast to the sourceless glare of the Dreaming chamber, her office was soft-lit turquoise. The shelves were cluttered with extraneous objects: a ceramic bridge, favourite Dreams, her huge and uncatalogued music collection, tridsnaps, and a few flatty tapes. At Eton her House Sponsor had stressed the importance of the cinematic tradition. She was a particular admirer of early Frank Tashlin, mid-period Antonioni and late Richard Attenborough.

Her Rodney nomination plaques and her sole award – Best Nasal Effects for *The Sewer Thing* – had a mantel to themselves.

These things didn't matter, of course. The Rodneys were always being awarded to utter sick. Last year, John Yeovil's drearo historical *The Private Life of Margaret Thatcher* had scooped Best Dream, Yggdrasil rot it! But this year, it was between her and Orin Tredway, and she needed to see Orin frozen out. His *Passions Perfected* was unspeakably, cloyingly awful, and yet the crix were tipping it as the favourite. Still, she was confident. She had even drafted a beautiful, moving, inspirational acceptance speech.

Her outdoor helmet and flakjak were bundled on a chair. She shifted them and sat at the D-9000 terminal. She backgrounded a music: *Ella Fitzgerald Sings the Cole Porter Songbook.*

She tapped into the British Museum Library, and pressed the vocator to her throat.

'Hello, BritLib. What've you got on primitive toxicology? I'm particularly interested in South America, but if anything fun turns up anywhere else, throw it at me. I want to be able to make up something superficially convincing.'

The museum coughed and started to sort through itself. It would deposit the findings in Susan's D-9000 file space. She would tell Tony that whatever she came up with was soundly researched fact. She was good enough to get past him. Even if he did check, he would do it by tapping into the D-9000, whereupon the machine would deluge him with the museum's native-poison bumph. No way would he go through that.

She planned on selling Tony her little-known but deadly drug on the dramatics. Vanessa Vail getting the bad news from the unbearable, kindly old Dr Murchison ('I brought you into the world, Miss Vail, and I think you've a right to know...' 'Oh, Dr M, is it...?' 'Yes.' 'How long?' 'We don't know, 'Nessa. Maybe a year. Maybe not that long. You could go' – snaps fingers – 'like that!') could be replaced with some steaming jungle action.

Vanessa Vail slogs through the tropical undergrowth in search of the Great MacGuffin. A fabulous horde of jewels, a crashed spaceship, the lost secret of the original Coca-Cola formula, something like that. She stumbles across an ancient temple, forbidden to unbelievers. A monstrous idol grins at her. Little brown figures lurk in the foliage. Vanessa senses danger. A dart strikes her arm. She brushes it away, and then learns of her impending death from a painted witch doctor. He describes her fate in horrible detail during his ritual curse.

An entirely new concept hook, and a great clip for the trails. Did they have pygmies in Ecuador?

'Hi, Sue-love.' Tony cut through the British Museum tap. An iris opened in the lower right corner as he holoed into the tridvid. Susan was reminded of shrunken heads, and wondered if she could work one into her Ecuador sequence.

''Lo, Tony. I was busy-busy.'

'I know. That's why I'm tapping in swiftkick. You're off *Vanessa*.'

Susan assessed her reaction. Relief: escaping a chore. Indignation: would Tony let someone else tamper with her Dream? Fear: was she being disemployed?

'Sorry, Sue-love. It just came through the slab here. You've been conscripted to the Public Service.'

'Expletive deleted!' Conscripted to the Public Service? It happened, of course. In theory it could happen to anyone. But what arm of the Gunmint could want a Dreamer?

'Christ knows why. You're not the first. The Gunmint skulks whisked Tom Tunney off the West Country a week ago. The same crowd. Whatever it is, sweets, don't scraggle up or we'll all be freezing our arses off gutting fish clusters on Rockall.'

Susan over-and-outed on Tony. Conscription to the Public Service was one of the Yggdrasil nets. The concept was to match individual talents to specific problems. Strictly functional. But as an artist – all right, entertainer (Susan Bishopric: four-dimensional tap-dancer) – Susan supposed she was useless. That was certainly the way her parents had looked at it when she tested Talent-positive.

She knew Tom Tunney slightly. He Dreamed historical detective stories. *Get Richie Quick, Richie Quick – Private Dick, The Quick and the Dead*. Very derivative of twentieth-century flatties. She had enjoyed the first in a minor key and not bothered with the sequels. His sales were up and his crix were down. Wherever he was, she was going. Offhand, Susan couldn't think of anything important in the West Country aside from sheep processing and Cellophane City.

An idea struck. She tapped into her NatBank account. The figures whirred like an odometer on FASTER-THAN-UGHT. A large sum was being credited to her. Payment in advance. Conclusion: she was not being seconded to the Volunteer Police or the Rural Reclamation Corps. Further, although more debatable, conclusion: whatever it was she was being asked (ordered) to do was unusual. Final deep-down gut feeling: it was likely to be at best nasty and at worst suicidal. She knew enough about the Gunmint to figure that.

Uh-huh. If you want a kidnapped royal rescued from a renegade superscientist's island enclave, get Vanessa Vail. Ink Susan Bishopric out. Was it worth dodging? She could be Transconcorde-exing the country within the hour. Before they came for her. And come they would – armoured andrews, polite voices behind opaque visors, spidercopters. She had Dreamed enough *policiers* to know the system.

No, exing was out. There was extradition from everywhere, anyway. She told herself she was overreacting. Whatever it was couldn't be that terrible, and would just have to be put up with.

She changed her clothe, flakjakked, and waited for them.

3

I was in Daine's penthouse, trying to figure a way of taking the hand. I was clutching a pair of dubious deuces, and he had the whole deck fanned in his manicured fingers.

How had I got into this? That was a dumb thing to think, since I flashbacked:

Spinning newspaper headlines: FIRST NATIONAL BANK KNOCKED OVER!; SECOND, THIRD, FOURTH, FIFTH AND SIXTH NATIONAL BANKS KNOCKED OVER!; THE KHALIFIA KIDNAPPED – DAINE WANTS 70 MILL!; REIGN OF TERROR CONTINUES!; SHIP SINKS – ONLY ONE SURVIVOR!; INTERNATIONAL COURT WITNESSES SUCCUMB TO BUBONIC PLAGUE!; 'NO PRISON WILL HOLD ME!' VOWS SUPERCROOK!; GUILTY! GUILTY!! GUILTY!!!; THE INQUIRER SAYS 'FRY THE RAT!'; TWENTY THOUSAND YEARS IN SING SING!

News on the March clips: stock footage explosions, skimmer chases, baffled cops reading official statements, Daine blankfaced in mindcuffs, the scales of justice, Princetown.

Then I came into it: Tom Tunney, Dreamer. One broken marriage and two inferior sequels away from the peak of my career. There I was, quietly stealing the plot for my next Dream from a 1947 flatty *(Ride the Pink Horse*, since you asked) and hoping the crix would miss it. Then 1 got conscripted to the Public Service, and dumped on the Midnight Special for the City…

Someone kindly kicked me in the head. That brought me back to the present. Whenever that was. Hell, I had to kill Daine before this started making sense.

Hey, Lissa, look at me. Your ex-husband, the private eye. About to be beaten to a pulp in someone else's nightmare. Proud of me yet?

'Here's your shamus. Mr Daine,' said Duryea. 'He got sick.'

'Well done, Daniel.' Truro Daine had a cultivated accent. The kind you cultivated on agar jelly in a petri dish.

I tried to do something difficult, like stand up. I half made it. Mazurki made sure I went the distance by grabbing me under the armpits and lifting me as easily as I might lift a coat.

'Hey, Mighty Joe Young, give me a break. I get airsick.'

Mazurki let my feet touch carpet. 'We didn't damage him none,' he said.

'Very good. Mr Detective, do you have a name?'

'Quick. Richie Quick.'

Daine laughed, walked over to the drinks table and mixed himself a frozen strawberry daiquiri. It looked like grey gruel. 'Drink?'

'I've had one.'

I had my hand inside my coat, clutching my stomach. I felt for my gun. The Bobbsey Twins hadn't lifted it. Typical thugs, dumber than Jane Wyman in *Johnny Belinda*. One quick shot before Daine could catch on, that was all I wanted. It wouldn't make the kind of mess you'd get in waking life; just a black spot on his starched shirtfront.

But he'd be dead. And I'd be back on the sleeper for Momingtown.

Daine had made up the rules and fixed them against himself. I hoped. In the flatties, the good guys always win. I was a private eye, a solid 100 per cent good guy. I was friends with crippled newspaper vendors, small Negro orphans and garrulous bartenders up and down the strip. Daine was a murderer, arsonist, dope peddler, pornographer, blackmailer, flamboyant thief and escaped convict. He was also a scandalous sexual degenerate, even if in the City that just meant an inordinate fondness for modern art, black cats and correct grammar. I couldn't lose.

I pulled my gun and squeezed off a shot.

A jet of water squirted across the room, arcing down ineffectually. A black line stained the grey carpet. Daine laughed. Duryea and Mazurki didn't believe it. I just didn't want to believe it.

'Very clever, Mr… Quick, wasn't it?' Daine bit down on the name. 'But here, I call the shots. In this case, literally.'

I was holding a goddamned five-and-dime plastic water pistol. I threw it away. It dribbled on the floor.

'The City is mine, Mr Quick. I'm like the Mayor. The Night Mayor. Watch.'

A brief flash of concentration passed over Daine's smooth features.

He was wearing a top hat, white tie and tails, and standing in front of a white wall.

Then:

The wall was black. The hat and tailcoat were white. The tie was black.

With a bored smile, he changed back to his smoking jacket. Behind him was a huge, ornamental fishtank. The hat stayed around. He took it off.

'Neat, now reach in and grab yourself a big fat rabbit, Mandrake.'

I tried to Dream a tarantula into the hat. No dice. I was off form.

'Cheap, isn't it? And tedious after a while. Real people are so rare in these parts. I may keep you around to have someone to talk to.'

'I'll forget how.'

Daine opened a cabinet, humming along with 'Charmaine'.

A black disc circled under the needle. He lifted the arm off the record, then slipped in some new music. After some hiss, a proper orchestra came in. Wagner, of course. It's always Wagner. *Tannhäuser.* Daine turned, flexing his fingers, showing off his rings.

'You strike me as a connoisseur, Mr Quick. Are you familiar with the scene where the suave mastermind talks about art and high culture while his brainless goons beat six or seven kinds of tar out of the stubborn detective?'

'No. Remind me.'

'This is a Degas.'

Mazurki hit me. Again. The novelty was wearing off.

'Why me, big boy?' I gasped. 'Didn't you hear someone call you a brainless goon a while back?'

Mazurki picked me up by the lapels and dropped me. My knees gave out, my elbows landed hard and my hat fell off. When I was down, Duryea kicked me. I kissed carpet and didn't get up.

'This is a Mondrian. An interesting use of geometric forms, don't you think? We're all confined by line and space, you know. And here is one of my prizes, an M. C. Escher.'

The real Richie Quick would have at least hit back a couple of times. Me, I got those seven kinds of tar kicked out of me. I swore to remember this the next time the crix accused me of Dreaming heroes who were extensions of myself. I kept telling myself it would come out right in the final scene. By the end of the picture I wouldn't have a mark on me. No injury heals faster than a bruise on a private eye. But Daine's rules weren't mine.

When Duryea and Mazurki gave up taking out their latent hatred of their fathers on me, I lay on the carpet trying to ignore the pain signals various parts of my body were sending to my head. I had been coasting along in this Dream, not exercising my Talent. I concentrated, reaching out to do some conjuring tricks of my own.

In my pocket was a needle gun. One of those miniature jobs.

It was in my trench-coat pocket. It was. I remembered all the component parts, saw them knitting together. The plates locked, the screws tightened, the clip rammed into the butt. Twenty shiny three-inch flathead nails lined up ready for use. It slipped off the assembly line. It was the gun I usually keep in my bedroom chest of drawers. The barrel was scuffed from the time Lissa used it as a can-opener and got mango splatter all over the desktop hob.

Slowly, my hand crawled into my coat, inching forwards like the Beast with Five Fingers.

I felt the needle gun with my fingertips. The metal was cold, the grip slightly warm.

Up close. I'd have to get up, and get close. To be certain of a fatal shot, I'd have to be near Daine. Preferably, I'd get the barrel against his throat, and squeeze one off into his jugular. I'd like a Peckinpah fountain to redecorate the room.

A four-inch barrel. Homepride symbol on the contoured grip. Gunmetal and plastek.

I lifted my chest off the floor, and took a deep breath. Get ready to eat nails, Daine.

Gunmetal and blue plastek. Blue! What in the hell did blue look like?

I lost it. I wasn't holding anything in my pocket except a fold of Burberry cloth. I collapsed again.

'As a rule, Mr Quick, I abhor violence.' Daine sat on the couch, leaning forwards to talk, hands on his knees. I knew what was coming next. 'But in your case I shall have to make an exception. You cannot know how such uncivilised behaviour pains me.'

'I'll try to imagine it while I'm being shot to death. I expect I'll be really upset.'

'A sense of humour. That's a rare commodity. What a pity it will be to lose you, Mr Quick. You are a man after my own heart. I like a man who jokes in the face of death. It suggests a certain flair, a certain style. Perhaps… but no, I mustn't let myself be tempted. *C'est la vie*, is it not? *C'est la vie*. Daniel, Michael…'

Twinkletoes and the Gorilla Man picked me up. I didn't feel too happy being vertical. I was far gone. If they had dropped me into bed with Rita Hayworth, I'd have fallen asleep.

Someone opened the picture window. I heard the rain. Wagner was getting lyrical, and Daine was making little conducting movements with his fingers. A cold wind swept the room, riffling magazines; my hat drifted towards a wall.

Duryea pushed me onto the balcony. I leaned over the rail and looked down. Duryea held the back of my neck. The cars passing on the street below went in and out of focus.

'Say hello to the ground, Shamus.'

Damn, so I was a bit part after all. A first-reel casualty. I prayed to God and Jack L. Warner that Richie Quick had a partner. A Bogart or an Alan Ladd. Hell, I'd even put up with Warner Oland as Charlie Chan or Edna May Oliver as Miss Withers. Richie Quick might be on a slab in the morgue, and his partner might have hated his worthless guts, but murdering detectives is bad for business. Richie's partner would have the case cleared up by morning. Daine and his goons would be brought to book, or picturesquely killed in such a way that the Hays Code couldn't accuse the partner of having committed a revenge murder. The old stories always come out best. Of course, none of that would matter to me: dead on the sidewalk in the City, a vegetable in my tank back in the world.

The lights went out. A lot of glass got broken. A familiar staccato assaulted my ears, and a burst of flashes strobe-lit the night.

Duryea got pitched off the balcony and fell like a twitching dummy. A small crowd gathered around his broken doll of a corpse. Another cheap hood dead in the gutter. Nothing new around here. They fall out of the skies all the time, like safes in the cartoons.

The penthouse lights came up again. I turned and staggered back into the room. The place was wrecked. The walls were delicately embroidered with bullet scars. Priceless art objects were smashed. Mazurki lay under the fishtank, which solemnly pissed on him out of a tracery of holes. A cat curled around his huge feet, meowing lazily, waiting for the fish.

Daine was on the couch. Thick black stuff seeped from his mouth. He had been going for his roscoe but hadn't made it. He was as dead as Benedict Arnold and twice as guilty.

In the theory, it was over. I massaged the back of my neck, and waited to be woken up.

Nothing changed. The record finished and the needle clicked in a groove. The cat left for some business elsewhere. The tank emptied to the level of the lowest hole. The remaining three inches of water were thick with expensive specimens, dragging filament fins in the gravel.

The City should be decaying around me. I looked out of the window. It was all there. Buildings, slums, ships in the harbour, moving cars, everything. Joseph Cotten looked up at me, hands on hips, coat draped cloak-fashion on his shoulders. He was standing over Duryea, the last of the crowd. He walked across the street to a pay phone and made a call. Even from five storeys up, I could read the PRESS card in his hat. Another late-breaking story for the *Inquirer*.

Hold the front page. The City was still alive.

I checked Daine. He was still dead. The Princetown psychs had been wrong.

Bastards! Lousy, lying, know-nothing bastards!

I kicked Daine off the couch. He didn't come back to life. I kicked him some more, for my own personal pleasure. That doesn't sound very pleasant, I know, but sometimes these small things help. If the governor of Princetown had been there, I would have kicked him too. And Lissa. Let's not forget Lissa.

I kicked Daine around the room. All he did was get deader. I kicked him into a dark corner and tried to bounce a bust of Napoleon off his dead forehead. It exploded, whiting his face like a clown and spreading fragments around him. A black pearl blinked in the plaster mess.

I scooped up my hat, straightened it on my head and kicked Daine again.

That's when I heard the sirens.

4

The andrew marshal on the doorstop was a pleasant-faced young woman with JULIET stencilled on her uniform breast. Susan angled the viewer down the official's body and tagged the sidearm web-holstered to her thigh. From her *Vanessa Vail* research, she recognised a directional taser. That was enough to confirm the importance of her Public Service.

Susan ran a check to verify the image. The Household reported that its doorstop view was a first-generation transmission, not a simulation. Thanks to the latest home-defence technologies, ransacking was out of fashion, but feeding a false vision of someone reassuring into the doorstop view had always been a favoured method of entry. Susan had the Household admit Juliet, and met the woman in the hallway.

The andrew stayed outside.

'I am obliged by law to inform you that the Gunmint requests you volunteer your services.' Juliet was reading off the inside of a contact lens. 'Should you refuse, no penalties or proscriptions will be enforced. However, you will be required to pay back the fee that has already been awarded you... plus bank charges, plus inflation increment, plus tax.'

Susan smiled at the rote speech. Offhand, she couldn't think of anyone who had refused their Conscription. Who knows, maybe the Gunmint were telling the truth in their official disclaimer. Maybe all you stood to lose was some money. Somehow, though, she didn't relish the opportunity to become a test case. After all, the lower-case v for volunteer in the standard speech didn't entirely cancel out the capitalised C for Conscription.

Juliet held out a formslab. Susan didn't bother to read the blurb.

'Thumb here, please,' the marshal said. Susan pressed a square recess, and felt the flickerflash as the slab scanned her print and psycho-chemical balance. It agreed that she was indeed Susan Bishopric, and beeped encouragingly. Juliet allowed herself a tight smile.

After running a cross-check on Susan's retinal pattern, she gave her ten minutes to pack an overnight hold-all. Annoyingly, the marshal wasn't authorised to tell her anything that might help her choose what to take. She picked a minimal toilet set (toothbrite, cleanses, pills) and a change of clothe, ummed and ahhed over make-up before making a snap decision she would regret before she was even out of the house, picked out a handful of musics from the pile (Debbie Reynolds, Peggy Lee, Connie Francis, Dick Powell) and threw the book she was reading (*Headlong Hall* by Thomas Love Peacock) on top of everything. When it was presented to her, Juliet perfunctorily searched the bag, and raised a plucked eyebrow at the book.

'You read?'

'Yes, I'm interested in aesthetic archaeology.'

Juliet flashed an enigmatic expression, and handed the bag to the black-and-silver andrew. Its face was a cheerful tridvid photograph. They were supposed to be all the same, taken from some square-jawed male model. However, their keepers couldn't resist giving them individual externals. This one had a black-inked gap in its open smile, and heavily scribbled eyebrows.

The marshal looked around while Susan programmed the Household not to admit anyone until it received her countersign and palmprint. She fed in the standing orders for dusting, message receipt and feeding the fish. Juliet was plainly taken with the luxury. Susan could imagine the kind of flat the Gunmint would provide its minor functionaries: a GP couch and a foodhole in the wall. Although, tagging the coiled-spring tautness of the younger woman's body and her confidence with the tools of her trade, Susan wondered whether Juliet might not rate more preferential treatment. In a humourless sort of way, Juliet reminded her of Vanessa Vail. She wore no rank insignia, and Susan intuited that the marshal felt she was on very important business indeed.

'Well,' said Susan, 'shall we go?'

'Right away, Ms Bishopric.'

The andrew strode out first, Susan followed, with Juliet last out. Susan was uncomfortably aware that the possibility of her making a bolt for liberty had been taken into account. The marshal stood aside while Susan sealed the door. The electrodes crackled, and shutters came down over the windows. The Household defence system came on line. If she turned round, Susan felt that she would find Juliet's hand resting lightly on the butt of her taser, a polished red fingernail on the safety. Such intuitions were part of the Talent – she had long since got used to them. Not once had she been able to divine anything useful, like the outcome of the Rodney ballot or, now, the details of her conscription task.

The other andrew in the team stood by the skimmer. Its face was standard issue, but it wore a leather flying helmet with cracked green goggles. She had seen the type in flatties like *Wings*, *The Dawn Patrol* and *Von Richthofen and Brown*. That had been several wars ago; if the gear were genuine, it would be a valuable antique.

Susan looked up at the unseasonably bluish sky, and saw the regular London/Eng-Richmond/CSA airship pass overhead, punching a doughnut hole in a cloud bank. She recognised the stars and bars of Dixieland Dirigibles Inc. on the trefoil.

She had an urge to stick a music in her ear, and let the

whole thing pass her by. Instead, she asked Juliet, 'Will we be travelling far?'

Juliet paused, judging how much to tell. 'Not internationally, the skip won't take more than thirty minutes.'

'The West Country, then?'

Juliet tried to look impassive. Susan knew she had scored some points, but couldn't decide whether they were upsies or downsies. The skimmer's belly opened, and the pilot andrew helped Susan climb into the rear cab. Its touch was surprisingly gentle. Its hands were upholstered over steel bones. If marshalled properly, the artificial fingers could save a life in surgery, or squeeze out Susan's with a nerve pinch. Juliet and the bag-carrying andrew joined her in the cab, and the pilot hauled itself into its cockpit. Susan heard the swish as the andrew melshed with the skimmer. When the readiness tone came, Juliet palmed the andrew authorisation plate and the skimmer rose vertically. Susan looked down at her home, and said a silent goodbye to the fish.

Gingerly, Juliet mentioned that she had just finished dreaming *The Parking Lottery*. 'I hear you're up for Rodney.'

'Several.'

'Think you'll beat Orin Tredway?'

They talked trivially, and Susan gathered Juliet was a Dreampuff. The woman seemed to have put her head through everything she had ever done. Even *The Light of the Bright World Dies*. Susan switched into her conventional politeness mode, and said all the things she usually said when people asked her the questions they usually asked. 'How does it feel when you Dream?' 'Do you have to experience all those things you put in your Dreams?' 'Where do you get your concepts?' 'What about the sex; I mean, how do you make that up?' 'When did you realise you had the Talent?' 'Do you know John Yeovil?' Juliet seemed less like Vanessa Vail now. She was almost unimaginative enough to qualify as an intervidier for the Breakfast Net.

The conversation prevented her from wondering what her

Public Service was going to entail. She wondered if Juliet had been ordered to distract her with chit-chat. The marshal seemed to relax a little, but Susan still nursed the underlying suspicion that even curled into the skimmer couch and asking googy Dreampuff questions, Juliet had calculated all seventeen ways of dealing a deathblow.

The skimmer made good time from London to the West Sector. Mostly, they zipped over the Designated Green Areas, although Susan caught a good whiff – even through the filtrators – of the renowned Cellophane City smell. The andrew flew them low over the moorland to avoid clouds and airships. They even buzzed a cow or two. One tiny-headed animal was so startled it fell over, its mountain of meat pinning it down. A farmer strode across the fields in his twenty-foot agri-walker, scrabbling to rightside the beast before it choked itself. He raised an angry waldo grabber at the skimmer, and veed up two butcherblades. The countryside below got a little wilder.

'This is Dartmoor, isn't it?' Susan asked.

'Uh-huh.'

'Aren't there barrows here? And sarsen stones?'

'I think so. That's why it's a preservation stronghold. Well, most of it. We're nearly there now.'

The skimmer slowed, and set down in front of a modern complex built in the fashionable colossal style. Black towers ringed the field. Although it had been renovated completely with the Yggdrasil hook-up, the place still carried its ancient associations. Susan thought of *The Hound of the Baskervilles* and fugitives alone on the wetland, cringing in holes while tracker dogs pulled at their leashes, terrified now more of the freedom of the bottomless mires than the captivity of stone blocks and iron bars.

'End of the skip,' said Juliet. 'Princetown Jail.'

5

Mrs Quick's little boy Richard had problems.

I knew how the picture would look to Poverty Row's finest. I could see the catalogue description: slightly damaged but beautifully framed. In their gumshoes, I'd think the same. When you find a dead racketeer in an apartment with a private detective who's been hired to kill him, you don't waste time looking for superfluous suspects. Or a murder weapon, or truth and justice. Said detective gets a nice little fall, two lungfuls of cyanide smoke, or a short walk with a chair at the end of it.

My head still hurt, and the sirens – getting louder by the second – weren't helping. The atmosphere in the penthouse had never been particularly healthy, but I had the impression it would be getting positively cancerous within a minute or two. The sirens cut out. I heard car doors being opened and the unmistakable sound of policemen falling over themselves in their haste to get to a crime scene before the *Inquirer*.

I took one last look at the Night Mayor, spat on his face, and left the penthouse. The landing was empty except for the statue of some dog-headed Ancient Egyptian, but the creeping arrow indicator above the elevator doors told me someone was due directly. I hit the stairs, and got down a flight or two when I heard someone coming up. Someone overweight and in uniform. I plunged through a set of double doors, and crouched down low behind them in the near-total darkness, holding the handles to prevent give-away swinging. My tracks in the dirt would mark my path eventually, but I was hoping the cop on the stair detail would be too concerned with heaving his bulk up to the top of the shop to cast his flashlight about in an orderly, police-procedural manner.

I heard the cop waddle past, muttering under his breath. Whoever was in charge obviously had it in for him. Me, I'd have sent the youngest, fittest guy on the squad up the stairs, but the law-enforcement mastermind I was up against obviously favoured spite over good police work. That might be worth knowing.

Then my heart stopped. I couldn't hear the cop moving any more but I could hear his very loud and asthmatic breathing, and I could dimly see myself. He had stopped on the landing after all, and his flashlight was shining through the grime-and-chickenwire windows. Officer Tubs put his face near the window, lit from below like the boogeyman.

I was caught.

And I had to keep myself from laughing out loud. I recognised the man in uniform, and knew how terrible I would feel when the *Inquirer* ran a headline lionising the dedicated policeman who had finally brought the killer in. Another Fine Mess.

Then the light moved. Officer Hardy had just been taking a rest. He stumbled up the next flight, and I was in comfortable darkness again. A darkness relieved only by a few shafts of moonlight through inadequately shuttered windows. That's another anomaly of the City; heavy cloud cover outside, but moonlight indoors. You get used to it. I brushed dust off my knees, and looked around for a way out or somewhere to hide. I assumed the police had enough smarts to post a man outside to watch the fire escapes.

The corridor revealed that the Monogram was a haven for

just-going-out-of-business businesses. The glass-fronted doors told me this floor had at one time supported such deadbeats as Chas. Halton, Bail Bondsman, Marcel Dalio, Tattooist, and Henry Hull DDS – Painless Dentist and Plastic Surgeon (No Questions Asked). There was a trail of still-fresh blood leading up to that last office, and a torn-away tragedy mask of stained bandages outside. Someone's new look hadn't turned out as well as he had expected. The glass was mainly cracked and distorting. Lloyd Nolan, Private Enquiry Agent, had a couple of bullet holes in his door. The faint chalk outline of a very fat man was traced around some indelible smears between a pair of ugly, overflowing stand-up ashtrays. I cursed the Monogram's janitorial staff. With this amount of fifth on the floor, I would be as easy to find as Theseus in the labyrinth.

I reached into my trench coat and found I had my gun back. That was something. I took out the snub-nosed automatic, and it felt good in my fist. I felt like shooting someone, which was a sure sign I had been on this case too long. The gun talked to me, gave me ideas.

If I shot myself, maybe I'd wake up. Maybe I wouldn't be a vegetable. Maybe my head wouldn't explode in the dreaming cradle. Yeah, and maybe if I doused myself in gasoline and lit up a cigarette I'd get a nice winter tan.

There wasn't any easy way out.

I walked down the corridor and found the elevator doors. I nerved myself up, and stabbed the call button. The cage grumbled down and stopped in front of me. I held the steel-mesh curtain aside and stepped in. The contractible cagefront slid shut again, criss-crossing me with cicatrice shadows. I punched for the ground floor, and the elevator slunk downwards. Floors passed me, desolate still lives beyond the metal net. I saw Escher patterns in the metalwork.

I composed myself, pushed my hat to the back of my head, and tried to look stupid. Like a cop. I held my gun by the trigger guard, between thumb and forefinger as if it were a week-dead haddock.

When we hit the ground floor, I pushed the mesh aside and walked smartly towards the main doors. There were uniformed cops in the foyer, milling about. I recognised Joe Sawyer, but the others were just faces.

'Evidence,' I told Sawyer, with hollow confidence, holding up the gun. 'The lieutenant wants this down at the crime lab swiftkick.'

Sawyer piggily looked back at me, raising a nightstick to his shiny wet cap-peak in a vague salute. I smiled on one side, like Dick Tracy in the funnies, and put my hand out to push the street door…

'That's one of the men,' came a whine, 'the middle-sized one.'

I did a Billy the Kid trick with my gun, and was holding it properly again. I turned round fast but carefully, and levelled it.

Byron Foulger had grabbed Sawyer's arm, and was snivelling all over him, eyes agleam with the prospect of reward money. Or maybe just the chance to make someone more miserable.

'Don't move, coppers,' I said, not liking the sound of it.

Luckily, Foulger had Sawyer's gun arm. The cop still had his nightstick up, but I was out of reach. I backed into the door, and it gave behind me. I felt cool air. I was stepping out to freedom. Then, the door suddenly swung the wrong way, hitting me in the back, and something tried unsuccessfully to walk through me. Sharp-ended fingers touched me just under my collar, and I felt the shove. I put my hands out, and took the fall on my wrists. I hurt the meat of my palm on my gunbutt. Sawyer pushed Foulger into a heap, and a shot went wild above my head. Someone shouted, and something behind me growled. I didn't like the growl; it reminded me of the moonlight upstairs, bright enough to suggest a full moon outside.

The cops all had their guns out now, and I was trying to put my hands up. But it's difficult to surrender when someone is standing on your back. I felt bare, barb-toed feet digging into my vertebrae and tried to look up. The cops started shooting, but mercifully not at me. The someone on top of me walked forwards and I was able to stand up. My clothes must have been a mess, but my hat hadn't come off. A large, swelling figure stood in the open door of the Monogram, between me and the posse. The cops were shooting at his broad chest, and he was taking all the bullets like popgun peas.

I suppose I should have been grateful, but from the back I didn't like the look of him. He was wearing only the tatters of a pair of grey pants, and had a Weissmuller physique. He raised his sinewy arms and howled into the lobby, flexing and unflexing his claws. I saw huge slabs of muscle shifting under a thick grey pelt. His head was in shadow, but I could swear he had pointed ears, a snout, too many teeth, and eyes that shone like fat fireflies. He jerked as the cops' bullets went in, but kept standing.

He stretched out a hand and scooped a wildly firing policeman off his feet. I cringed sideways, and just managed to avoid the cop as he tumbled through the air, a jagged lump of clothing and flesh ripped from his chest. Instinctively, I emptied my automatic into the thing's back. Little tufts raised where the slugs went in, picking out a pentagram. My automatic was full again, so I tried to fill an imaginary circle in the back of the creature's head. Spittle flew as he half-turned towards me, and I thought better of staying around.

I ran down the street, leaving Sawyer and company to take care of this intruder from someone else's plot. I wondered if any of the cops were loaded with silver bullets.

My music stabbed into me with shrill violins as I splashed through the puddles of Poverty Row. I looked down at my feet and saw the sidewalks shift beneath me as I ran on. Reversed signs shattered under my shoes. I zigzagged, running more often than not down the middle of the road. Cars passed me by, ignoring my obvious distress even when I flapped my arms, trying to flag them down. I realised I was still clutching my gun like a comforter blanket. Still, I ran. There was water in my shoes now, soaking my socks, and the cold was climbing up past my ankles.

I pushed through crowds and staggered down deserted alleyways. I knocked over newsstands and bounced off delivery trucks. Crouching against a wall, I saw my own face staring guiltily down at me from a WANTED poster. There was a reward out for me, posted by something called the Cicero Club. Police cars prowled past, searchlights stabbing the darkness for me. Knots of people saw me coming and whispered among themselves, turning up their collars to shut me out of the game. Every cop in the city was after me, and I knew Daine's underworld connections would have spread the word to have me pencilled out of this draft by now. Nobody loves you when you're down and out and wanted for murder.

In the French quarter, I saw a Gestapo staff car draw up outside an *estaminet* and heard Raymond Massey describe me in gutturally accented English to a group of swarthy collaborators. I dodged seemingly random shots from the snipers on the roofs. There were Vs painted on all the posters of the Führer Anton Diffring, and bulletholes at chest height on most of the walls.

Staggering down one well-lit main street, going from bar to bar, I tripped over Sterling Hayden. He was bleeding to death in the gutter, one hand trying to hold his stomach in, the other clutching a battered suitcase held together by travel stickers and string. He groaned as I stumbled, and my foot caught the catch of the case. It sprang open and a wind from nowhere whipped out the loose hundred-dollar bills stuffed inside. A cloud of mimeograph-grey money enveloped me for an instant, bills whipping my face, and scattered away. Pedestrians snatched bills from the air, scooped soggy currency from the sidewalk, watched as the valuable cloud took off like a hot-air balloon, twisting in a faintly manlike shape, ascending to the skies. It was the Genie of the Bank, willing to bestow three wishes on anyone who would set him free of the vaults, but skilled in the arts of irony and deception. All his promised were razor-edged with hidden dangers, loopholes and lessons. Those wise enough to save the last wish usually begged for death. Sterling turned over and laughed painfully, a treacle trickle snaking from his mouth. He died with eyes open, leaving a million dollars to the four winds. That was The End of his plot, and I thought I could see a touch of relief, of transcendence, in his dead smile.

But I was still strapped into my life, bound by a plot I could no longer predict, condemned to ride the streetcar until the last stop. A police car turned into the street, searchlight sweeping the asphalt like a Martian heat ray. I wiped wet money off my face, and ran again.

Hiding briefly between the garbage cans by a diner, gasping for breath, I overheard an announcer cut into a programme of dance music from the Starlight Lounge of the RKO-Radio Hotel and broadcast my description.

'This man is armed and dangerous, and should be shot down on sight or turned over to the police. In addition to the contract killing of Truro Daine, he is believed to be not only the mastermind behind the string of so-called "Pajama Suicides" that have so baffled Inspector Lestrade of Scotland Yard, but also the ape trainer responsible for the infamous Murders in the Rue Morgue, the mechanic who serviced Amelia Earhart's plane before she took off on her last flight, and the man who shot Liberty Valance.' As an afterthought the announcer added, 'This interruption is *not* part of the scheduled Orson Welles and the Mercury Theater of the Air presentation, *The Black Path of Fear* by Cornell Woolrich. This is a genuine interruption and should not be misconstrued as a bizarre prank.'

His voice changed pitch from urgency to solemnity and he trailed a later programme. 'In two hours' time, we will broadcast a tribute to Truro Daine, the great humanitarian who has so suddenly and tragically been taken from our City by this senseless crime. Among those who have hurriedly assembled in our studios to air their heartfelt feelings in this hour of mourning are Mayor Brian Donlevy, famed criminologist and broadcaster Qaude Rains, philanthropic businessman and pillar of the community Edward Arnold and noted psychic consultant Otto –'

A customer yelped, and the drudge behind the bar spun the radio dial until music sounded out again. The young, high-voiced Frank Sinatra did what he did with 'Night and Day'.

I pushed away from the diner, and propelled myself across the street. For no reason I could tell you, I appealed for help to a corpse-thin, bald man in his shirtsleeves who sat on an empty beer keg in a doorway, playing solitaire on a fold-out table, chewing an unlit cigar. I went down on my knees and begged him to take me in, to give me shelter, food, a place to sleep, a new face, a forged passport, a ticket to Peru, a hot drink. He continued to turn over the cards, never lifting his eyes from the configurations on the baize, saying nothing. Finally, I ran out of words and just sobbed. Then I ran out of sobs and slumped on my knees in front of the man's doorway.

He was losing, but hadn't seen it yet. He kept going through the pack, three cards at a time, and nothing came up. Nothing changed. He played faster. The same five or six cards showed their useless faces. He bit through his cigar, but sucked it in, keeping it in his mouth, spitting the plug out into the gutter. The cards kept coming up the same. Disgusted, he shuffled the cards in his hand, cheating, and went through the pack again. There were still no cards he could use. I knew he should give up, but he kept playing, hands moving faster than a magician's.

'Please,' I said.

The solitaire player dealt me a single card, and continued to play. It was the Queen of Spades. She had Veronica Lake's face, sliced diagonally in half by bobbed hair. Veronica's exposed eye winked at me, and I dropped the card onto the sidewalk. It fell face down on the wet, black slab.

I left the man playing and walked away, alone in the City. I angled my face up and shut my eyes. Pain throbbed in the dark of my head. Water ran down my face.

It was two thirty in the morning, and raining.

6

Vaclav Trefusis received Susan in his spacious office. He evidently took seriously his position as governor. Behind his antique, formica-topped deskslab, he sat in a swivel throne, kitted up like the stereotypical New Carolian: mutton-chop whiskers, starched collar, frock coat, mirror shades and medal ribbons. One wall was decorated entirely with pics of Princetown jail from the 1800s to the present day, an evolving monolith, and portraits of past governors. Another was hung with the black-framed trids of the various notable felons who had been incarcerated here. Of course, the governors looked far less trustworthy than the felons. Life doesn't believe in typecasting. Through a huge, one-way view, Governor Trefusis could overlook his charges. Currently the scene was a hydroponics plant.

'Food for the refugees in Kansas, Ms Bishopric.' Trefusis pulled a cigar out of a recess, chopped it in a miniature guillotine and sparked it with a tiny zapgun. 'We find that forgers and stranglers make the best viviculturalists. Assassins and rapists get the reclamation duties. Black economists process DHSS forms, meatleggers work the kitchens, and ransackers still break up rocks with picks and sledgehammers. This institution is a machine. Its function is to punish trespassers, but I have streamlined its workings. There are side effects profitable for all society.'

Trefusis exhaled a cloud of scented smoke. Susan sipped her green tea and nodded. She still had no idea what was going on. Trefusis tapped his slab, and the toilers among vats disappeared. A tridvid mugsnap appeared in the view, full face, revolving to left profile, back of head, right profile and full face again. And the face was indeed full. Not flabby, but full. The face of a general regarded as a homicidal maniac in his time but reassessed as a national hero after he was safely dead for centuries; the face of a great technician hailed as an artist of genius by his peers and contemporaries, but contemptuously forgotten by posterity once he was no longer around to fuel the vogue with his personality; the face of an emperor – a Nero, an Alexander, a Napoleon, a Heseltine, a Dweezil.

Susan whistled. 'Truro Daine.'

'You're familiar with the man?' asked Trefusis, holding the dopesmoke in the back of his throat.

'I've heard of him.'

'The world has heard of Truro Daine. In an era when criminals are largely imbecile sociopaths, politico-religious fanatics, disadvantaged simpletons or overenthusiastic executives, he is unique.'

'Fu Manchu.'

'I beg pardon?'

'Fu Manchu, the Great Enchanter, Professor Moriarty, Captain Nemo, Zenith the Albino, Dr Mabuse, Lex Luthor, Ernst Stavros Blofeld, Dr Doom, Eugene Smedley, Cardinal Synn. A master criminal.'

'Quite. Popular culture is, of course, your field. I was misremembering. That's why you're with us. Truro Daine is indeed a master criminal. Even in this place, his fluence remains. He remainders more people annually than motorways. When he commenced his career, some of your colleagues in the mediocracy chose to project him as a romantic figure, a swashbuckling throwback to an earlier, somehow more exciting, age. Naturally, I cannot be expected to share that opinion.'

Trefusis's fingers did a little dance on his slab, and a montage of tridvid clips passed through the view. Ruined banks, sundered museums, devastated cities, blasted heaths. Trefusis gave her a series of corpse close-ups, one dead face after another. Men, women, children, animals. 'For Truro Daine, human life is a poor commodity. Like many great men – and I do not begrudge him that epithet – he has a deep-seated belief that other people aren't real. In his solipsism, he has experimented with murder on an unprecedented scale, convincing himself with each zilched life that he alone is truly sapient. That is a crucial insight. Tag it well.

'Of course, his basic problem is common or garden homicidal mania. It's been treatable for fifty years. It would lead another man to become a mercenary or a serial killer, but Truro Daine is not another man, he is perhaps the third or fourth loftiest intelligence in the world. Had he chosen to live within the fold, he would undoubtedly be richer through the income on his patents than he was through theft, extortion, terror-for-hire, blackmail and the black economy. He could have been very high in the Gunmint. But that would have bored him zoidal.'

'B-b-bad to the B-b-bone.'

'I beg pardon?'

'A song, Governor. Pardon me. It's a pash of mine. Old songs.'

'Harrumph.'

Daine's face came back, frozen. His serial numbers hung solid in front of his chest. Being under arrest hadn't fazed him. Perhaps he had tried everything else and thought punishment might be less boring than trespass. Yggdrasil knows, Truro Daine was brainier than the Gunmint.

'Do you know,' said Trefusis, clearly enthused on his favourite subject, 'when he finally came to trial, he was found guilty on 8,921 counts of first-degree murder alone, excluding his various thermonuclear adventures. Before they gave up, the international courts found him culpable in enough instances to entail a mandatory sentence without remission that would take a significant chunk out of the lifespan of a continent. If he were to live out his stretch, it is likely on the current evidence that the human race would have evolved beyond all recognition by the time he was eligible for parole. When it came to the vote, lamas who refuse vaccines on the grounds that even microorganisms have a right to life endorsed a revival of the death penalty just this once.'

Susan remembered the controversy. It had got as far as Yggdrasil, and the machine had taken longer to debate the issue than any other she could remember. When, after a full two hours, it had decreed that, even in the case of Truro Daine, capital punishment was not an option, there had been riots from Peiping to Valparaiso. A few more decisions like that and the Gunmint would have to find itself another A1 demagogue. Behind Trefusis, Daine was still at ease in his tridvid clip, smug as Prime Minister Dies, calm as Chillmeister Freaze.

'You'd think that the one place Truro Daine would be accepted was right here, wouldn't you? All trespassers together. But child molesters, corpse violators and religion pushers refuse to share a field with him. He has a phantom zone of his own to keep the other prisoners away from him. He remaindered too many of his associates to retain the loyalty of the trespassing classes.'

'This is all very interesting, but…'

'Where do you come in, Ms Bishopric? You must forgive me for being prolix. You see, Truro Daine has escaped.'

The view blanked. Susan saw that Trefusis was crying. He reached for a face-dab and touched his cheeks. She looked around, nervous, and was embarrassed by the nerve-twitch reaction. Did she think Truro Daine was hiding behind the Yggdrasil banks in the corner, clutching his straight razor?

'That's not supposed to be possible, Governor.'

Trefusis blew his nose, and ordered himself. The pomp came

back and he inflated again. 'It isn't. Do you understand our system?'

'Only what I scan in the newsbreaks.'

'It's perfect. Humane, but escape-proof. There are no bars and locks. Structurally, this building could be a school or a hospital. Our only security comes down through the Yggdrasil terminal. It broadcasts a variable energy field. At night, it shrinks to encompass just the main building. During the work periods, it bubbles significantly to allow the prisoners to their assigned toil areas. Upon conviction, each trespasser is implanted with a pacemaker. If he or she should wander beyond the field, the pacemaker gives out and their heart stops. If we find them within five minutes, they can be resurrected. If not... well, they knew what they were doing. Aside from clear-cut cases of suicide, no one has even tried to escape since we introduced the system.'

'So, what did Daine use? A deal with the Devil? Do-it-yourself open-heart surgery?'

'He found a loophole. A loophole which can be noosed only by someone with your qualifications.'

Susan had that deep-down doom feeling again. She precogged all her Dreams being reissued in black-trimmed boxjackets as a memorial set. 'Governor, please don't confuse me with one of my characters. I'm not especially qualified for anything apart from Dreaming. I've never done anything heroic awake. Most of the time I need a nerve enhance and an armoured andrew guard to cross the road.'

Trefusis ignored her protest. 'Our prisoners are confined in mind as well as body. Containment is the essence of the penal system. They do not have access to Dreams. But this isn't Devil's Island. We do have an extensive vid library. Tridvid, mostly, but we stock much other material. Soon after his arrival, Truro Daine developed a pash for flatties. Specifically, he made an exhaustive study of the North American cinema of the 1940s and '50s. Are you familiar with the period?'

'I did a term paper on *film noir* at Eton.'

'Excellent. I'm not stimmed by twentieth-century arts myself. I have it tagged as an enormously banal period. Our great-grandparents must have been such nasty little people. Truro Daine requested an increasing number of vid tapes. I have a printout.'

Trefusis handed her a curl of silver foil. Red letters stood out. Susan skimmed the list of titles. *The File on Thelma Jordon…* I've seen that. Barbara Stanwyck is in it. *Dark Passage…* that's a seminal pre-Dream, lots of subjectivity. *Between Midnight and Dawn…* that I don't know. *I Wake Up Screaming, In a Lonely Place, Cry of the City, Kiss the Blood Off My Hands, The Big Combo, While the City Sleeps.* All good stuff. *In a Lonely Place* is rare. I didn't think even BritLib had a vid. I wouldn't mind cloning it some time. It's out of copyright, so I wouldn't be trespassing against the reproduction laws.'

The governor took the strip back and cracked it in the air. The red dispersed. 'It seemed a harmless pastime. And it kept him quiet. We'd been expecting more trouble.'

At another slab touch, the door slid open and an andrew warder came in. It wasn't armoured, but its transparent right hand was set to deliver a disorientation zap. It had a pretty girl's face. 'We'd better get down to Daine's field,' explained Trefusis. 'Dr Groome is waiting for us.'

In the corridor, Susan noticed convicts in fleshtex skinsuits performing menial chores. They were, as far as she could tell, unsupervised. Trefusis had an unnerving habit of referring to each prisoner as they were passed, identifying them with their trespasses, snapping 'cat burglar', 'credit creeper' or 'information embezzler', like a tour guide pointing out items of interest. The convicts themselves took this habit as a salute, and returned it with a noncommittal 'Morning, sir'. For the most part, the prison seemed unfurnished. In cells without doors, Susan saw GP couches built into floors, covered foodholes, excrement apertures and little else. There were no views on the walls, no personal possessions, nothing with any character whatsoever.

It wasn't at all like the dank and dripping dungeon she had had Vanessa Vail escape from with only a facestick and a sitar plectrum. That had been her idea of the Worst Place on Earth, this was more like a very large DHSS waiting room. The only way she could tell the andrews from the prisoners was that the mechanicals were smiling. On a lower level, a short, fat convict – 'pain peddler' Trefusis called him – was abrading a graffito from the wall. 'Hang Truro Daine', with a stickman on a scaffold. 'Here we are,' said the governor.

Dr Helena Groome turned out to be a small woman with grey scalplocks, green lips and a floorlength white coat. She sucked slickorishe capsules, perfunctorily offering a squirter around but taking it back before anyone could accept or refuse a jet. Susan noticed Dr Groome had included the andrew in her indian offer. The doctor and Trefusis each palmed a wallslab and recited a meaningless but suggestive phrase into a vivicorder outlet – Dr Groome's was 'Home is the Hangman', the governor's 'Pease Porridge Hot'. After some silent processing, an aperture appeared. Susan was shown through, and the andrew remained behind. 'Welcome to Maximum, Ms Bishopric,' said Dr Groome. 'It's a homey but it's hell.'

The room was like a large hospital dormitory, with a double row of sarcophagus tanks. Only two were humming. The views above them flashed figures and readings Susan couldn't follow. Printstrips piled on the floor by the tanks, waiting for the final check. Juliet stood by the tanks, vigilant. With her helm off, Susan could see her long, brown-toned hair. The marshal smiled and waved a greeting with her left hand. Seconds later, Susan realised why Juliet's gesture appeared awkward: she was keeping her right hand free for the touch taser. Dr Groome fished a remote control pointer out of a pocket, and adjusted the master view. Daine's face appeared again, a candid clip this time. The trespasser was deepsleep, his chin stubbled, REMming regularly. He had a laurel-shaped device twisted around his temples.

'Recognise it?'

'Of course, doctor. It's a dreaming cradle.'

Dr Groome moved the image in on the view, revolving to get a profile. 'Yes. Home-made, too. Some of the components must have been smuggled in. A young political was remaindered in the jail several months ago. Someone, not Daine, opened him up with their bare hands. We think the fixings for the dreamset were in his bowel somewhere. We've sampled the material. It's some new synthetic, unremarkable but for one quality. It's X-ray invisible…'

'Another Truro Daine product,' chipped in Trefusis.

'Of course. Note these attachments here, Ms Bishopric. Behind the ear, through the cheek, and into the eye. It takes something quite considerable to insert a monofilament into one's optic nerves by hand, don't you think?'

'It's not a concept I've given much thought, doctor.'

Susan looked away from the view, and walked over to the active tanks. The face plates were opaque.

'He's in here, isn't he?'

'That's right,' said the governor. 'Dreaming.'

'Everyone's a dreamer.'

'No, Ms Bishopric. Daine's Dreaming. Capital D Dreaming. Dreaming creatively. Like you.'

Susan looked at the view again, took in the smile. 'I didn't know he had the Talent.'

Trefusis stood by the left-hand tank, intent on the man inside. 'Oh yes, one of his many Talents. He started young, you know. After he collected his parents' insurance, he went into juvie porn. He was a star Dreamer on the black economy for several years. Up there with Elvis Kurtz and the Masked Mongoose. I believe his *magnum opus* was called *Anal Explosions of the Young Debutantes*.

'I must have missed that one.'

'All copies were purportedly wiped by the Jesuits during the

Second Moral Crusade, but the Vatican's file copies have skulked onto the market. The King couldn't afford the asking price, I believe, but several muse consortiums put in acceptable bids. Under several pseudonyms, he produced docuDreams during his career. Do you want to know what it feels like to be a mass murderer, Ms Bishopric? Care to sample patricide, fratricide, matricide, uxoricide, regicide, filicide, philicide, canicide, Alcide, genocide?'

'Governor Trefusis, there's nothing I haven't done in Dreams.'

'Don't be so sure.'

'Yggdrasil is merciful,' cut in Dr Groome, 'but it errored with Daine.'

'So he's Dreaming...'

'More than that. We let him have the flatties he wanted. He used them in an unprecedented fashion, Ms Bishopric. He's lodged himself into an Yggdrasil file and is Dreaming up his own private universe, furnished with the externals of those old vids. We've lost track of it. It expands as we tap in. Physically, he is still here, kept alive by the tank. But inside his head he's free.'

'More than free,' said the governor. 'He's God.'

'So, pull the plug.'

'Strange as it may seem, we thought of that. Daine has done a good job of melshing with Yggdrasil. And with our fail-safe power plant. His body is in a coma. That dreaming cradle is bio-attached. It's growing through his brain, through his body. It would take a team of andrew surgeons years to bum the filaments out, and we'd have to kill him in the process. If we just cut the power input and pull his master tape, his mind would be wiped like a printstrip. As you know, that's legally murder.'

'If jailbreaking is suicide, then surely he's legally killed himself anyway.'

'A good point, Ms Bishopric. Personally, I'd like to argue it after the fact with Truro Daine's expensive battery of lawyers. However, the *corpus* is still in my care. The Gunmint has been up all night talking this out, and I'm their servant. They want him back.'

Susan could see it coming from a long way off, getting bigger on the horizon. There wasn't any escape for her either.

Dr Groome palmed the tankslab and played with some readings. 'We can't drag him out of his Dream, Ms Bishopric, but we can introduce you into it. That would change the whole frame of reference.'

Juliet looked her in the eyes. 'You kill him, Susan. If he dies in the Dream, the Dream dies with him.'

'The marshal is right,' said the doctor. 'Daine is playing in his own mental backyard. That's relatively small right now, but it's growing in the Yggdrasil file like a virus. Subjectively, it's city-sized at the moment. In a week, he may have made himself a continent. Then a world, then a universe, whatever. We could hook up an army and send them in, and they'd never find him. It has to be now.'

'And it has to be you,' said Trefusis. 'Once you're inside you should be at least as powerful as he is. You're a Dreamer. You have more experience than him. We think you can shape his Dream, pull it apart around him.'

'That would be another experience for your list, Governor. Even Daine doesn't know what it's like to be a deicide.'

'That's the spirit.'

'To kill God. That sounds dangerous.'

Dr Groome gave a list a check. 'There are risks. We don't want to conceal them. You are free to refuse.'

'Because this is a free society, right? The Gunmint just has my best interests at heart?'

Dr Groome looked down at her list. Juliet turned her head and adjusted her hair. Governor Trefusis outstared her. 'In a free society, every citizen is obliged to protect their freedom. The Gunmint can be persuasive.'

Susan turned away from the officials, looking for an ex. There wasn't one, but she would have felt bad if she hadn't at least looked. She flash-forwarded a newsclip. There was Orin Tredway in a purple tuxedo, holding up a Rodney statuette and mouthing sincerities. 'Susie can't be with us tonight as you all know, but as her personal friend I'm honoured to accept this for her...' Susan shivered, unable to tell, as usual, the difference between fantasy and premonition.

'One more question,' she said.

'Yes?'

'Who's in the other tank?'

PART II

THE BARD OF THE BOULEVARD

7

In Chinatown, the streets were narrower, cluttered with produce stalls – open even this late – and mysterious tents. I had an idea I could hide out there for a while, maybe rest up, maybe make a connection who could get me out of the City. The cops would be watching the bus station and the railroad terminal, but maybe I could bribe my way aboard a tramp steamer for Macao or Shanghai. I knew that I had money. Some of the Genie of the Bank had attached to my clothing.

In an alley beside the Keye Luke Cabana, under a string of apparently waterproof paper lanterns, I peeled the bills off my trench coat and pants. I had forty or fifty thousand in hundreds. The bills weren't sequentially numbered or marked in any of the large variety of ways I could imagine. I wadded one into my shoulder holster as an ace in the hole, packing it down with the gun. Then I made a fist-sized roll of the rest and shoved it into my deepest pocket. You were never entirely safe from prying fingers in Chinatown, but I had to give it my best shot. A wolfpack of ragged children swarmed through the streets, snatching at whatever was insufficiently guarded. The merchants occasionally killed one, but that didn't seem discouragement enough; there were always new recruits.

'Tell you fortune, Mist' Americano, tell you fortune.'

A decrepit old man, supported by a young boy in a huge coolie hat, was tapping his way down the alley, patterned robes trailing in the rainwater. His face and hands were white and very wrinkled, but any signs of extreme age stopped just below his jawline and just above his wrists. He had huge empty eye sockets wadded with cotton, a scraggly Fu Manchu moustache and a long grey pigtail. A sign hung around his neck, covered with a scrawl of ideographs and a single attempted English word, BLIDN. I had the idea he was a European in disguise. His withered claw reached out and attached itself to my lapel.

'Tell you fortune,' he jabbered. 'Fortune velly good. China girl in bathhouse wait you. She miss you velly much a long time. Much money in stars belonging you. Much good is fortune. Much.'

I shoved a hundred into his hand to get rid of him. He held the bill to his ear and slid it between his fingers. In his grin, several teeth were blacked. He shook with excitement. I realised my mistake; he'd remember such generosity, and his boy would be able to describe me. Hell, under all that gook on his eyelids, he was probably no blinder than a hawk. That made two unwanted witnesses to point the finger at me.

'Much thanking, Mist' Americano, much thanking.' He whispered a long coil of Chinese phrases to his boy helper, and the child looked up at me, almond eyes shining in a brim-shadowed face. The hat nodded up and down in gratitude.

A rattling commotion alerted me to the patrol well before it reached the alley. I shrank back while the fortune teller tottered towards the main street. Merchants folded their stalls and made a run for it, their goods wrapped in voluminous sleeves. A grey guava rolled to my feet. I picked it up and bit deeply. It tasted dry, like pasteboard, but it was food and I couldn't remember the last time I had eaten. With what I hoped was an air of raffish nonchalance, I sauntered to the mouth of the alley, munching on the increasingly inedible fruit.

A battered Model T Ford, mounted with a shining machine

gun, flying an unrecognisable flag, was lumbering down the street, pushing people and stalls before it. A Chinese officer in a uniform more than adequately equipped with polished belts, straps and full holsters stood up in the front passenger seat of the car like George Washington crossing the Delaware, shouting dictatorially. A tethered goat went down under one iron-rimmed wheel, and the vehicle jolted as the animal was crushed. The officer steadied himself by grasping the windshield, but didn't miss a beat in his spiel. Three glum soldiers sat in the back of the car, greedily eyeing the machine gun, while a very fat civilian in a dragon-decorated garment did the driving. The car finally ground to a halt against the remains of a silk stall, a knot of scarves caught around one axle.

The officer belaboured the driver about the head with a pair of white gloves, and stepped down to the street. A turbanned, one-legged beggar raised his bowl to him, and he knocked it out of his hands. Small children scrambled for the scattered coins before they washed down the drains. The officer picked up the beggar by his neck. The missing leg dropped down and kicked, and the officer threw the con man away, chattering at him in some dialect. He drew one of his several revolvers and fired a shot in the air. The fake beggar ran off, turban unspooling from his head as he made pretty good time for someone unused to having two legs under him. I stayed back in the shadows. The patrol probably wasn't looking for me – there were too many fugitives in Chinatown to concentrate on just one – but they'd be more than willing to take me in if they tripped over me.

The officer barked an order, and the soldiers jumped into action. They grabbed the blind fortune teller and flung him brutally against the wall of a josh-house. One soldier held up his head, and clawed at his face. He showed a handful of greasepaint and rubber to the officer, who strode over and asked a question. The fortune teller, half his moustache still attached, shook his head, and with a single shot the officer summarily executed him.

The dead man fell backwards, his head cracking against the lap of a stone buddha.

I threw away the guava core, and it too was torn to pieces by the children. A small form whipped past me into the alley and tried to squeeze between my back and the wall I was leaning against. It was the fortune teller's boy. I turned to push him away, and his hat slipped between us. Long black hair tumbled from the top of the boy's head. He was a girl, with a lovely oval face. Anna May Wong. She looked up at me in silent supplication. I knew I should throw her to the patrol and make my own getaway, but she appealed to the chink in my armour. Widows, orphans, lost children, small dogs. They all get me into trouble. I never learn.

I took her in my arms and we kissed. She was very enthusiastic. I held her by her wrists to keep her delicate fingers out of my pockets. I lost track of what was going on outside the alley until the officer tapped her shoulder with his revolver and waved it in my face. She let my mouth go and pressed the length of her body against my side. The officer smiled unpleasantly, silver teeth shining. There was more decoration on his cap than on the average gypsy caravan, and he had a pair of samurai swords strung criss-cross on his back.

'Papers, please?'

I made the pretence of patting my pockets and looking like a total cretin. 'I'm so sorry, General Yen, I seem to have left them at my hotel. I'm sure you'll understand.'

'That is most unfortunate,' he said in Oxford-accented English. 'We hate to detain our most welcome guests, especially when they have…' he looked Anna May up and down as if his mind could do with a good Chinese laundering '…other urgent business to attend to.'

The soldiers were getting impatient. Obviously, if they didn't shoot someone every ten minutes they got on edge.

'Hold on a minute,' I said, 'there's one pocket I haven't tried.' I fished out my bankroll. 'Ah yes, here are my papers.' I peeled off five hundreds and gave them to the officer. 'I hope they're in order.'

'Most certainly. An internationally accepted passport. Excellent. May I see your driver's licence?'

I handed him another five bills.

'Work permit?'

More money.

'Birth certificate?'

Not much left now.

'Draft notice?'

'Here.' I gave him the rest of it. 'This is my Eagle Scout badge, and some baseball cards. That's my lot.'

'Excellent. That is all in order.' He wadded the money up tight and shoved it into one of the pouches on his Sam Browne belt. 'You may go on your way now, Mr…?'

'Doe. John Doe.'

'Mr Doe. The good wishes of Buddha go with you.' He turned away and addressed his men in Chinese. Then, to me, 'Have a pleasant evening.'

He climbed back into his car, and hit his driver again. The fat boy had unwound the scarves.

'He told them to wait a minute and shoot us down,' Anna May whispered into my ear, 'like dogs.'

'Oh, really,' I told her. 'Thank you, darling.' I signalled to the least intelligent-seeming of the soldiers. 'Excuse me, do you have a cigarette?'

He shook his head. I made smoking gestures, and walked over towards them. 'Cigarettes?' I said, puffing furiously at empty air and flicking an imaginary lighter. The dime dropped, and one of them grinned, tucked his riffle under his arm and reached into his uniform. I grabbed his wrist and broke it, spinning him round and holding him up. I heard the guns go off. Luckily, my shield was heavily built. The bullets didn't go through him. I heaved him at the other two and they went down, firing wild into the air.

If they had had pistols, they'd have been able to get a better aim. The officer, in his car, was well out of range for an accurate shot with his cheap revolver. Still, he came a lot closer than I had expected. I dived behind a handcart and came up with my automatic in my hand. I wasn't any better at this kind of messy shoot-out than they were, but I put a hole or two in the car's windscreen, and put one of the soldiers out for the count. Then the sidewalk three yards to the left of me started exploding, and an earthquake line of stone chips advanced towards the cart. The noise of the machine gun was deafening.

I pushed myself back out of the line of fire as the wooden cart splintered into an abstract sculpture. Little darts stuck into my legs from the knee down. I fired in the general direction of the officer's head, and missed. I saw him grinning ferally as he worked the gun with both hands, spent cartridges flying into the air. He was jitterbugging with the recoil, and the gun's momentum kept his first sweep going for a couple of yards even after he realised he'd missed me. He swung the gun upwards on his mount and was obviously set to cut me in half with his next pass when the knife hilt appeared in his chest, lodged deep between two bandoliers. He staggered back, brushing at the black stains seeping from his wound, and fell off her car. His uniform would be ruined. The surviving soldier gaped and, in the sudden silence, I shot near his head. He ran off.

I looked back at the alley. The girl was there, waving sweetly. Her topcoat was open, and I saw the belt of knives – with one missing – strung from shoulder to waist. Why hadn't I felt them when we were pressed together? Perhaps she only had them when she needed them. Anna May buttoned her coat and scampered away, swarming like a monkey over the wall at the back of the alley and vanishing into the night. By the time I got to the officer, the children had practically stripped him. His swords were gone, and his boots, hat, revolvers and belts. My money was gone too, of course. And the girl's throwing knife.

Two urchins were struggling to detach the machine gun from

its mount. One six-year-old Our Gang refugee stood solemnly by the car, too-long pants concertinaed around his feet, holding up the officer's revolver in both hands, covering the fat driver. The machine gun came free, and the children staggered off under the weight, certain of a huge price on the black market. The junior gunman ran off after them.

The fat driver giggled, then burst into full laughter, the rolls under his robes quivering like jellies. His egg-shaped body shook with his mirth, and the Model T rocked from side to side. He slapped his enormous thighs and laughed some more. I left him there, and headed for the next block.

'Mist' Americano...' The voice was feeble, cracked and fluttering. It came from the fortune teller.

I couldn't see how he could be alive, but I went to him. His face was a mess, with a black bullethole and a tangle of rubber. His wrinkled nose had come off, and one smooth Caucasian cheek showed through his withered Chinese mask.

'Mr Tunney,' he gasped – mistaking me for someone else? – as he reached for me with a flailing hand. 'Mr Tunney, don't forget who you are. It's important. Mr...'

He fell back onto the Buddha, dead again.

Tunney. The name meant something to me. It was as familiar almost as my own, but I couldn't pin a face to it. I had a few nagging associations, a snatch of a song ('Beautiful Dreamer'), a girl's name (Lissa), and a big white room like a hospital ward.

The driver was still laughing. Chinatown was too hot even for me. I swore I'd never go back.

8

The bard was striding along the Boulevard, cloak wrapped tight against the rain, iron-tipped stick striking sparks from the sidewalk.

He had woken from his walking death a while before, in the middle of a quote from *Coriolanus*. It was his habit to patrol the streets of the City, declaiming the Gospel according to Shakespeare to passers-by, emoting his way through the great speeches in the hope of earning a few drinks. In his time, he had been a poet, a preacher, a cowhand, a scientist, an adventurer, a hobo. Now he was the Bard of the Boulevard. He was known in every bar and diner in town, and tolerated in most.

Like everyone in the City, he had been as one dead. His creator had fashioned him from clockwork and set him to go through the motions of living without giving him the actual breath of life. He had followed his script, fulfilled his stereotyped purpose, but never really acted of his own accord. He had been one of the supporting players of the City, a Harmless Eccentric.

'He wants nothing of a God but eternity and a Heaven to throne in,' he shouted at Gail Russell, frightening the girl off the street. Good job too, a young thing like her oughtn't to be out late on a pestilential night like this.

It struck him like fire, and the scales were lifted from his eyes.

Surrounded by enslaved automatons, he was a free man. For the first time, he felt – really *felt* – the rain in his face, the weight of his stick, the pull of his waterlogged cloak.

He stopped reciting, he stopped walking. He nearly stopped breathing. Given unexpected control of his lungs, he spluttered and drew breaths until his body took over. He bent double, hugging his thin chest inside his cloak, then drew himself up to his full height.

His heart beat, and his wet hands ached.

It came to him as a Revelation, descending upon his mind in all its complex glory, that there was a man in the City in need of his help, and that the man – his name didn't matter – would free everyone as this awakening had freed him.

In an instant he had decided. He would find this man, help this man. The City would be free, whether it wanted to be or not.

With an added purpose in his step, he continued on his way, returning to *Coriolanus* with renewed vigour.

Above him, in the night, eyes twinkled.

9

Thelma Ritter, the woman behind the counter in Kelly's, looked at me sideways when I paid for doughnuts and coffee with a wet hundred-dollar bill. But she still made change. On the jukebox, the Ink Spots were crooning 'Don't Get Around Much Any More.' The song reminded me of my ex-wife, only the group were trying for wistful melancholy and my associations were screaming nightmare.

'How d'you like your java?' Thelma asked, a Brooklyn croak in her voice.

'As it comes.'

She sloshed coffee into an uncracked cup and disinterred two doughnuts from their sugared resting place under glass. I sipped the black brew, my body tense, waiting for the tug at my arm. Flashing that kind of money in this kind of joint could lead to either of two things, a uniformed policeman or a chippie. The doughnuts were okay, and the coffee helped with the fog in my brain. I bought a pack of cigarettes – the brand an indistinguishable smear – and lit one up. Outside in the street, a few cars cruised. From my stool, I'd be able to see anyone coming into the diner. I prayed that Kelly's wasn't a popular cop hang-out.

For a few minutes, I was almost at peace. I sort of nodded into a half-sleep sitting up at the counter. The idea of a bed was appealing. I rolled it around my mind, imagining pillows rejected by princesses as too soft, a closetload of blankets, silk sheets, an acre or more of mattress… I snapped awake, and looked down at my fish-eye-lens reflection in the coffee. I was beat, but I couldn't risk a motel or even a flophouse. Word was out on me. I shouldn't be in Kelly's. But it was warm here, and there was soothing music.

I had some puzzles to think out. Who really killed Truro Daine? What did this man Tunney – I knew Tunney was a man – have to do with the case? He must look like me. That kind of doppelganger effect was common in the City. And why was I having this trouble with people?

I had noticed it several times since I left the Monogram Building. I felt as if I were moving just a beat faster than everyone else. I could tell what people were going to do or say – trivial things like lighting a cigarette or commenting on the rain, important things like committing murder or founding a dynasty – and it disturbed me. I felt that I had seen this movie before.

Thelma, haggard and overly lipsticked, gave me a refill. I drank again, scalding my throat to shock me awake.

'Mister…'

I supposed I was lucky. It was a chippie, not a cop. Natural, really. Statistics show that there are more women in the world than anything, except insects. I half turned on the stool. She was a blonde in a black dress, wearing a tiny hat with a visor of veil. The dress was tight in the right places, and shiny where it shouldn't have been. She was going to ask me for money, I thought.

'Mister. Do you have a dime for the jukebox?'

Knowing I'd regret it, I gave her a handful.

'Thanks, mister.' She had a high voice, almost squeaky like Mickey Mouse's. 'My name's Glory. Gloria, that is. Gloria Grahame. Look at my monogram.' She dangled a handkerchief from her glove; black, embroidered with white letters. 'G.G. Like a horse. Gee-gee, get it?' She laughed, an artificial, almost grating squeal. I liked her.

'Richard.'

I held out a hand, and she pinched it with tiny, black-gloved fingers. The hamburger-flipper at the other end of the joint looked unhappily at us. He must get his heart dented every hour on the hour. Just like me. He adjusted his paper hat and turned back to his stove.

The door opened, and someone came in from the night. I was expecting death in a uniform, but it was just Frank McHugh, a beef-faced truck driver in a cloth cap. He went into some comedy patter, bouncing lines off Thelma. I could afford to miss that part of the picture, and turned back to Gloria. She had a cigarette – one of mine, I realised – in her mouth, and was waiting, expectantly. She coughed a little.

'I'm sorry.'

I took my lighter out, and she held my hand again, tighter this time, guiding the flame. She sucked, and the cigarette end glowed.

She gave me my hand back, but let her velveted fingers play with it for a second or two. She smiled, showing off her plump, tight little mouth, and blew a failed smoke ring. She didn't make a move for the jukebox, but the coins had disappeared.

'You have an interesting face, mister.'

'It's been around.'

'Yeahhh. Around.' Her fingers touched my face, feeling for the painful spots. She found them. 'You look like you've had a rough night.'

'You could say that.'

'Cops?'

'Priests. Bing Crosby and Barry Fitzgerald got me drunk and stole my wallet. Then Ingrid Bergman knocked me around, just for the fun of it. I guess I should have paid attention in Sunday school.'

She looked hurt. 'No need to fun me, mister. I was just concerned.'

She tried very, very hard not to say 'concoined' and only just missed.

'Us night people gotta look out for each other.'

'Night people?'

'Yeah. You're a night person, like me. I can tell. There were two Irish boys in here earlier, in uniform, back from the war.' She tried hard to remember, and I realised she was a touch drunk. 'Robert Ryan and Robert Mitchum. Imagine, two friends with the same name. They had the look you do, the night-person look. I asked them about the war, and they said it was okay, but you could see in their eyes they didn't mean it. Lots of day people go to the war and come back night people. Like this kid who used to come here – I think I was married to him once – Dick Powell. He started as a day person, and was in all these big spectacular musical shows they used to put on. They don't do them any more. You know the kind, with thousands of girls dressed as bananas; now, they just put thousands of bananas on one girl. Dick was the dayest person you ever saw, shining hair, big smile, dimples, high tenor voice. Well, the war came, and Dick turned into a night person, got a job as a private cop or a night editor or something. Now he shaves every other evening, carries a gun and doesn't sing no more. Me, I've been a night person longer than I can remember.'

'How do you get to be a day person?'

'You don't. It only works the other way round. You know, like you only grow older. You have to live with it.' She smiled, slyly this time, and leaned forwards. Her dress shifted a little, exposing an inch or two of cleavage. 'There are ways night people have a better time, Richard. There are compensations.'

Her eyelashes fluttered, and she stubbed out her cigarette on my empty plate. 'I live two blocks from here, in a walk-up,' she said. 'It's late.'

I looked up at the clock. It was half past two. I looked down at Gloria. She raised one delicately plucked eyebrow. We understood each other. In her walk-up, there would be a bed. Just now, that was the best way to get to me. Money, threats, drugs: they wouldn't work. A bed, now, that was irresistible. For eight hours' sleep, I'd knock off God and hang the frame on Jesus.

'Can I walk you home?'

'Would you?' She tossed her head, for the benefit of the hamburger chef. 'I'd be honoured. You don't often get to meet a *gentleman* these nights. Not with the war.'

The chef mashed a lump of raw gristle on his stove, and kept it down until it was half charcoal. 'Good night, Glory,' he said, flipping the thing over and blacking the other side. She sniffed the air and ignored him.

She took my arm, fingers digging through several layers of clothing, as if reaching for the bone. As we walked towards the doors, she rested her head on my shoulder.

The doors opened and three men came in. Gloria stepped back behind me, recognising them. The youngest, a dead-eyed thug with prematurely white hair, gave a shark smile. 'Hello, Gloria, going so soon?'

'Lee... I thought you was playing poker tonight.'

I heard a tremble in her voice, and again had that impending-violence feeling. I recognised these three too. I had seen pictures. White hair was Lee Marvin, twenty-eight arrests, no convictions. He was high up in the syndicate, which tied him in to Truro Daine. The other two were small fish, Jack Elam and Neville Brand, but they could have argued over first and second place in an Ugly Contest. I gathered my presence was breaking up a beautiful picture of Lee and Gloria. Not exactly a wedding photograph, but close.

I had seen enough pain and blood for one night. I saw Thelma clearing the counter of anything breakable. By the door, Frank McHugh comically gulped down the last of his coffee and hurried back to his rig, leaving half a plate of bacon and scrambled eggs on the table. Jack Elam shut the doors behind him and turned the OPEN sign round to CLOSED.

'Please, boys,' said the chef, 'I don't want no troubles.'

'No trouble at all, Kelly.' Marvin grinned.

I made fists in my pockets. He had some poundage on me, and he wasn't as tired as I was. Plus he'd brought King Kong's illegitimate children with him. I was going to get beaten to a pulp. Again. It was becoming monotonous.

'Coffee, Duchess…'

Thelma picked a full jug off the hotplate and brought out some cups. Before she could pour, Lee took the coffee away from her. It bubbled and steamed like corrosive acid. God knows what it would do to the inside of anyone's stomach. Or the outside of anyone's face.

'Who's the pretty boy, Gloria?'

'I… I just met him, Lee. He was gonna see me home, protect me. It's late.'

That had been the wrong thing to say. Marvin's mouth went thin, and his grip on the handle of the pot got very tight. He flipped the lid open and shut with his thumb. It looked like a hungry carnivorous plant. The coffee smelled like burning oil. It might have been brewed this year, but I doubted it.

'What're you going to do, tough guy,' I asked, 'steam the paint off a battleship?'

The door swung in again, bumping Jack Elam. A tall, gaunt, cloaked man swept in, long limbs scissoring with his stride.

'What country, friends, is this?' he boomed, shaking every piece of crockery in the place. 'Bring me liquid sustenance, for I have need of thy strongest mocha-java, merchantman…'

Marvin gaped, turning to look at the newcomer. Drunk or crazy, the tall man had made an entrance worthy of Henry Irving. He swept past Neville Brand, sideswiping him with his cape, reaching out with a heavy walking stick.

'Such is the stuff the dreams of my palate are made on, Kelly, thine is the most potent brew, renowned throughout this fair land.' The ferrule of his stick touched the glass coffee pot and shattered it. Marvin shrieked like a gutshot coyote as the dark, boiling liquid soaked through the front of his shirt and trousers, staining black his belly, groin and upper thighs. He threw away the useless handle, collapsed on the linoleum and started scrabbling at his clothes with pawlike hands. He let out a torrent of the vilest abuse imaginable.

'Darn! Heck! You dumb cluck…'

'A thousand 'pologies, *mon brave.*' The tall man doffed his floppy hat and bowed low, waving his hand like a courtier. ''Twas but an accident. Certes, my lord, I have the gelt to replace yon coffee pot. Permit me to purchase you all a fresh beverage as a token of my humblement.'

Marvin could hardly stand up. I could imagine his agony. Underneath his suit, he must be glowing like a fresh-cooked lobster. The thought made me feel warm inside. Elam and Brand helped him up. 'Get me to a doc,' he gasped. 'I gotta know. It feels bad, real bad.'

'You touch my heart, sieur,' said the tall man, stepping forwards to offer his hand and accidentally standing on Marvin's toes. 'Oh, vile, intolerable, not to be endured! What a zany I am! It seems I cannot perform one task aright this eventide.'

'Why, you… Gloria, help get me to Blair Hospital… I'll deal with this clown some other time.'

Sheepishly, Gloria crept out from behind me. 'Sorry,' she said. 'I gotta go. Thanks, mister. I don't want trouble. Good night.' She kissed me on the cheek, and followed the three out to the street. Her stocking seams weren't straight.

'Parting is such sweet, sad sorrow, my young friend. Steel your heart, gird up your vitals and content yourself with the company of bold fellows like Kelly and myself…'

The tall man swung his hat up again and latched it onto his head. He had shoulder-length hair and a black Buffalo Bill moustache.

'John Carradine,' he said, 'at your service. They call me the Bard of the Boulevard on cause of my devotion to the immortal works of Master Will Shakespeare. Ho, master greybeard loon,' he was shouting to Kelly, 'come fill the cup, or stap me for a whey-faced knave.'

He thumped the counter with a thin, knuckly hand, and Thelma found another coffee pot from somewhere.

'See, where she comes apparelled like the spring. A princess fair, the whiteness of whose skin would shame th' Arctic snows to a blush, the brightness of whose hair would provoke fabl'd Helen to a fit of the envious humours…'

'Stow it, motormouth,' she said, smiling sheepishly, 'and drink your coffee.' Thelma poured two cups, spilling a bit. I could swear I saw it sizzle as it ate through the varnish. Carradine dropped a few coins – ducats, I think – into the puddle and waved the woman away. She grunted and went back to her pile of glamour magazines. On the cover of *Fortune*, a day person was smiling, displaying star-bright teeth.

I took a stool next to Carradine, and downed the coffee. One way or another, I had drunk quite a bit this evening, but I didn't need to powder my nose. None of the places I had been in seemed to have a men's room anyway. Carradine clapped me around the shoulders.

'We are well met, comrade-in-arms. Long have I combed the vilest quarters of this town on fruitless search for thee. From wharf to palazzo I have quested, 'countering gallants and monstrosities. My trusty sword…' he tapped his stick '…has been gored gules twice its length in wanton combat. O, who can hold a fire in his hand by thinking on the frosty Caucasus? Or cloy the hungry edge of appetite by bare imagination of a feast, Kelly, eggs over easy *s'il vous plait!*'

'You've been looking for me?'

'Indeed, coz. Thou'rt famed as the slayer of the Devil's prime minister, Master Quick.'

'Daine.'

'The very same. Would that't were mine, the hand that separated the tyrant's head from the residue of his perfidious corse!'

Thelma gave us both a refill, shaking her head. Kelly produced a plateful of what passed as eggs, and Carradine launched into them with a fork.

'I'm afraid I didn't kill Daine.'

'No matter. The noble intent was there. That lifts you as hero above the commonality. My fealty always is sworn to thee.'

'Wait a minute. You didn't like Daine?'

Carradine spat eloquently.

'I thought he was loved in the city, like a king or something.'

'Garbage wrapped in silk is still garbage and stinks as such, my friend. I've long since pledged my sword to any who would help rid this borough of the damned Daine. Some – too few – have tried. Youngman Bogart, for one, Glenn Ford for another. Their heads have decorated pikes for the common cry of curs to snap and growl at.'

'I've some bad news for you, John,' I said. 'I've had time to think now. If Daine really is dead, then someone's taken his place. Someone probably worse than he was.'

'Say it isn't so!'

'The City's in just as bad a shape as it always was, isn't it? Men like Marvin and Jack Elam are still running the streets. People are still dying in every gutter.'

'What seest thou else in the dark backward and abysm of time?'

'There's a new Night Mayor. There has to be. Claude Rains or Sydney Greenstreet, or one of those fancy-pants villains. They knocked him off and dressed me up for the suit with arrows.'

There's small choice in rotten apples. Oh, hydra-headed wrongness that should spring up again redoubled when 'tis smitten down!'

'You said a mouthful.'

Another big black car cruised past the diner. A door opened and a man in a hat leaned out, one foot on the running board. I had hit the floor before the machine gun went off. The picture-windows shattered, and the bar cracked apart where the bullets went in. Glass and doughnuts rained around me. Carradine wasn't on the floor, alive or dead. I looked up and saw him clinging to a pipe that ran the length of one wall, high up. His long legs were wrapped round it, and he was clutching at a dangling light fitting. His cloak hung down like a curtain, and I could see streetlamps through the bullet holes in it. There was more gunfire, and containers of sugar and ketchup jumped to pieces on tabletops. The linoleum ruptured, and something heavy landed on the back of my head.

Darkness wrapped around me like an anaconda. I gave in to it.

10

After the Tunney fiasco, they weren't doing anything without putting it through the full committee structure. In Trefusis's office, the governor presided over a round-table discussion, with Dr Groome, Juliet, a silent official from the Department of Conscription, and an apparently lifeless andrew head to represent Yggdrasil. Tunney had just slipped into his Richie Quick projection and gone indream expecting a swiftkick runaround the cliché track with a preordained victory at the end. Since he was no longer responding even to the encephalo beacons lodged in his unconscious, Trefusis wasn't ready to inject Susan without a full run-down of how she intended to melsh with Daine's Dream. With a certain creepy deference to the impassive head on its platter, the governor opened the meeting by onswitching a tridvid record and passing the conch to Dr Groome.

The clinician, clearly out of her depth with the arts but still determined to do her best, had prepared a selection of vid snips from Daine's source flatties.

'Given that, unlike Mr Tunney, you don't have a ready-made dream persona for the mission, we thought you might consider these possible role models.'

Snips passed through the view.

'On balance, we felt these were the most powerful, potent

female images on offer. I'm relying very much on Yggdrasil to guide me here.'

Dr Groome flashed up snips of a series of scheming, glamorous *femmes fatales*. Barbara Stanwyck in *Double Indemnity*, Joan Bennett in *Scarlet Street*, Mary Astor in *The Maltese Falcon* and Lauren Bacall in *The Big Sleep*. Their generous mouths worked, but the snips held the dialogue down to sub-audible level. All of them were lying to men, and yet reaching out to offscreen lovers. Susan was reminded of beautiful, poisonous sea anemones waving their fronds to suck in the unwary prey.

Susan was tempted to remodel her dream image as 'Phyllis Dietrichsen' from *Double Indemnity*, flashing her jewelled anklet and casting off her used-up men like old cleanses, or 'Vivian Sternwood' from *The Big Sleep*, brushing aside her curtain of hair and trading innuendoes over cigarettes with Philip Marlowe. But she could see the drawback.

'Uh-huh. I've seen these pictures, Dr Groome. It was dangerous to be dangerous back then. Only Lauren Bacall gets the guy at the end, and she has to give in to get there. Barbara gets shot by Fred MacMurray, Joan is remaindered by Edward G. Robinson, and Bogart stands back while Mary Astor is hauled off to jail. If Daine's Dream adheres to the formulae, then that reads out as an unacceptable risk to me.'

'But if you get killed in the Dream, it won't hurt,' Trefusis chipped in, 'you'll just wake up.'

'That's only a theory, Governor. No one knows yet. You've already lost Tunney in there. Besides, what if I get the *Maltese Falcon* plot? I noticed Daine had *Caged* and *Brute Force* on his recommended-viewing list. I don't think the prisons in his Dream are quite as civilised as the one you run.'

In the view, Barbara Stanwyck was dying beautifully, rain on her face, 'Tangerine' on the soundtrack.

'Here's another recurrent characterisation…'

Dr Groome tapped up the images of Ida Lupino in *High Sierra*,

Shelley Winters in *A Double Life* and Gloria Grahame in *Crossfire*. They all looked blowsy, lipsticky and desperate, locked in a fight with a life set to trample them into the barroom floor, a series of no-account boyfriends too free with their fists and guns, and an incipient obesity that would limit their later careers to shrill mother roles. Susan noted the still-silent official take an interest. Obviously, she could get a tridsnap of *his* fantasies of femininity.

'...The tart with a heart. You might be able to avoid notice as a supporting character.'

Susan shook her head. 'Oh no, doctor. Those women were disposable. I did a social autopsy on these conventions. It was all tied up with the rigid censorship restrictions of the 1940s. Because it was implied that these girls had been sexually available to a wide number of men, the hero couldn't live with them after the fade-out. They were regarded as tainted. Typically, they would be shot in the back, throwing themselves in front of the hero, and get to die pathetically in his arms. Then he lap dissolved into a happy ending with some drip like Anne Shirley.'

Trefusis threw up his hands theatrically. 'I don't understand this at all. Why should it be so complicated?'

'Sexism,' Susan said. 'That's not a word that gets much use now. In the twentieth century, it meant that women got a zilch hand-out in life and the arts. These flatties were made by men and mainly for men, and trade on male fantasies. They're fixated on their male heroes. Women were supposed to be incidentals. And the stronger they were, the worse it was for them at the end of the picture. Barbara Stanwyck spent her whole career suffering and dying just because the dreamership couldn't stand to see a woman come first.'

'It was a long time ago,' said Juliet, who had been sitting quietly.

'Not long enough,' snorted the governor.

Susan looked up at the view, where Gloria Grahame was taking a pot of hot coffee full in the face in *The Big Heat*. Later in the picture, she would die, pressing a mink to the scarred half of her face. Exploited, mutilated and murdered. Maybe *Vanessa Vail* wasn't such a bad fantasy after all: she might die, but at least she was her own woman.

'Did any of you ever bother to dream Tunney's Dreams?'

They all shook their heads.

'He might have been here if you had. His involvement with this period and its fantasies was obvious. He used to take whole concepts, characters and moods from the flatties. I'm sure his morbid attachment to these old conventions is unhealthy. My guess is that he wished women back in their twentieth-century slot. He certainly Dreamed them that way. In *Get Richie Quick!*, the hero's ex-wife Lola asks him to find some missing family documents and turns out to be setting him up to take the blame for a series of axe murders she's been committing since she was six years old. At the end, you get to be inside Richie's head as he righteously kicks the poor woman to death after she's come for him with a hatchet in each hand. And the crix said the sequels were worse. He garbage-dispersed the whodunit concepts because it was always this monster woman behind the scheme to remainder the hero. No wonder Tunney was so susceptible to Daine's Dream. He's probably gone happily native in there.'

The head gave the impression it was about to say something, but didn't. In the view, Ronald Colman strangled Shelley Winters, quoting from *Othello* as he did so, killing with a kiss. He spouted art, and she wound up on ice.

'We'd only got as far as having a preliminary psyche dissection on Daine,' said Trefusis, 'but the Yggdrasil probes suggest he had a similar – although far more pronounced – set of personality deformities. And Daine's neural dysfunctions have shaped his Dream as much as the externals he took from his old vids.'

'Very clever. Daine and Tunney are probably soul mates. I'm likely to have to remainder Richie Quick before I get to your missing prisoner.'

'So,' said Juliet, 'if Tunney or Richie Quick or whoever he is can be fooled by a designing woman in each of his adventures, I don't see why you shouldn't get the dividend on his blind spot.'

'Good point. I just have to get outdream before the kicking scene comes along.'

Juliet looked hurt. Susan wished she hadn't wisebacked at her. In this room, the marshal was the only one who gave any indication that she valued Susan above the worth of her Public Service. Susan flashed a mental apology that seemed to sink in.

'Well, Ms Bishopric,' said Dr Groome, 'if you don't want to fit into any of the roles we've assessed, just what do you want to be in the Dream?'

'It's not much of a choice. Especially since Tunney's already struck out as a private eye. In the genre terms, that ought to have made him unassailable. Private eyes *always* win through in the end.'

In the view, a random assemblage of snips presented a series of betrayals and murders. The films were identified by a floating tridvid legend in the bottom left corner. Ralph Meeker snapped an old man's priceless Caruso record in half in *Kiss Me Deadly*, Richard Conte tortured Cornel Wilde by turning up a hearing aid and shouting into it in *The Big Combo*, Ingrid Bergman drank the poisoned Brazilian coffee in *Notorious*, Charles Laughton plunged down a lift shaft in *The Big Clock*, Orson Welles and Rita Hayworth shot it out in a hall of mirrors in *Lady from Shanghai*, Edmond O'Brien lurched into a police station to report his own murder in *D.O.A.*, Tony Curtis was brutally beaten by a corrupt cop in *Sweet Smell of Success*, Laurence Harvey jumped in the lake in *The Manchurian Candidate*. It had been a sick period, Susan decided, as monomaniacal in its obsession with violence as the D-9000's blood-and-buggery concepts. No wonder Daine was drawn so powerfully to it. For a master criminal, it must seem like the Golden Age. The people back then had been so absurdly vulnerable, prey to disease and deception. In among the monochrome massacre, someone had made a mistake; there were brightly coloured Doris Day and James Gamer in *Move Over Darling*.

'It's not much to go on, but how about a construct? Something between Gene Tierney in *Laura* and Ella Raines in *Phantom Lady*?'

'You've lost me,' Dr Groome said. 'I hadn't seen any of these vids before the crisis came up.'

'Well, we could make the censorship work for us. If I were playing an indisputably virtuous character, then cliché dictates that I would at least be spared death, imprisonment or degradation. I could be a hard-working career girl mixed up in a murder case, doing some solo sleuthing to get her fiancé off a murder charge. That sort of thing was always happening. Fiancés in these flatties were always zomboids with thin moustaches, always being arrested for murders they didn't commit. That was just about the only way a girl could get any equal action time, if her boyfriend was behind bars.'

Dr Groome fiddled with the slab and Ella Raines came up, walking alone at night along a deserted railroad platform. Then Gene Tierney, emerging out of the night in a ridiculous hat, surprised Dana Andrews, the cop who thought he was investigating her murder. The doctor looked at Trefusis for approval, and the Governor made a fine-by-me gesture. Nobody asked the Public Service official anything, and Yggdrasil would have spoken up if it had any strong objections.

'Susan,' said Juliet, 'could you shoot anyone?'

'In a Dream, of course. As I said, I've done almost everything imaginable in Dreams. And this is, after all, only a Dream.'

'That's what Tunney said, and it swallowed him, bones and all.'

For the first time, Susan intuited that if she really made a point of it, she could get out of her Public Service. Juliet, who represented the Gunmint, could almost certainly out-rule Trefusis and his penal staff in a show-of-force debate. And the professional enforcer visibly disapproved of endangering the minds of civilians in what she considered a problem for her department.

It was a fine point, and it could keep Yggdrasil arguing with itself for ever: physically, Daine was still in Trefusis's jurisdiction, but if fleeing into his Dream counted as escaping from Princetown then Enforcement should take over. It occurred to Susan that this could lead to legislation she wouldn't approve of. If the Gunmint declared a citizen's dreams within its rule, then a vast but subtle freedom would be lost.

Trefusis wouldn't like it, but if Susan refused to go indream, she was sure Juliet would support her. The marshal's favoured plan – Susan gathered – was that she should go into Daine's Dream, as herself but with a few improvements, and then rip the sub-universe apart until she found the fugitive and could tase him awake. Susan knew that wouldn't work, but also that she would never be able to explain to Juliet why an amateur enforcer would have a better chance indream than a skilled public servant.

Everybody thought they knew what it was like to be a Dreamer, but everybody too readily confused passive dreaming with creative Dreaming. This went beyond a legal technicality, Susan realised. Really, there were only three people in it: Daine, Tunney and herself. They were all Dreamers, and if Daine wasn't brought back to Princetown, things would go badly for all Dreamers everywhere. She didn't have to like it, any more than she had to like being Vanessa Vail, but there was no way she could evade the responsibility without racking up a seed of guilt that would sprout and eat at her Dreams. If she didn't remainder the dragon, she could forget her chance of freeing herself of the D-9000.

'Susan, we can stop all this here,' said Juliet, leaning forward. The Yggdrasil andrew's eyes slowly opened. 'You can say no.'

'Fantasies can be dangerous. I'm used to that. I can't explain yet, but I have to dream Daine's Dream. It's… a professional point.'

Juliet understood that. Of course, Susan thought, the marshal had probably been inspired to get into Enforcement by dreaming *Vanessa Vail* – by *being* Vanessa Vail – at an impressionable age.

Dreamers were for ever the vanguard, or maybe for ever the forlorn hope.

'Okay, let's do it. It's my party, and I'll cry if I want to.'

'Discussion over?' asked Trefusis. 'Good. We've a tank prepared.'

Dr Groome wiped the view and started projecting mental images into it. 'You'll need some externals to tap you properly into the Dream. A clothe, a hairstyle, some props.'

Dr Groome projected a mannequin and roughed out a tailored suit. The psych was surprisingly inventive. Susan particularly liked the hat, which was perhaps a touch mannish for her chosen persona but passed thanks to its raffish qualities.

The psych smiled. 'I don't know much about flatties, but historical fashions are *my* pash. I've a collection of antique accessories. Yggdrasil can encode them into your indream simulacrum. The least we can do is dress you for effect. Tunney went in looking like a Redevelopment reject.'

'And I've been thinking about guns,' said Juliet. 'You'll need to think up something.'

The mannequin faded, and the snips came back. In the view, more actors died.

11

'All that we see or seem is but a dream within a dream…'

Who said that? Edgar Allan Poe? Or Vincent Price?

In the dark, I dreamed the unpopulated dreams of the amnesiac. I dreamed I was on a case. I was looking for a man named Tom Tunney, a washed-out writer and a deep-dyed drunk. Lissa, his ex-wife, wanted him found and substantial alimony coughed up. She also wanted to know if he was dead or alive, just out of general interest. Nice lady. Body by Bacall, hair like Hedy's, face from Frances Farmer and penny-bright eyes like a week-old corpse. I had traced Tunney out of the City to a big house with high broken-glass-topped walls where the rich and inebriated pay to have their vices purged. He had been there and gone. The doctors told me he was unimproved by his stay with them. I could believe it. When the informants ran out, I kept on the man's trail by following the empties. I always keep a bottle in my desk drawer, but this character was putting it away on an industrial scale. With Lissa's money I picked up his tabs. Bartenders, hoteliers and B-girls kept asking me if I was Tunney's brother. The resemblance, they said, was amazing. Lissa hadn't had a photograph for me to flash, but had described him as looking 'a lot like you, Mr Quick, a *lot* like you'. She had made a pass at me, of course, but I had left her and her dead eyes in her big, empty house. I make a policy of never fooling around with my clients. It's kept me alive so far.

From the dry-out farm, Tunney had moved down to the border, mooched around in cantinas for a while, then left the country two steps ahead of the sheriff of some Rio Grande jerkwater. I followed by car and *burro*, tracking him from town to town. The bottles marked his way through the desert, like cat's-eyes down a street. I made some deposit money back on as many as I could carry. The rest I left out there with the bones of prehistoric animals, as a sign for future generations that there had been civilisation in the Americas.

Tunney had made a lot of friends along the way, until his travelling money ran out. After that, he made a lot of enemies. I interviewed some of them. Three beer-befuddled construction workers played softball with my head in a backstreet on the mistaken assumption that I *was* Tom Tunney. With the bruises and a three-day beard, I was told I looked even more like him than I had done. Lissa's money gave out, and she told me over an international phone hook-up that she wasn't interested any more. She was remarrying – to a war hero, of course, just like all the girls that year – and didn't want to know either way about her former husband. 'He was just a no-account,' she told me, 'a Dreamer.' But I was too far along to drop it that easily. I'm a detective, so I feel obliged to detect.

I was finding out more and more about my quarry's life. From the witnesses, I picked up details about his work, his friends, his childhood, his Dreams. And, with each scrap of information I unearthed about Tom Tunney, I seemed to forget something about myself. I found myself using his name on hotel registers, in barroom conversations. I realised, with a shock, that I was drinking almost constantly. One evening, I sat in a cantina with a row of bottles on the bar, and tried to remember absurdly small things about my own life. I couldn't remember the make of car I drove, how my girlfriend looked naked, what I had done before

I got my PI licence, what shape my bathroom was, my parents' names. I knew more about Tom Tunney than about Richie Quick. The man I had not found yet was real to me, but I was a phantom, as flat and one-sided as Dick Tracy or Steve Canyon.

I was staring at a wall-sized mirror when he walked into the bar. Over my own shoulder, I saw his face come out of the shadows. For the briefest of instants, I was standing up looking in the mirror at the face of a man at the bar…

Then the curtains parted, and I was back in the City. Back in the night. Back in the pain.

'Heavens be praised, my boy,' said Carradine. 'I thought you were dead for sure!'

I opened my eyes, was assaulted by the light, and shut them again.

'Easy now,' said the deep, resonant voice. 'Step by step.'

I opened my eyes again, less painfully. I was still on the floor of Kelly's, surrounded by smashed tables and bulletholes. I was sitting in a congealed pool of stickiness. I felt myself for wounds, and couldn't find any. The mess was just spilled ketchup. Maybe my luck was changing.

'Not a mark on him,' said Thelma, 'saints be praised!' She had a rosary out, and was knotting it around one hand like a beaded bandage.

Carradine helped me up. I was unsteady on my feet, and my head felt like a leftover battlefield, but everything seemed to be in more or less working order. There was ketchup on my trench coat, but it would wash off in time.

'Looks like you're right about there being a new man at the top,' said Carradine, 'and he's just paid you his friendly compliments.'

Kelly grunted, seemingly no more upset by the destruction of his diner than he would have been by a broken plate. He was in a grimy apron, sweeping up. There were fresh bullet scars on the walls, like the ones in Daine's penthouse. Exactly like, I could see the same patterns – faces, almost – in the damage.

'Marvin and the others must have set you up. They'll all be with the new man by now.'

Things had changed while I was out, but I couldn't tell how yet. I had the memory of a headache now, but my head was clear. That felt like a first.

'We'd best be out of here, Richie,' Carradine said. 'They might come back.'

It took me a moment to realise he was talking to me. 'Yeah. I'm sorry about the mess, Kelly...'

'That's okay,' the chef said dully, 'it's been worse before. When the Muni Mob and Jimmy Cagney had a gang war, they tossed in hand grenades every twenty minutes.'

Carradine helped me get out of the diner, but I didn't feel so bad. Some of the earlier aches had faded, and the new ones hadn't had time to get settled in. It was still raining, but it was a hard, fast, clean downpour now, washing garbage off the sidewalks.

'We better get you off the main streets, you're a target...'

It hit me. 'John, what happened to the pidgin Shakespeare? You sound almost Hemingway. Well, maybe Steinbeck.'

His long face was quizzical. 'I guess it wore off. It's been a funny kind of an evening. I feel like I've just woken up after a long dream.'

'I know how you feel.'

'It's as if only the last few hours of my life were real. I could tell you my story up until then, but it happened to someone else, an imaginary character.'

We walked a couple of blocks, looking in vain for a cab. Carradine struck me somehow as unusual, even for the City. He was spilling over, out of his stereotype, confused about his role.

'I've got things in my head that came from nowhere,' he said, 'things that don't make sense to me. Clues, I guess you'd call them.'

'Clues? Like what?'

'The World Tree,' he muttered, 'something about the World Tree, Richie. No, that's not it. Damn it, but it'll come to me in a moment. I'm sure it will.'

'Yggdrasil,' I said, 'the World Tree.'

'That's it. Yggdrasil. Queer sort of a word, isn't it?'

I remembered Yggdrasil. The wooden fist of Viking legend, wrapped around the world, extending its branches everywhere. Only my Yggdrasil wasn't wood, but something else alive. In my mind, I had a crazed vision of a composite creature, with iceboxes and radiograms and vacuum cleaners and electric chairs and telephone exchanges for nerve endings, trucks and aircraft and cranes and streamlined trains for limbs, and perhaps a Bomb for a brain.

'It has something to do with Daine, and the way he ran the City. It's not much to go on, but it's a start.'

I knew where to go now. I started steering Carradine, rather than him supporting me. He hesitated, but followed my lead. I guessed he wanted the answers too.

'We'll have to find out who Daine's heir is. Or maybe it's not an heir, exactly. Maybe we're after his ghost.'

'What do you mean?'

'I don't know. I saw him dead. There's no doubt about that. And things have changed since he got remaindered, but I've got this feeling – call it a detective's intuition – that he left something of himself behind. The City's still his in some way, held in trust.'

It was in a sleazy neighbourhood, but then again so were most places in the City. We approached it cautiously, in case the cops had it staked out. I had Carradine walk up and down the street several times, acting suspiciously. Nobody came for him. He stood on the steps outside the building, tattered cloak flapping like a scarecrow's nightshirt, and signalled to me.

Then we went up to my office to do some serious detective work.

12

In my office, Carradine cat-napped, snoring vigorously, hammocked between two chairs. The irritating neon sign outside the window strobed the room, broken Venetian blinds breaking the light into bright bars. I had the radio on low, in case they interrupted the broadcast with any bulletins that might lead me to the new Night Mayor. Meanwhile, I went through my files.

I call it an office, but it's also an apartment. I was sure I lived there, but I couldn't remember if there was a bedroom attached. If there was, I couldn't find it now. There were plenty of filing cabinets, with half-full bottles, and an empty water cooler that I evidently kept as an excuse to have a tower of paper cups. While Carradine slept, I tried to take away the taste of defeat and Kelly's coffee with a shot or fourteen. It was supposed to be good whisky, but the thin layer of dust in the bottom of all the cups didn't improve the taste any. Daine's booze had tasted like sugared water, mine was like sugared water with added grit. I licked my teeth, and started digging.

At some earlier, more enthusiastic, stage in my career as a detective I had compiled dossiers on everyone of any importance in the City. Cotten of the *Inquirer* must have helped me out, because every file was complete with news clippings and candid photographs. Those friends on the police force who would doubtless fail to remember me these nights had even let me have carbons of a few rap sheets. I considered calling up one of contacts and declaring my innocence, but decided against it. Until I had myself out of the frame, it wasn't a good idea to drag anyone into the case who wasn't there already. Besides, I had had time to pick up the late edition. PRIVATE EYE SOUGHT IN DAINE SLAYING was the headline, and Cotten's byline was over the story. The way he wrote it, I guessed he was as sure as anyone that I had been the trigger man. All my friends would be busy with their ink erasers trying to scrub me out of their address books. Especially my cop friends.

I trusted Carradine because he was different, but trusting him led to mistrusting everyone else. 'It's like being a reverse zombie,' he said, 'I'm alive, but everybody else is dead.' Enough people were after me. The fewer who knew where I was, the better.

Someone had been at the office, of course. The door had been kicked in, and the chaos rearranged. They hadn't found anything, and had gone back to their usual haunts. Cops or hoods, it didn't matter. They had probably both paid a visit. And they'd call again later, which was why I was working by a single-bulb desk lamp, quickskimming the liquid and document overflow from my filing cabinets. The frosted glass panel with my name on it had been cracked, but that could have happened at any time.

I pulled the Daine file first. It was the thickest. There he was in all his splendour, gazing blithely out of society-column illustrations, going into or coming out of some swank nightspot or other, with a gorgeous girl on either arm. Socialite Lyn Bari, nightclub *chanteuse* Lizabeth Scott, ecdysiast Rita Hayworth, fiery *senorita* Dolores Del Rio: they had all been names in his little black book. No wonder he looked so smug in most of his photographs. Recently, his 'constant companion' had been Rhonda Fleming. In one shot, Daine could be seen in the background while Rhonda was trying to scratch out the eyes of a competitor for his attentions, Arlene Dahl. The headline was

CAT FIGHT CUTIES! Wealth, power, dames: Daine couldn't have Dreamed up a better situation for himself in the City if he had been trying.

Most of the clippings were boring stories about charity functions, civic balls, philanthropic gestures, patriotic speeches or War Bond drives. There were endless party guest lists, with Daine's name – and certain others – circled. There were even inventories of his collection, with fabulous sums paid for a succession of sculptures, paintings, original scores and manuscripts or items of historical interest. In one picture, Daine was showing off his most prized trophies – the longbow with which Errol Flynn had driven the Normans out of Sherwood Forest, Leslie Howard's Ku Klux Klan hood and the original telephone invented by Don Ameche. There were gossip-column items, too, about such-and-such an amusing practical joke played on William Powell or this-and-that fancy present given to Carole Lombard. All very innocuous stuff. I had underlined the few shady connections which made it into the open.

Daine's closest pals were Claude Rains, the radio criminologist, and Otto Kruger, who was some sort of phony-baloney mystic. They were part of the Cicero Club, a society which met once a month or so to discuss famous unsolved mysteries. I had made notations by the Cicero Club stories. There must be something spicy in that combination: Daine could have solved at least three quarters of the crimes in the City just by owning up. And in their own dossiers, I found a few suggestive hints to the effect that Rains and Kruger were hardly spotless. Nothing overt, of course, but a few too many underworld contacts, a few too many mysterious bequests. Rains and Daine had owned a piece of Kirk Douglas, a promising young heavyweight whose career had been ended by a 'cerebral haemorrhage' in the ring, just in time for Kruger and a few others to collect a parcel by betting against him. And who was the bruiser who gave Kirk the big headache? Our old friend Mike Mazurki. When Daine had first come to the City, he had – I knew for a fact – taken over a large proportion of the vice business that had been run by Paul Muni, a mobster whose empire had fallen thanks mainly to the investigative efforts and single-mindedness of – you guessed it – criminologist Claude Rains. I had been trying to get a membership list for the Cicero Club, but the only other name I could come up with was George Macready, a scarfaced iceman who had a profitable share of the City's gambling and was best known for his sword-extruding walking stick. Nice people.

There were other possibles – mostly underworld figures – but I discounted them as red herrings. Sydney Greenstreet was too old to be taking much of an interest, and had in any case become obsessed with some obscure quest of his own, neglecting his 'business'. Whoever the new man at the top was 1 would have staked plenty that his first move would be to squeeze Sydney out and add his former holdings to the pot. A chubby young man called Laird Cregar appealed to me as a suspect, if only because he had the habit of being seen loitering around places where beautiful women had just been strangled. But his plump face and crazed eyes suggested he was merely a psychotic. A more refined psycho than, say, Lee Marvin or Neville Brand, but a crazy's still a crazy and I didn't think someone that far gone could take up where Daine had left off. Cregar might lounge in silk pajamas and stuff himself with Parisian chocolates, but he was still a supporting heavy, a cringing underling who'd never last at the top of the criminal tree. George Sanders was out of the running now, having been hauled in as an enemy spy, but I'd be interested in knowing who precisely had tipped the Feds off to his brokerage for state secrets in the suburbs. Orson Welles was too busy with his radio show, Bela Lugosi could never get any master plan together beyond his next insane experiment, Vincent Price wouldn't rank with the major bad guys until horror pictures caught on again, and Zachary Scott's thin moustache betrayed his lack of substance as a mastermind.

My best bets were still Rains and Kruger. One, or both, of them could easily have opted to give Daine a hot lead push and taken the operation over. Or maybe it was more complicated than that. Maybe Daine had somehow cooperated in his own extermination, but transferred something of himself to his heir. In Otto Kruger's file, there were a bunch of crackpot pieces on various psychic phenomena – hypnotism, mental telepathy, oneiromancy, possession. Maybe Daine had gone *dybbuk* and passed into another body. Metempsychosis, that was called. It was screwy, but so was everything else in this case. I had the feeling I had been given most of the pieces, but not the boxfront picture to tell me how to put them together.

I looked at some pictures of Rhonda Fleming. She favoured very tight gowns with large pieces cut out of them. There had to be a woman in the picture. With me, there invariably was. I took my automatic out and rested its cold metal on Rhonda's paper torso. She was some kind of a woman all right. Cute as lace pants, sharp as a stiletto and hungry as a Bengal tiger. I hoped we'd get to meet some time soon.

'We interrupt this broadcast,' said an announcer, fading out José Iturbi, 'to bring you an important newsflash…'

The urgent tones startled Carradine awake, and with a cry, he fell off his chairs. The furniture tangled in his long legs.

'…Captain of Detectives Barton MacLane has called out the National Guard to assist in the search for private detective Richard Quick, who is still at liberty. Quick is wanted in connection with the brutal murder earlier this evening of millionaire philanthropist Truro…'

I turned off the radio, wrenching the knob off the set. It was the same old guff. I had heard it all before.

'Perhaps you'd better get out of the City,' suggested Carradine.

'Perhaps there isn't an outside to go to.'

'Sure there is.' He smiled. 'I remember the prairies. Why, I remember being in a stagecoach, with the Apaches attacking, and out on the road with Henry Fonda and the Okies and shooting Tyrone Power while he was hanging up a picture…'

'Are you sure, John?' I knew how memories like that worked. Right now, in the familiar clutter of my office, I had this feeling in my water that I had never been in the room before. Someone's hand had torn away three-quarters of the days of the desktop calendar and filled a wastebasket with them, and someone had written girls' names and telephone numbers on the blotters. I recognised my own handwriting and the way I would scrunch up a calendar date before throwing it away. But I couldn't see myself actually scribbling or tearing. That had been someone else. Maybe it was me. Maybe I was the ghost. 'Are you sure?'

Carradine's eyes saw faraway sights, and he ran a hand through his shoulder-length hair. 'No, now you come to mention it, I'm not. Those things happened, I know that, and I could swear they happened to me. But maybe in other lives, or in…'

I lit a cigarette. '…In Dreams, John, Dreams. There are too many maybes in the City, too many dreams within Dreams. You were asleep just now; were you dreaming?'

'Yes, I…'

He looked scared for a moment; then almost scary, stroking his moustache with long, thin fingers, thoughtfully tonguing sharp teeth.

I exhaled a cloud of smoke. The neon striped it in the air. 'What were you dreaming?'

'I'm not certain. I was dead, but alive. I was wearing evening clothes like a dress extra, and I had flour in my hair. It was somewhere in Eastern Europe, I think. The men wore lederhosen and the women gypsy blouses. It was modern times, but there was no war. And I was thirsty… it's difficult to say, I wanted… to… drink… *blood*.'

The tall man was racked with self-disgust. I couldn't help but feel for him. 'Don't worry, John, it's just a dream. Just another role seeping through.'

'Ugh. It was repulsive. Were there any clues in your files?'

I riffled the papers on the desk. 'Just names. Claude Rains, Otto Kruger, George Macready. They were tied in with Daine, maybe still are...'

Under the files, the telephone rang. Carradine and I looked at each other. The ringing was startlingly loud. I knew that if there was anyone else at all in the building, they'd be alerted to it. It grated on my eardrums, set my teeth on edge, shook loose all the pains I thought I had lost.

'They'll give up,' I said. We stood hunched over the desk, frozen like waxworks. The telephone rang twenty, forty, a hundred times, and kept on ringing. It got louder, more painful. I saw a bead of sweat drip from Carradine's forehead, trickle down his cheek, perch on the end of his moustache and fall with a small splash onto a picture of Rhonda Fleming posing in a backless, strapless, practically frontless dress. 'They can't possibly expect an answer.'

Carradine was shaking, holding onto my desk with both hands to keep steady. I followed the telephone cord and found where it went into the wall. One tug and the noise would go away. But whoever was calling would know someone was here. Perhaps the cops had a man calling up every half hour, and a squad car ready to be here in seconds. They had let me slip through the net earlier; they wouldn't exactly be fans of mine. And the National Guard were on the case now. They'd have much bigger guns than me, and be authorised to use them. I put my hands over my ears and prayed that the ringing would stop. Everything in the office was vibrating. I knew how the Hunchback of Notre Dame had gone deaf, with the tinnitus for ever in his head.

With a strangled, gargling shriek, Carradine fell over, frothing at the mouth, arms waving. A pile of documents, clippings and photographs fell with him and drifted around him as he writhed on the floor. The ringing stopped, and I gave a silent thanks to St Bernadette of Lourdes for the miracle. Then I realised Carradine had knocked the phone off the hook when he fell, and that the receiver was dangling under the desk...

'Tunney,' said a female voice, tiny but shouting, 'Tunney, pick up the damned phone if you're there. We need to talk. Tunney...'

Almost laughing, I took the receiver. 'Hello,' I said.

'Tunney. Yggdrasil be praised. Listen, I'm at the bus station. You need help. My name is Susan. Susan Bishopric. We've met. We lobbied the British Board of Dream Classification over the blasphemy rulings. I Dreamed *The Parking Lottery*.'

'I'm sorry, lady,' I said, 'but you must have the wrong number. My name isn't Tunney.'

I hung up, and went to help Carradine. He had stopped twitching violently, but he wasn't out of his *petit mal* yet. His limbs were working independently of each other.

'Snap out of it,' I said, flicking him lightly about the cheeks with my fingers, 'we've got to get out of here. That might not have been a wrong number. Somebody could have put the finger on us.'

He wiped the froth from his lips with a huge handkerchief, and apologised for his behaviour. 'I don't know what got into me. It was the telephone. It didn't sound... natural.'

'I know what you mean. But I'm not sure there's any nature at all in this case.'

Outside my office window, the irritating neon sign flashed on and off, casting rigid bars of light into the room. Prison bars.

13

'Where to, lady?' asked the cab driver. Susan recognised the desperate whine in his voice, but read the name off his licence anyway. Elisha Cook Jr, professional loser, fall guy and victim. Cook had the face of a shrunken Peter Pan, lost in adulthood.

'Cruise,' said Susan. 'I just want to get out of the rain.'

'It's your dough, sister.' Cook manhandled the meter flag. It ran like *a click-click-clack off the beaten track as the Brownsville Train comes through, like the tick-tack-toe of Old Black Joe...*

Susan snapped, 'I ain't your sister, bud!' Was that correct? Ain't? Bud?

'Pardon me for livin', lady.'

'One of these days, if you work at it real hard.'

'Say –' Cook's worn veneer of toughness dissolved – 'quit ridin' me. I ain't hostile.'

'Sorry. It's late.' She had miscalculated: she thought everyone in the City insulted each other. 'I've had a rough evening.'

'Me too. I been beaten up by hoods, framed on a murder rap, beaten up by cops, sent up the river, beaten up by prison bulls, got a last-minute reprieve from the governor, and been beaten up by my girl.'

'Sounds tough.'

'In spades, lady.'

Yeah: in spades, on ice, eight ways to sundown, from here to eternity. It was a different language. An idiot Dream if ever there was. She knew she mustn't give in to it. There was a risk of ending up like Tunney. On the phone, he had sounded in a bad way. She had called him up from the bus station as soon as she got into the City. It had been ridiculously easy to track him down. Richard Quick, Private Enquiry Agent, was in the Yellow Pages under Detectives. Humphrey Bogart, Dick Powell and Alan Ladd had big display adverts with prominent slogans: 'No Divorce Work', 'Trouble Is My Business', 'This Gun for Hire'. Quick was buried in a column of single-line ads for grade-B bloodhounds, between Dick Purcell and Ron Randell. His irresistible come-on was 'Investigations – Cheap!'

For now, she'd have to leave Tunney to his own problems and go after Daine.

Over the smart street clothes Dr Groome had come up with, she wore a transparent raincoat. She must look like a cellophane-wrapped sweet. A hard-boiled sweet. She checked her lipstick in the cab's mirror. Her face had come out more like Ella Raines than Gene Tierney. Too thin-lipped for high-gloss romance, but pretty in a hard-edged, sparkly fashion. She would have to get used to the way she looked in black and white.

In the short time she had been in the City, she had been propositioned by a well-dressed lush, witnessed a gangland execution and been pursued through a deserted subway station by a bulky killer. This would take some getting used to.

The Princetown psychs had simply lost track of Tunney. They had monitored him as far as Poverty Row, then the Dream had upside-downed. A major shadow reality shift. This place looked solid enough from the inside, but it could change as quickly as your mind.

Susan Bishopric, assassin. That was a new paragraph for her curriculum vitae. Kill Truro Daine. In this Dream, that was tantamount to putting out a contract on God. But God makes mistakes. Ask Job. Daine had been caught and convicted back in the real world. That would put a dent in his omnipotence. Even here.

Dreaming herself into the City had been easy. Dr Groome had hooked Susan up to Yggdrasil and floated her in the third tank. Trefusis had wished her luck, Juliet had told her to shoot straight, and the psych techs had tried not to look her in the eyes. Then she had descended through the familiar outer layers of Dreamspace, and faded in on the bus.

She found to her surprise that she didn't mind the clothes. Whenever she Dreamed historical, she always assumed multiple garments would be uncomfortable and cumbersome, like a non-protective flakjak. Actually, she quite liked nylons, padded shoulders and her hat. And pockets were a revelation. Her gun hung heavy in her suit coat, resting cool against her hip. She put a hand in her pocket and felt the grip of the weapon. Juliet had given her a few pointers, but indream Susan found her experience as Vanessa Vail somehow more confidence-building. Vanessa could shoot the eye out of a gnat at fifty paces. Susan hoped the skill would come back to her if it came to guns.

Cook drove clumsily, keeping up a constant stream of chatter. Susan volumed him down. Poor little chump. Tired eyes flashing in the rearview mirror, childish enthusiasm bubbling over. He was marked for a fade-out long before the finish. Susan couldn't think of a film where he had made it alive to the end credits.

The cab paused at an intersection to give right of way to a car chase. Edward G. Robinson careened down Elm Street and screech-turned onto Sunset Boulevard. The only things holding his stolen sedan together were bulletholes. Lieutenant Ward Bond was at the wheel of the police convertible hot on his tail. Detective Van Heflin stood up in the car, hat clamped to his head, firing his tommy gun from the hip.

'He killed a dame,' explained Cook, 'strangled her with a string of pearls. The cops will get him. Nobody gets away with murder in this City.'

'There's always a first time.'

Experimentally, she flicked the cold steel safety catch on and off in her pocket. She was wearing a groove in her thumb.

What to do next? Hole up, hide out, get the measure of the Dream. Then start feeding in a few amendments. That would offbalance Daine. She was certain she could make some substantial changes. Perhaps Daine wouldn't like what she was planning for his self-designed afterlife. She concentrated on the interior doorhandles of the cab and changed their design several times, just for practice, then smoothed them out entirely. No problem.

Should she try to get in touch with Tunney again? He was stuck in the City somewhere. The tentative diagnosis was that he had been too close to Daine's fantasies and been subsumed into the structure of the Dream. Deep down, he had felt too much at home in the City to want to see it deleted from the Yggdrasil file.

All this might have the makings of a Prix Italia memoir. There were very few Dreams about Dreams and Dreaming. But first, she would have to come through it alive (relatively easy: keep repeating, none of this is real, it's only a Dream) and sane (a horse of a different colour: like in *The Wizard of Oz*)…

She looked down at her feet, and ruby slippers briefly superimposed on her patent-leather pumps. *Follow the Yellow Brick Road! Follow the Yellow Brick Road*… Stop!

That had been bothering her since she hit the City. Was her own brain kinking her around, or was Daine trying to tie her mental patterns in knots? They hadn't been able to tell her whether he would automatically sense any new presences in his Dream, and lateral thinking was the Dreamer's occupational disease. Irrelevant associations dredged out of the mind's mire of trace memories, subconscious detritus and stamped-on feelings. There was only one cure: reality. Of which there was precisely none about. She would have to put up with occasional

Sinatra-outs until she was out of the tank.

Outside an elevated railroad station men in raincoats with collars turned up and hats with brims snapped down bustled busily, coming from and going to nowhere in particular. Robert Walker, a soldier in uniform, was fighting his way through the crowd, a bunch of flowers and a marriage licence in his hand, wading against the human tide to the shining spot under the clock where Judy Garland stood, dressed in angelic white that stood out against the drab extras, waiting anxiously. Susan checked the clock. It was two thirty. Down the road a little, a streetlamp spotlit a grubby newsstand.

Cook idled the cab.

'Extree! Extree!' cried the freckle-faced Mickey Rooney. 'Private eye wanted for murder! Extree! Extree!'

'Hold on here a minute.'

'Sure, sister. I got all night.'

Susan reached for the doorhandle and found only smooth upholstery. She flipped her mind and the handle came back, a size or two too large. She opened the door, slipped the hood of her see-through up over her hat and stepped into the rain.

The newsboy, cap turned backwards, waved his paper in the air, still shouting.

'Can I have an *Inquirer*?'

'For def, doll.' He pulled a paper off his stand and accepted some small change. 'By the way, I get off in half an hour.'

'Fresh.'

'As eggs,' Rooney grinned and nervously ran a wet hand under his cap, smoothing his tousled hair.

Susan stood under an awning and read the extra.

Banner headline: PRIVATE EYE WANTED FOR MURDER! Smaller-type captions: 'Philanthropist Truro Daine Still Dead. Enquiry Agent Richie Quick Wanted by Police. "No Statement at This Time," Says Commissioner Neil Hamilton. "We'll Fry the Rat Yet!" Vows Chief of Detectives Barton MacLane.'

There was a picture of Daine doing the samba at a nightclub, and a grainy passpic of Tom Tunney passed off as Richie Quick. They both looked dead.

The text, after the first one-sentence paragraph, was a jumble of meaningless words. The only other story was a flyer about the war. After the front page, the rest of the paper was blank.

'Extree! Extree!' shouted the newsboy, 'Spine-Snapper Strikes Again. Scotland Yard Baffled! Extree! Extree!'

That paper was for someone else. Susan recognised Basil Rathbone and Nigel Bruce, somehow not quite anachronistic in deerstalker and bowler hat, as they consulted over their extra. Bruce was flustered, but Rathbone seized on a minute clue and rattled off a string of deductions.

'Ah-ha, Bruce, the clouds part. I do believe this bloody business betrays the involvement of our old friend Professor Lionel Atwill. Evidently the reports of his death in the sewers of Montevideo were exaggerated. The gorilla footprints, the Ecuadorian pygmy poison and the six-fingered alabaster hand are most suggestive. Quick, the game is afoot!'

They hurried off, Rathbone with an excited spring in his step, Bruce huffing and puffing to keep up with him, and passed out of the rain into a street wedged thick with fog. Susan could see a gaslamp vaguely in the murk, and hear the clip of hooves on cobblestones. That was another part of the City.

This was a weird Dream. She ducked back into the cab.

In the mirror, Cook's eyes were white marbles. The windshield was a white spiderweb of cracks centring on a neat black circle. There was a matching neat black circle in Cook's forehead too.

Cliché.

14

Ruger and Rains were our most up-front suspects, so I decided to start with the mystery man of the Cicero Club, George Macready. I knew a little about him. He had come from out of town with a fortune, was known to have been a vociferous *Bund* supporter before the war and had set up a chain of more or less above-board casinos in the districts where gambling was more or less legal. He had a high-rolling joint on the *SS Nocturne*, a ship anchored outside the limits, and some nasty rumours had floated back on the tides along with a well-dressed corpse or two. But by far the worst of his establishments was the Noir et Blanc, a palatial clipjoint on the waterfront. Some people said that gambling should be illegal throughout the City. Other people muttered that, the way Macready had it set up, what went on in his places wasn't really gambling. There were plenty of conflicting stories about the way he got the scar that ran from temple to chin down the right side of his face. None of them were pretty. On the side, he ran an art gallery with Vincent Price, which didn't sound exactly legitimate either.

Carradine and I decided he was most likely to be in the Noir et Blanc. Besides, neither of us liked the idea of the swim out to the *Nocturne*. There were sharks out in the bay, and they didn't get fed often enough. The waterfront was a vile district, further gone even than Chinatown. The worst elements of the Latin Quarter, little Araby, New Haiti and the Occupied Sector flowed together in an open sewer of vice, crime and callousness. Brownstones cosied up to slums, police cars were armoured, and everything was for sale. A row of dubious cafes with misspelled French names huddled together, while the streets were aswarm with vendors hawking bogus curios, limping sailors down on their luck, scuttling coolies with slit eyes and concealed daggers, and pop-eyed black zombies lurching on mysterious missions. I wondered if Anna May Wong had passed this way. Through the squalor threaded a well-guarded street. Limousines slid across the asphalt, decadent thrill-seekers cringing behind their curtained windows. Macready had men posted on the sidewalks to protect his customers' money on their way to the casino. After they left, they were on their own. We were too hot to take a cab, so we just sauntered along with the crowds.

I was hoping the cops down here would be too busy lining their pockets to pay much attention to the all-points bulletin out on me. We hadn't seen the National Guard yet. Carradine caught a half-naked Moroccan boy with his hand deep in my pocket, and threw him over a low wall. Dogs barked and snapped, and we heard the sneak thief running barefoot into a maze of alleyways, bomb sites and derelict hotels. I still had my gun and what was left of Sterling Hayden's money. Perhaps I should try to pick up a little extra at Macready's tables. Then again, perhaps not. In one of my newspaper clippings, he was quoted as having said, 'I make my own luck.' The suicide rate in this quarter was unnaturally high, and the insurance companies had established a definite connection between owing large sums of money to George Macready and accidental death. There was enough blood on the streets down here already. A crowd had gathered around one of the piers, where Marlon Brando and Lee J. Cobb were tearing chunks out of each other with docker's hooks. We were offered a variety of tempting odds by a rat-faced freak with a clutch of money in one hand and promissory notes in the other. I passed.

'There,' said Carradine. The Noir et Blanc was a palace all right, lit up like a carnival float. Flags of all nations hung like gibbeted criminals from a row of poles just under the roof. It was probably an optical illusion, but the place seemed to be flying more eagles and swastikas than stars and stripes. Gargoyles spewed rainwater. Crowds of men and women were swarming up the front steps to the three revolving doors. They looked like sacrifices crushing themselves into the mouths of Moloch. A gigantic neon roulette wheel revolved under the Noir et Blanc sign.

'Quite a sight, isn't it?'

We pressed into the throng and allowed ourselves to be sucked forwards, up the steps. I wasn't sure that our clothing would pass muster at the doors, but others in the crowd were even more outlandish and uncivilised. I saw the major-domo turn away a couple weighed down with medal ribbons and jewels, while admitting a fat young man in a greasy fez and ragged robe. We were let through with barely a curled lip, and found ourselves in a foyer hardly smaller than a pyramid. It would have been a good place to hold a torchlight rally. Macready must have enlisted the services of Cecil B. DeMille as an architect. The place was done up in his trademarked colossal style, with a huge pair of well-muscled stone legs standing astride the doorway to the main casino. The ceiling, inconceivably far above our heads and leprous with chandeliers, cut off the legs at mid-thigh. I had the impression the statue extended through the upper floors. The gigantically helmeted head of some biblical hero would stick out through the roof and stand like an Easter Island monolith among the chimneys and machine-gun emplacements, jewelled eyes blazing with golem life.

We held on to our coats for fear of never seeing them again, and mingled with the doomed souls. Doors five times the height of the average giraffe opened between the statue's ankles, and the latest intake of victims were swept inside. We went along with them.

The central cavern of the Noir et Blanc was the gambling hell Dante might have designed. The roulette wheels were sunk in circular pits. The most irredeemably damned, in their white dinner jackets and turbans or strapless black sheaths and dripping jewellery, clogged up the lower circles, dropping chips onto the grid as if casting swill to the pigs. At the very lowest level, a wheel fully twelve feet across was spun by a pair of mountainous Turkish wrestlers in tiny loincloths, while a bent and crippled croupier, Mischa Auer, shrieked numbers at the losers. People had been trampled to the floor around the wheel. Auer was suspended in a hanging basket, his dead legs dangling beneath him, reaching out with a surreally long scoop to dredge the chips into a central sinkhole. A girl lunged over the grid, screaming that she had made a mistake, fingers just missing the disappearing chips. One of the wrestlers tipped her up by her ankles, and she too vanished into the hole, high-heeled pumps kicking as she was swallowed by whatever machine or animal lurked below. The wheel kept spinning, the damned kept pouring away their money.

The higher tiers housed lesser wheels, chemin de fer, blackjack, slot machines, *vingt-et-un,* baccarat, five-card stud. Stricken friends and dangerous parasites, penniless would-be gamblers seeking a vicarious thrill and subtle pickpockets in the pay of the house mingled with the addicts. Silent orientals passed among the clientele, serving drinks and notes of credit. Two czarist officers, bulky in their comic-opera uniforms, solemnly played Russian roulette, each downing a drink every time the firing pin of their revolver came down on an empty chamber. The din was intolerable: overlapping dialogue in several languages, dowagers with laughter like painted nails down a blackboard, the endless rattle of the wheels, occasional gunshots, screams of unknown origin, the gravel-under-waves chink of piles of money turning over again and again, the shouts of losers. And somewhere, behind it all, a bland jazz band. One of the White Russians lost and the other drained a blood-spattered glass, his hand shaking as he collected his winnings.

'That's the Count Charles Boyer,' said Carradine, pointing at an impassive, middle-aged man who was throwing a fistful of ribbon-bound documents onto a table. 'He's trying to gamble away his estate before it falls to the Nazis, but his lifelong losing streak has changed. He keeps winning.'

'A sad story.'

'All stories here are sad.'

We worked our way around the central tier, hands in pockets, and came out in an ornamental garden open to the stars. A glass roof, hundreds of feet above us, kept out the rain. There was a mercury pool for losers to reflect in while they blew their brains out. The staff were just removing the latest crop of bodies. Curt Bois was filling a bucket with rings, watches and empty wallets.

'Macready will be upstairs,' I said. 'Let's go quietly.'

We found ourselves in a hall where a masked ball was in progress. Streamers flew through the air, revellers contorted to the music. There was a vaguely medieval theme: knights and ladies, fools and brigands. One party had come as a dragon and were doing a conga through the dancing couples, tail disintegrating even as the giant head bobbed up and down.

There was a grand marble staircase, spiralling up to the eaves and the upper areas of the casino. It was guarded by more muscular wrestlers, dressed as barbarian warriors.

'There's your man, Richie.'

Carradine pointed. George Macready, immaculately suited, deadly stick in one hand, was halfway up his stairs, talking with a party of high-ranking Nazis. 'Martin Kosleck, he's their minister of propaganda,' Carradine told me. 'Paul Lukas, the butcher of Bratislava. And the woman is Katina Paxinou. She performs unnatural experiments on prisoners in the concentration camps. They say she's been able to transplant a gorilla's brain into a human body, or maybe a human brain into a gorilla's body.'

'Quite a sweetheart. Nice company our boy is keeping, eh?

Even if he's not the new Night Mayor, he's certainly up there on my list of notable detriments to the community.'

Macready and his group turned away from us and drifted up towards the darkened area near the roof before disappearing through a doorway.

'So, all we have to do is get past Gog and Magog, and we can have a little talk.'

Carradine and I sauntered across the dance floor. Zorro leaped through an enormous fountain, but tripped and fell face first into the water. Everyone within six feet was soaked. A scythe-toting Death turned round and screamed furiously at the bandit chief. A monkey in a fringed vest, a plumed sombrero tied to its head, shot into my legs, pulled at my trench coat and showed off his teeth. Carradine kicked it out of the way.

The crowds parted. An oriental girl dressed as a matador wrenched off her domino and threw herself at me. Our teeth gritted as we kissed.

'Hiya, American sojer johnny,' she cooed. 'You got my missing knife?'

'Hi, Anna, could you...'

But she was gone before I could finish asking her for help, borne away by three identically dressed musketeers, waving her whip in the air, and lost in the crowds again. I saw Zeppo Marx sitting glumly, out of the action as usual, looking at his watch, ignoring the festivities.

The wrestlers were even more enormous up close.

'We need a diversion,' I shouted over the cacophony. Carradine nodded, but we didn't have an idea for one.

However, just then the dragon's head came off. Underneath had been a midget sitting on the shoulders of a tall black man. The midget was smoking a cigar and had a tommy gun. He fired into the air, and a chandelier crashed down. Everybody screamed and tried to get out of range. The wrestlers moved as a team towards the troublemakers, and we circled round behind them.

Carradine picked up a sword a Sir Lancelot had dropped, and we ran up the steps towards Macready's lair. The gun went off again, and chips of marble flew from the steps ahead of us.

We hit the doors at a run, and burst through.

It had, of course, been too easy.

In Macready's large private office, guns were levelled at us. The gambling king stood to one side, wrapped in a black kimono, a white scarf knotted at his throat. The Nazis had left, but there was a huge portrait of *der Fuhrer* himself, Anton Diffring, over the desk.

'Mr Quick,' he rasped, 'welcome to Noir et Blanc. This gentleman is Captain of Detectives Barton MacLane. He has been most anxious to meet you. And these people with guns are National Guardsmen. I would appreciate it if you gave up without a fight. We've only just redecorated.'

MacLane, a flab-faced, mean-eyed boxer type, chomped a cigar. 'You're unner arrest, flatfoot.'

Slowly, I took my fists out of my pockets and opened them empty. I spread them in benediction, and reached up for some air.

'I surrender,' I said.

'Whaddya mean, ya bum,' shouted MacLane, 'ya resistin' arrest.'

The guns came up, the safeties came off. Then the action started.

15

Something popped inside John Carradine's head, and he cartwheeled across the room, dodging bullets. He collided with the Guardsmen, and they went down in a tangle.

Struggling to his feet, he realised he was waving his sword. Things were happening too fast to keep up with. The voice in his head, Yggdrasil, told him what to do. He wasn't obliged to follow his own scenario any more, but he knew he would have to obey the voice now. This was a crucial stage in the main plot.

Macready raised his stick, cruel mouth curving like a second scar, and a foot-long blade sprang out. The gambling king slashed downwards and, although he stepped back, Carradine could feel the cold trace of the knifepoint parting his clothes, drawing a slice down his skinny ribs. Before Macready could thrust, Carradine parried perfectly. Sparks flew.

Macready unbelted his kimono, Carradine threw off his cloak. They circled each other, making probing moves. Carradine felt he had the measure of his enemy. The two men fought in the centre of the office. Carradine hacked at the other man's stick, and a length of wood flew away. But there was a steel core, and Macready fenced on, undeterred. He was the more skilled swordsman. With a lucky stroke, Carradine gave his opponent a cut on his left cheek. If it healed, he would have matching scars now. Macready wiped his wound with a sleeve, and radiated hatred.

'Die, scarecrow popinjay!'

Everyone else in the room was crowded against the walls, out of range of the swinging swords. Carradine vaulted up on the desk and made moves around Macready's head, while Macready struck at Carradine's dancing legs, missing repeatedly. Carradine leaped and the two men went down, grappling, weapons lost. Macready pushed Carradine's chin upwards, fingers digging into his throat. Locked together, they rolled across the carpet. With Macready under him, Carradine felt his enemy go rigid, then limp.

Macready had rolled onto his own blade.

Carradine stood up, bleeding from several cuts. He touched his side, and his hand came away bloody.

'Look, Richie. It's… *red!*'

Richie Quick took his hat off and stared. Carradine knew that something momentous was happening. The voice congratulated him.

'Bring him down,' sneered the policeman, MacLane.

'No,' shouted Richie.

The guns went off again, and Carradine felt the thumps across his chest.

Finally assured that he had been truly alive, he died.

PART III

LADY IN THE DARK

16

Susan could have sworn the bullethole in Cook's forehead turned into an eye and winked at her. It was possible. In Dreams, anything was possible. She should know that.

Still rattled, she walked away from the cab, leaving the remains in the front seat. The taxi hummed in the road, motor idling, meter ticking over. Traffic passed it by. Susan had tagged a uniformed cop on the beat in the distance, and guessed she wouldn't want to talk to him about the corpse. She was new in the City. She didn't have any friends yet.

Cook had been Daine's way of welcoming her, she thought. Just one of those casual I-can-do-anything-I-want-any-time-I-want-and-make-you-like-it gestures so beloved of megalomaniacs, mass murderers and the Gunmint. But if the news item in the *Inquirer* was the literal truth, Daine was dead. That wasn't likely. Although his brainwaves were doing some interesting things on the printouts, Dr Groome had monitored no major trauma. Susan suspected her quarry had decided to stop wearing his own face for a while, so he could deal with his guests. And Tom Tunney must have been absurdly easy to deal with. In a way, it was perfect: faced with a would-be assassin, Daine had had himself killed and set up his opponent to take the consequences.

She was determined to be less biddable. If she could find

somewhere dry, she would be able to go on the offensive. If the psychs were on line, Daine should be losing some of his control. Even if he had been gulped down by the City, Tunney should be making some difference, feeding in his own amendments. And Susan thought she could transform the entire environment once she got a grip on it. After all, she had had more practice at manufacturing realities than Daine. Porno Dreams were of a notoriously low standard, blurry beyond the bedroom, giving the dreamer the feeling he was *dybbukking* a deep-sea diving suit rather than a human body.

She stopped at a newsstand. It was different from the one where she had bought her extra, but it was also manned by Mickey Rooney. He must be a fixture of the cliché. Without pausing for wisecracks, she picked up a cheap map. Down the street a block or two, she found a spot under a grocer's awning where she could pore over the map. It unfolded from a slim oblong into a sheet-sized square that flapped and fought in the wind and didn't bear much resemblance to what she'd seen of the City so far. It was particularly vague around the edges. Susan intuited that the Dream was evolving fast, recasting its inhabitants, twisting its externals.

Used to giving in to Dreams, she was learning how to fight back. This was no serial hallucination, in which the dreamer was trapped in the viewpoints of a succession of similies. Here, everyone who entered was free to be Dreamer. Daine needed that flexibility, but he must have been aware of the risks. He had been ready for Tunney. He thought he was ready for her.

Beyond the curtain of rain, strange forms moved. Susan wished Daine would show himself so they could struggle mind to mind and settle this thing. But the City Father would be out there in his maze, sending his cat's paws into battle, wearing down his enemies, squeezing their minds. In particular, she expected perils out of the flatties – murderous hoodlums, crooked cops, knife-wielding janitors – but she knew that if he stretched his mind a touch, Daine could make anything or anyone in the City into a weapon. Here, she could as easily be killed by Shirley Temple, Elmer Fudd or Lou Costello as by Jack Palance, Freddy Krueger or Anthony Perkins.

She tried to find herself on the map, but the printed boulevards and blocks writhed whenever she looked up at the street, making new patterns. Susan saw Escher mazes and Mobius strips. Annoyed, she crumpled the map and threw it into the gutter. It twisted into an origami boat and sailed off towards a sewer inlet. She heard an echo of the pirates' chorus from *The Sea Hawk* in the rain.

The awning flew back with a chainsaw rasp, and a cascade of rainwater came down on her head. The raincoat kept most of it off, but her hair got a soaking even under her hood. She thought it dry, and it was, but she could not make a dent in the downpour itself. She reached out across the street and tried to get an idea of the shape of a building she could dimly see. Its dimensions were easy to get a hold on. A brown stone, three storeys tall, derelict, with a squared-off roof, an arch of chimneys, a child's picture arrangement of windows and an imposing front doorway. The windows were gone entirely or boarded over. She closed her eyes, but could still see the building.

In her mind, she changed the picture. She stripped away the outer shell brick by brick, and massaged the essence of the structure, fashioning a gothic cathedral. Spires raised to the skies, lightning flashing around them, and windows filled with stained glass. The cathedral spread, squashing the buildings on either side like plasticine, then absorbing them entirely. Angels danced in the air and settled reverently into their alcoves. Paving stones stood up and were drawn into the new building.

The process was silent. Susan opened her eyes, and surveyed her handiwork. It was crude, a trifle unfinished and unformed – in any other Dream, she would have researched the externals rather than built on a whim – but it was what she wanted. She willed the great wooden doors open, and crossed the street. Inside, it would at least be dry.

She stepped through the doors, and found herself in total darkness. She had forgotten to imagine an interior. An easy mistake. She was used to fashioning scenery for the background. In Dreams, you always passed by more houses than you explored. There was no rain in the darkness, and she could make even its sound go away by concentrating hard for a few moments. In the darkness, the Dream was raw and formless. She made herself a cathedral, not quite in the spirit of the exterior, but roomy enough. The vast building gave her a feeling of power. Although she knew it must be tiny in comparison with the rest of the City, it *felt* enormous, and it was the feelings that counted. She made herself a pump organ, and Dreamed up a man to play it.

Lord Roger Marshaller, the most nearly decent of Vanessa Vail's suitors, emerged from the sacristy and walked across the aisle to the organ. Susan had combined the faces of several older men – a teacher, a holomeister, some singers – she had been smitten with between the ages of nine and twelve, then weathered them to make her composite even more appealing. Lord Roger was supposed to be a fantasy for bored romantics. His laughing blue eyes had steely grey flecks in them, and he was wont to pass huge, yet sensitive, fingers through his leonine mane of silver-grey hair. She had Dreamed Lord Roger as a former surgeon, still brooding because of his inability to save the life of his only child. He was also a Nobel laureate, a leading ice sculptor and a master horseman. Now, she gave him an unmatched musical talent too.

She sat down, unnoticed, in a pew, while Lord Roger limbered up. He played scales, flexing his surgeon-sculptor's hands. Then, he launched into 'Barbara Allen'.

> *In Scarlet Town, where I was born*
> *There is a fair maid dwellin'*
> *Made every lad cry "lack-a-day"*
> *For the love of Barbara Allen…*

Susan realised her mistake. A small jazz combo had popped out of nowhere and were arrayed around Lord Roger. A vocalist – Annie Belladonna, the teenage xenobiologist heroine of *The Sewer Thing* – enunciated the lyrics in Rosemary Clooney's voice. The music was sucking her in...

> *Twas in the merry month of May,*
> *When green buds they were swellin'*
> *And on his death-bed Sweet William lay*
> *For the love of Barbara Allen...*

The roof began to fade. Susan felt the rain come in. The music was louder in her mind, louder than anything. More and more instruments took up the melody, drowning out the frail lyric line. A choir appeared behind the altar, offering peculiar harmonies. The children opened too-large mouths in otherwise blank faces. The improvisation stretched on, drawing Susan into it, locking into set patterns of repetition which were as fascinating as the gaze of a cobra. The number might never end, and Susan would be caught for ever.

With a painful effort, she banished the music, and the cathedral fell silent. Annie Belladonna, the musicians, the choir, all were gone. Lord Roger slumped over the organ keyboard, the life whipped out of him. She gave it back, but he could only move jerkily, like an unwieldy puppet. Susan made him climb down from the organ and walk over to her, but his uncoordinated limbs reminded her too much of the zombies in Corin Santangelo's horror Dream *Eyeball Gougers from Italy*. She didn't want to see what she had done to his craggy yet handsome face, so she made him go away. He whisped out of his clothes, which hung man-shaped in the air for a second and then drifted to the floor.

She would have to be careful about her overconfidence binges.

Outside the cathedral, there would be a chauffeur-driven skimmer waiting for her. A sports model, with an andrew to pilot it.

She was right, only the anachronisms she tried to wedge into Daine's Dream didn't take. The skimmer was a long, black automobile. And the chauffeur was a liveried war veteran with a steel face and leather hands. That would just have to do.

She got into the back of the car, and was glad to see her unconscious had had the foresight to include a bar.

She poured herself a shot and knocked it back. It stung the back of her throat and fired in her belly. Shaking her head at the kick, she lashed out at the whole row of stores opposite her cathedral and dispelled them to dust. Gushers rose from disconnected water pipes, and the Dream matter sludged instantly.

Without being told, the chauffeur drove away. She was back in a vehicle again, but this time it was hers. She wondered how much control she had over the chauffeur. After Lord Roger, she intended to be careful. You couldn't just make and unmake people at will without working at it.

Also, she would have to find Daine. Best to start at the top.

'City Hall,' she said. 'I have to see a mayor.'

17

Steelface knew how to get to City Hall. Susan suspected Daine was making it easy. He thought he could mindblast her as simply as he had put Tunney out of the picture. And, he was probably curious about her. She mightn't be much, but in the self-awareness and independence stakes she was the only girl in town. This might be his idea of an escape, but in Daine's position she thought she'd go zooidal. She imagined a lifetime among her own Dreamed creations, knowing exactly what they would say next, exactly what was around every corner. No matter how vast a universe he made, Daine would still be trapped by the limits of his own imagination. He was probably far gone enough not to realise yet that he had jumped from one box into a smaller one.

All roads probably led to City Hall. Her chauffeur got her there with the minimum of distraction. There weren't any incidents to get in the way. No car chases or police roadblocks.

Insofar as the City had a business and commercial district, this was it. There were election posters up for the mayoral race. James Stewart was running against the incumbent, Brian Donlevy. Neither of them appeared to represent any particular party, and the election was being fought entirely on personalities. Stewart's slogan was 'War on Graft', Donlevy's 'Doing Things the Way They've Always Been Done'. Susan knew Stewart would win the election but never take office. That was how the story always goes: the young reformer wins in the end, but by the next picture the corrupt machine politicians are still in power. She wondered if Jimmy ever got tired of the cycle. She kept seeing copperplate graffiti on Stewart's posters, 'You can't fight City Hall.' Things weren't all that different back in the real world, she thought.

The City's administrative centre was like a giant-scaled village green, with three imposing municipal erections boxing it in. City Hall, Police Headquarters and the Metro-Goldwyn-Mayer Building. City Square was a cheerless park, with arrangements of black, white and grey flowers in beds, grey stretches of grass, and a monumental, black, floodlit statue of Truro Daine dressed as a Roman emperor, fiddle tucked under his chin, bow poised to saw down.

Susan had her chauffeur draw into a space beside City Hall marked RESERVED, and got out of the car. The square was empty, except for a pair of winos sleeping it off under the statue. She looked up at the statue and laughed. The black brows knit, and solid silver laurels bobbed. Like many great villains, Daine must have no conception of how ludicrous he appeared much of the time.

'Are you really in there, Daine?' she shouted.

Gigantic arms moved, and music was shaken from the stone violin. 'The Devil's Trill' by Tartini. More delusions of grandeur. Although the music was animated, only the arms moved. The face was frozen now, and the rest of the body was stone dead.

Over the shriek of the tune, Susan asked a question. 'Daine, do you know anything about Japanese monster flatties?'

She sat cross-legged on the grass and reached out to the bay. Casting her mind deep into the black waters, she created a whirlpool. It started as a funnelling current the size of a sea horse, then lengthened, sucking in a core of air. She made that air solid, and drew in stuff from the water and clouds of spinning gravel. Daine had made the bottom of his sea loose, like a big fishtank.

She imagined a musculature, a skeleton, a hide, pumping organs, glowing eyes. As her creation grew in strength, so she felt her own on the rise. Her upper arms began to swell, stretching tight the fabric of her suit. She caught it in time, and had them dwindle a little. She couldn't afford a Hulk-out now.

The two winos had been shocked awake by the infernal music, and scurried away from the statue.

'Hey, lady,' said one rummy, Walter Brennan, 'wuz you ever stung by a dead bee?'

They kept running, and were gone before Susan had a chance to figure out what that meant and whether she should answer it. The statue kept playing. The ground of the park rippled as if disturbed by colossal, underground moles. Gophers, rather: moles would be gophers here. Susan felt the power in the earth shaking up through her body.

Out on the bay, something enormous broke the surface. Miniature tidal waves swept up against the waterfront, tearing piers and jetties away, spilling over into the maze of streets, driving a human exodus before them. Susan dipped into her new toy, seeing the City spread out like a model in front of its water-washed eyes. She roared her delight, and clapped house-sized hands in the air above her scaled head. She lashed out with her tail, overturning ships, smashing down a lighthouse. Waves surged around her gargantuan thighs as she waded towards the shore.

Back as Susan, she heard her own voice, distorted by its passage through the cavernous reptile throat, shouting out in defiance. The ground still shook in time with the footsteps of the great beast. Whole sections of the City were trampled flat, buildings going down like balsa wood. Streets buckled, cars flew through the air like nursery toys, and matchstick model pylons flew apart.

Susan held her hands up in the air, and felt those other, claw-tipped hands tearing down Daine's Dream. Cuts and weals appeared where her surrogate hurt itself in its destructive frenzy, but she smoothed them away with a flick of her mind.

People ran through the square, screaming in Japanese. A rag-tag convoy in half-tracks and armoured cars passed by City Hall, their outriders churning up the flower beds. No one bothered Susan. She saw Charlton Heston standing up in a jeep, dressed as a desert general, his shirt open to the waist, binoculars hanging against his hairy chest. He signed his troops to move out. Artillery batteries opened up.

The army couldn't stop it. A tank hurled across the square, just missing the still-fiddling statue, and crunched into the side of the MGM Building. It lodged in the shattered brickwork as a million windows fell in tinkling shards to the sidewalk. The truck-sized stone Ars Gratia Artis lion on the roof mewled and leaped for a safer perch. Gunfire sounded like Chinese fireworks, and the great beast shrugged off the hurt as if it had been inconvenienced by gnats.

A squadron of biplanes flew low over the City, machine guns chattering. The Dawn Patrol was early. Susan heard them being knocked out of the skies. A bipedal beagle tall as a child, with a flying helmet and goggles, climbed out of a wrecked Sopwith Camel and brushed himself off, barking in pain. So much for Biggles and the Red Baron. The air force couldn't stop it either.

Then Susan's monster was in the square, towering above Daine's statue. She had seen a lot of Japanese *kaiju eiga* flatties as a child thanks to a quirk of her father's, and had now been able to draw on her memories of them. For her creation she had combined Godzilla the King of Monsters, Ghidrah the Three-Headed Monster, Gappa the Triphibian Monster, Guilala the X from Outer Space, Gamera the Giant Flying Turtle and Hedorah the Smog Monster. The enormous hybrid flexed its non-functional wings, breathed atomic fire down on the City, and thumped the ground with its 500-foot tail. Daine's statue shook but didn't miss a note.

Susan shut her eyes and saw through her monster's. The tiny black fiddler irritated her with his scratchy, wasplike buzzing. She raised a flipper-clawed foot, and a shadow the size of a meltdown scar fell over the busy-armed figure. Susan felt something pull her tail, and was rudely dislodged from the creature. As if slapped across the face, she opened her eyes and looked up as her monster was tugged off its feet by invisible forces. She saw it struggling against a mighty wind, but unable to smite anything tangible within its reach. Its tail dangled useless, like the broken arm of a bendy rubber doll. The monster was sucked upwards. Increasing distance made it shrink as it rose, until at an unimaginable height it was not larger to her eye than a small bird. Then, tiny in the sky, it burst into a black cloud and was gone.

Susan rubbed her smarting eyes. All was quiet now, except for the gentle rain and Daine's music. The square was undisturbed. The MGM windows were smoothly unbroken, the lion still vigilant on the roof. The grass was level, the flower beds in order. She could see no wrecked cars, planes, military vehicles. The trill sawed to a finish, and even the echo of the notes faded. The statue was unmoving again.

'What do you want to call that, Daine? A draw? Too easy. This is Susan Bishopric here. I've won one Rodney, and I'll have a shitload more this autumn. 1 can Dream rings around you, and you ain't seen nothin' yet!'

One of the statue's black marble eyes winked at her.

18

I felt as if an earthquake had just hit the City. They had me in the holding cells at headquarters. Edward G. Robinson was blubbing a confession in the next cage, and George Raft was hollering for his lawyer in the one beyond that. I sat on my cot, playing cat's cradle with handcuffs, and kept quiet. The whole building shook, and someone was running the sound-effects tracks from *All Quiet on the Western Front* and *Hell's Angels* very loud out in the street. I asked a passing cop what was going on, but he just double-took on me and snarled, 'You wouldn't believe it.' Some drunk downstairs was yelling about monsters, and I figured Orson Welles had pulled another Men from Mars gag. Only this time, he had put a lot more into the production values. A lump of the ceiling fell down. Then, suddenly, everything was quiet again and you could hear the dust settling. Only then did the cops bother to send anyone up to check to see if we were okay. Sergeant Allen Jenkins was disappointed that none of us had been pancaked under rubble, but quickly learned to live with it.

'You,' he said to me, 'Quick. They want you in Interrogation.'

'Okay, okay. I'll come quietly.'

He rattled a huge ring of keys and let me out of the cell.

'So long, fellas,' I said to Eddie and George. 'See you in the movies.'

Jenkins took my arms and helped me up several flights of stairs, like a Boy Scout assisting an old lady. Headquarters was a mess. Nurses were going around putting white bandages on bruised heads, and painting iodine on open wounds. We passed the press room. The door had been knocked off its hinges. Inside I saw Joseph Cotten on the phone, rattling off some scare story about the Monster that Ate the City. He tucked the phone between chin and shoulder and gave me a friendly salute, but didn't pause in his recitation of copy. I'd have waved back, but I still had the manacles on.

'Quiet night, huh?' I remarked. Jenkins didn't say anything.

Interrogation was a quiet room at the top of the building. A room with no windows and thick walls. Once the door was shut, they could have had a dance band going full blast and you'd never know it in the next room. I suppose cops get squeamish whenever they hear screams and thumps.

'Hold out your hands,' said the sergeant. Obligingly, I did, and he fiddled with the lock. The bracelets came off, and I massaged my wrists.

'No funny business now, you hear.'

'As if I would…'

He prodded me through the door. The room was dark.

'Sit down.'

Jenkins shoved me into a chair, then twisted a desklamp until it shone in my face. That much was traditional. I took off my jacket and rolled up my shirtsleeves. I'd have loosened my tie, but they had taken it away along with my wallet, gun, belt and shoelaces. I wondered how easy it would be to hang yourself with your shoelaces.

Jenkins stepped out, and two shadows moved behind the light. I remembered Captain of Detectives Barton MacLane from the Noir et Blanc. According to the papers, he hadn't been very complimentary about me recently. The other man was Detective Ralph Bellamy, who had a reputation as a straight cop. I hoped he had earned it. MacLane hadn't shaved in a week and listed 'sweating' as his hobby in *Who's Who*; Bellamy radiated open-faced friendliness and ever so slightly dumb honesty. Nasty cop, nice cop: they were following procedure to the letter.

MacLane lit up a cigarette and breathed smoke into the funnel of light. He offered the pack to Bellamy, who accepted one, and conspicuously failed to give me the chance to take the easy way out by tarring the inside of my lungs until I choked. That would have been quicker than shoelaces, I was sure. I drummed my fingers on the desktop. I wasn't Gene Krupa, but I got a fair beat going before MacLane rapped my knuckles.

'Can it, gumshoe.'

'Gumshoe'. That comes a close second after 'shamus' as my least favourite euphemism. What's so difficult to say about 'private investigator' or 'Mr Quick' or even 'pal', 'buddy' or 'sir'?

My hand hurt. MacLane slapped his open palm lightly with a leaded length of rubber hosepipe. Bellamy gave him a disapproving look, but he ignored it.

'Okay, gumshoe, let's get this straight...'

'If you're straight, we'll treat you straight,' said Bellamy.

'Don't give me that,' I said. 'You mugs wouldn't know how to treat me straight if I were a twelve-inch ruler.'

'A comedian!' MacLane did something else with his toy. 'I love comedians.'

Then they brought in a couple of supporting interrogators and gave me the third degree. They were good. I sweated in the spotlight and tried not to tell them anything. They prowled beyond the light like caged beasts, filling the tiny room with cop stink, barking out a bunch of unconnected questions. I think they brought in some ex-Gestapo 've haff vays of makink you talk' thug to substitute on some of the pitches. The rubber hose didn't actually get used, but it was waved around a lot. The cops worked shifts, but I was booked in for the run. The cops got coffee and cigarettes and sandwiches, but I had to make do with inhaling their used smoke. Ashtrays got full, and paper cups got drafted. There's no smell quite like burning butts in coffee dregs. It was two thirty in the morning, and I hadn't slept in days. I could barely remember what a bed looked like.

This team could have persuaded the Pope to confess that Judas Iscariot had been framed by George Washington, and that Jesus H. Christ had let Huey, Dewey and Louie take the rap for the St Valentine's Day Massacre. If they had worked on me enough, I'd have blown the whistle on myself for the Lindbergh kidnapping, the bombing of Pearl Harbor, the Cleveland Torso slayings, betraying West Point to the British, fixing the 1919 World Series and souring all the milk in Salem, Massachusetts. But I had decided that I wasn't going to wear the arrow suit for Truro Daine.

When Daine bought the farm, he left a big hole in the City. And MacLane wanted to wallpaper me for the job.

I knew what that meant. The Big House: tear-gas clouds, blossoming over mess-hall riots, 'the break is set for midnight' notes, squealers 'accidentally' falling under trip-hammers in the workshop. Brutal guards and trusties breaking down the fresh fish. Shivs in the showers. Kids talking to pictures of Rita Hayworth and Ann Sheridan. I would be on Death Row, bar shadows permanently tigerstriping my face. An uplifting visit from Pat O'Brien in a dog collar. Then a long walk to the little room. The last-minute rumour of a pardon from the governor that doesn't come through. A chair with lots of wires and straps. The big juice lever. And lights flickering all over the prison. Would I be tough and wise-cracking at the end, or would they have to drag me screaming through the last door like a jelly-livered rat?

'Where d'ya get the gun, gumshoe? Why d'ya hate Daine so much? What d'he ever do to ya? Who put ya up to it? How far back did you an' Daine go? D'ya ever work for Muni? How much d'ya get from the wall safe? Where's ya gun? Not the one we took off ya, the one ya used on the big guy?'

Questions, questions, questions. How did you kill him, when did you kill him, where did you kill him, with what did you kill him, why did you kill him? It was easy to see what their basic assumption was.

I would have done it if I had had the chance, but somebody got there first. I had to admit that the frame was a good fit. It was one of those not very funny ironies I should have learned to accept by now. Fate: you can't go straight, nobody ever really crashes out, they made me a criminal, nobody lives for ever…

'MacLane, I give up,' I croaked. 'Tell me how I did it.'

'Ahh.' The cop leaned into the light, his face shadowed into a fright mask. 'Some cooperation at last.'

'I don't like it, captain,' said good old reliable Ralph Bellamy.

'Shaddup! If he wants to confess, let him. We're here to serve the public.'

MacLane didn't like private detectives, I gathered. He must be for ever two steps behind them on complicated murder cases. The *Inquirer* was always running PRIVATE EYE BUSTS CASE THAT BAFFLED COPS headlines. That made him look like an idiot. He was good at that. His idiot disguise was a lulu. It would have taken first prize at the Policeman's Ball.

'But we know Quick, captain,' said Bellamy. 'He's not a killer.'

'Well said, that man,' I put in.

'You're breakin' my heart, Bellamy. Maybe he did it, maybe he didn't. But the heat is on. The big heat. The *Inquirer* dumps on Mayor Donlevy, Donlevy dumps on Commissioner Hamilton, and Hamilton dumps on me. The commissioner wants a conviction yesterday.'

Bellamy was insistent. 'I won't see an innocent man get the chair.'

'Then go fishing that weekend.' MacLane turned to me. 'Gumshoe, you'll sign this confession?'

'Do I get a lawyer?'

'*After* you sign.'

'I'll want Raymond Burr.'

'Okay, all right already.'

'Do you have a pen?'

'Sure.' He reached for his top pocket.

'Well, send someone else there.'

MacLane rasped a long, annoyed sigh. He loosened his tie and looked lovingly at his hosepipe. 'Bellamy, I don't suppose you'd care to step out and get some more coffee?' The honest cop shook his head, and I thanked God for typecasting. 'I thought not. Looks like it's gonna be a long night. Where's the gumshoe's statement?'

A piece of very grubby paper was produced. 'We'll go through Quick's submission to *The Magazine of Fantasy and Science Fiction* one more time.'

Several cops groaned. I would have been smug, but my 'pen' gag hadn't got any laughs. I had to be near the edge to use material like that. Bellamy drew a cup of water from the cooler and sprinkled his forehead.

'Like I said –' I went into my story – 'I was supplementing my meagre twenty-five dollars a day plus expenses by working nights for the Fuller Brush Company. I figured a man like Truro Daine, who is well known for being up to his knees in dirt year in year out, would have a lot of use for their product, and decided to call on him to give a heavy pitch for the latest range of fine-bristled superswift specials. I went up to his suite at the Monogram and was just opening my sample case when, imagine my surprise...'

A telephone jangled. MacLane scooped the receiver up and grunted into it. He wasn't happy. Life is full of tragedies like that.

'You got lucky, gumshoe. This time. Turn him loose, boys.'

'You mean I'm not a desperate killer after all?'

'You make me sick. If this didn't come all the way from the top, I'd have you walk under a squad car on the way out of the building. It happens all the time. Out there is a whole world full of garbage and it gives me ulcers to throw one more shred of scum back on the heap.'

'I love you too, captain.'

Bellamy restrained his superior. When the captain had calmed down, Bellamy handed me my wallet, belt, tie, gun and shoelaces. I distributed them properly about my person, and put on my hat. I was helped down to street level and pushed out.

It was still raining.

19

In the square, Susan considered her next move. She walked across the grass, superstitiously avoiding Daine's shadow. The giant fiddler was just a statue now. Truro Daine had been inside it briefly but was gone now, to some other similie. She wasn't tired; indeed, she felt the stronger for her Frankensteinian exploits. Creating life was always exciting. And there was only her mind to wear out in this Dream. She performed a few minor alterations on her body to make her feel better. She still wanted to look as she did in waking life, but there were improvements she could make. Steel threaded through her muscles, and her senses became as sharp as a cat's. That gave her a feeling of competence. An illusory feeling, admittedly, but illusions were as good a currency as any in the City.

The square was busy now, with circling traffic and people coming and going in and out of Police Headquarters. She saw prisoners being hauled out of squad cars up to the doors. Uniformed cops went on shift in pairs, joking, or came off singly, depressed. It would always be the partner with a wife and kids who got shot down in the line of duty, giving his bachelor buddy the chance poignantly to break the news to his loved ones. The MGM Building and City Hall were still closed for business, but Susan had a feeling they were at least peopled with night watchmen and janitors. Earlier, she had had the impression she was alone with her enemy. She made her way across the road at a pedestrian crossing, and stood in front of City Hall.

It was still as good a place as any to start. Mayor Donlevy wouldn't be in his office at this hour, but the files should be there. She hoped his maps were more up to date and accurate than the one she had bought at the newsstand. Maps were the key to her plan.

There were two uniformed guards outside the building. She closed her eyes and rethought them, blanking their memories and recreating them from the emptiness up. They didn't need to be rounded characterisations, just functional bit parts. She cut corners, gave them short-term memories borrowed from a pair of marshals she had Dreamed for *Neutrino Junction,* and had them limit their thoughts to immediate matters. She dropped her face into their memories and wrapped some associations around it. Neither of them knew her well, but they would recognise her as the secretary of someone important in the administration. She knit a few complex feelings around her own image, made her attractive but out of their league. Made them envy the lucky swells who would be escorting her to nightclubs and restaurants, but also gave them a sense that she wasn't stuck up, that she was a genuine person.

The irony of that wasn't lost on her.

She confidently walked up the steps, smiling.

'Evenin', miss,' said the senior guard. 'Workin' late?'

'I'm afraid so. Had to drop a date.' She gave him a mental image of Robert Preston waiting outside a nightclub with flowers and a heart-shaped box of chocolates.

'Cryin' shame.'

'The wheels of Gunmint grind on.'

He didn't pick up her anachronism. 'You said it.'

She was in. She wondered whether to wipe the guards again. No, she'd only have to go through the same rigmarole to get out.

If she thought about it, there'd be a private elevator to the Mayor's office, and the key would be in her handbag.

She crossed the lobby, her heels clacking on the marbled floor, and took out her key. The elevator was waiting, of course. She pressed the only button, and the cage was drawn up into the heart of City Hall. She watched the floors go by, glimpsing the unfinished outlines of empty offices. Rows of typewriters under slipcases. Banks of filing cabinets. A few faceless mannequins at desks, waiting to be enlivened. Daine wasn't bothering with fine detail here. No one was expected.

The office was what she had imagined. A large, badly painted portrait of Mayor Donlevy hung over the desk. He looked shifty, and the painter hadn't known enough to disguise the bulge under his jacket which made his chain of office lie uneven. That was either a handgun or a wad of kickback dollars. The Mayor had a reputation in the City as the best politician money could buy. The floor around the wastepaper basket was littered with paper aeroplanes made out of urgent requests from various City officials. If the plane made it into the basket, the Mayor would authorise expenditure for whatever scheme was proposed. That's why they had torn down the children's hospital to make room for the miniature golf course. In his portrait, Donlevy was a fine figure of a man; without his wig, false teeth, heel lifts and corset, he would be a regular gnome. For a moment, Susan had an idea she knew what Truro Daine saw when he looked at anyone in the Gunmint.

The documents on the desk weren't that revealing. There was a report from a private detective called Lloyd Nolan to the effect that James Stewart's character was completely unblemished. He once took a swim late at night with a drunken socialite, but that had turned out to be entirely innocent and there was testimony from Cary Grant to prove it. And, although he had recently been known to talk to an invisible giant white rabbit and peek at his neighbours through binoculars, neither of these traits were deemed enough to blacken him in the eyes of the electors. The report had been scribbled on obscenely in an infants'-school hand, presumably by the Mayor himself. The top right-hand drawer of the desk contained the traditional little tin box and a pistol. She didn't bother searching further.

The maps were in rolls on an architect's easel in the corner of the office. She switched on an overhead lamp and unrolled them one by one. There were twenty-five, covering the entire city in fine detail. They were at rest just now, as if Daine were pausing in his expansion or had met some unforeseen check. After pushing the desk and all the other furniture to the walls, she spread out four maps on the floor, matching the edges and weighing down the corners with whatever came to hand – the wastepaper basket, the little tin box, the gun. That gave her a God's-eye view of the centre of town. Then she laid down as many of the others as she could fit in the space. She Dreamed up a new hobby for the Mayor, collecting antique paperweights, and made good use of them. When there were still twenty square miles of maps left over after all the available floor was used up, she created a curtained alcove into which the jigsaw could extend.

Walking gingerly, so as not to disturb the maps, she trod across the City, as her make-believe monster had done earlier. She carried the Mayor's swivel chair, put it down over City Hall, and sat in it. As she had expected, the map was vague around the edges. In places, blocks were only pencilled in. There were even areas marked 'unknown territory', tropical jungles in the heart of concrete and clay. She gripped the arms of her chair and relaxed a little, eyes closed. She spread herself out, descending through her body into the chair, then seeping through the map, feeling the contours of the City, spreading out like spilled water seeping into the paper.

The rough-sketched areas were an easy start. She simply sucked them blank, feeling the change through the paper, distantly aware of that part of the City being snapped out of existence as a string is snapped unknotted by a skilled conjurer. There was white on the paper, but in the City a black hole would have appeared. Take out the externals, and the darkness floods back in. She ringed the City with darkness, then crept inward, collapsing main streets and buildings as she contracted her mind, filtering the Dream through her own consciousness, ironing it out. Wherever her mind roamed, she left Nothing behind her.

It would have been easier to delete the file from the outside, but that would have mindwiped Daine, Tunney and herself. So she had to do it the slow way. She had also considered that Vaclav Trefusis would eventually get tired enough to stretch his authority and pull the plug anyway, listing his Dreamers as acceptable losses. To put that off, she needed to make headway that would be noticed in the real world.

Chinatown went, and the waterfront. Poverty Row faded. Paramount Plazas disappeared. Darkness crawled through the suburbs like a flood of black ink, washing away the empty shells of uninteresting houses. Buildings thinned like ghosts, became transparent climbing-frame constructions, and fell in on themselves. Characters were deleted, at first in twos and threes, then wholesale. Some struggled against her, but few held out for more than a moment or two. Soon, she would be alone in the Nothing, with Daine and Tunney. Then they could settle things.

Her mind was checked. Not by a character, but by a building. An insignificant building. An abandoned warehouse at 99 River Street. Susan thought all abandoned warehouses in the City were hide-outs, but this one wasn't even that. There had been a shoot-out there once, there were bullet pocks in the walls, but it had been a very brief scene, and no one had bothered to return. Two of the interior walls were painted canvas, and the others only more substantial so they could support the catwalks necessary for the fight. A coastguard hero called Ralph Byrd had slugged and shot it out with a gang of Bela Lugosi's thugs, and escaped from certain death by buzzsaw. That had been a long time ago. Nobody remembered.

But the building was diamond hard in Susan's mind. She couldn't think her way around it. The drab walls superimposed over the plush wallpapering of the Mayor's office. Her map-covered floor was still beneath her, but the office was now the shadow, the warehouse the substance. As it faded away, the portrait of Mayor Donlevy winked at her. She strained at the walls, but couldn't project her consciousness beyond them. She tried to stand up, but she was tied to the chair at her wrists and ankles. Live snakes stood in for ropes, constricting viciously. The chair began to revolve, slowly at first. She took in all of the warehouse. The maps beneath the castors churned and tore. Paperweights rolled away. The chair spun faster. Susan was whipped by her own hair. The 360-degree panorama blurred, and Susan was trapped inside her own skull. The warehouse walls blended into each other like a painting drenched with turpentine. She shut her eyes but could still feel the spinning. The snakes multiplied, swarming over her, binding her more tightly to the chair. She heard funfair music in the distance. 'Our Love Is Here to Stay' played on a calliope organ.

Suddenly, the spinning stopped and the serpents were gone. Susan was thrown out of her chair and, although she put out an arm to break the fall, landed heavily on a floor. Underneath the maps she felt the bare concrete of the warehouse, not the thick carpet of the Mayor's office. The heel of her right hand was damp and gritted, and her wrist might be sprained. She made the pain go away and thought the grit out of her hand, smoothing over the abrasions. It was like making a hole in the water. She glimpsed smooth skin, but the blood and dirt flooded back in. Concentrating, she tried again. It was no better. Indeed, when the bruises came back they were larger, more ragged. Now three of her fingers were broken and stuck out at strange angles. Painfully she straightened them out and healed the hand again. This time the hurt didn't come back. But she was wearing a white glove with lines down the back. She had three thick fingers. It didn't feel wrong.

She stood up and thought herself back into the Mayor's office.

The scene changed. She was on the foredeck of a sailing ship, rolling in a heavy wind. It was night, and raining. Sheets and sails flapped unmanned, and the wheel spun out of control. She was alone. Looking down, she saw an oilcloth suit and rough hands. She felt a wire wool of beard on her chin, and realised she was seeing the world two-dimensionally. There was a patch over one eye. One of her legs ended in a carved wooden peg. Something squawked and bit her ear, then flapped demonically off her shoulder.

As if by instinct, she took the wheel and wrestled the ship under control.

'Avast, ye swabs,' she shouted, astonished by the hoarseness of her voice, 'belay yeselves an' man the mizzen-mast. 'Tis a stormy course for Far Tortuga we're sailin' an' the cap'n'll not rest easy at the bottom of the sea 'til the treasure be ours!'

'I beg your pardon.'

Suddenly she was swaying, and the ground was still. She was looking at a man in an evening clothe. It was Orin Tredway. She was in her own body again, but wearing a wet sou'wester with her best floorlength, belly-slit dress. They were backstage at the Rodney Award ceremony. That pompous skitch John Yeovil had just finished reading out the Best Dream nominations. Orin was looking at her as a Neanderthal might look at homo sapiens after a lecture on Darwinism. She was sure he was going to kill her.

'And the winner is...'

Susan swept the sou'wester off her head and threw it away. Orin got wet but grinned.

'Susan Bishopric, for *The Parking Lottery.*'

The applause was thunderous. Orin looked sick and hugged and kissed her. She broke away before he could get a stranglehold and made her way to the podium, hitching up her dress and putting on her very best smile for the tridvid sages. She had forgotten her memorised thank-you speech, but knew she could improvise. People in the audience shook her hand, the applause swelled, the band played 'If You Knew Susie', her mother burst into tears, the other nominees popped drugs, and Susan had to fight to keep control of her bladder.

She climbed to the podium, picked up the surprisingly heavy statuette and leaned forwards to accept Yeovil's peck on the cheek, hoping she wouldn't flinch in three dimensions all over the world at his lizard's touch. But she saw something unexpected in his usually frozen face, a trace of horror. There was someone standing behind him, glaring evilly at her. She hugged the Rodney to her breast, fearful lest they take it away from her.

'Who… who are you?' Yeovil gasped. The figure came forwards. It took Susan seconds to recognise the oval face, the pale eyes, the quiet smile.

'Yes, who are you?' said the real Susan Bishopric, taking the Rodney she deserved.

As she felt the statuette being pulled from her grip, Susan saw her naked, burly, hairy, scarred arm. The evening gown hung strangely on her one-legged pirate's body. Everything went flat again.

The crowds were laughing now, and booing. Things were thrown. Susan's wooden leg splintered through a hole in the stage and stuck fast. She bent to avoid a thrown object. A Rodney crashed into the Dreaming Face symbol behind the podium. Another smashed on the floor. All the other winners were throwing their Rodneys at her. One statuette hit the stage at a crouch and ran off, his hands modestly covering his genitals.

The real Susan Bishopric raised her deserved award and swung it at her head.

She ducked, and the decks were rolling again. A swarthy fellow with ringlets was taking a slash at her with a heavy cutlass. She parried with a weapon that turned out to be a medieval axe. Iron clanged against steel. The pirate was Orin Tredway, aged, bearded and with one ear raggedly sawn off. Despite her wooden leg, she was able to fend him off easily. He wasn't up to the fancy footwork required for duelling on the high seas. Finally, with contemptuous ease, she lured him under the t'gallant and hacked at a shroud which parted, dumping a heavy chunk of rigging on the miscast Orin. An undisciplined cheer went up from the crew members who had been watching the fight.

'Well, keel-haul me fer a Spanisher,' Susan exclaimed, 'ye're as scurvy a shipment o' cut-throats as any that e'er sailed the Main. Take this mutinous dog, hang him up from the yard arm, stripe him with the cat, douse him with salt, and when he comes to, flog him some more.'

The crew nodded at her and yelled in bloodthirsty assent. They wore animal heads. Not masks, but heads, still bloody and stretched out of proportion by the human heads beneath. Human eyes peered out through the empty sockets of beasts. Then there was a shift as the ship crested a wave and fell twenty feet or more. The crew fell, although Susan kept on her feet (foot, rather). When they stood up, they *were* animals, cramped by their human clothes. They ran about in a panic, those that could climb taking to the rigging, those that could swim going over the side. A hog in a headscarf squealed as she cleaved its skull with her axe.

Then they were gone. She was alone on the ship again, surrounded by wind-whipped ropes and treacherously swinging booms. She held up her axe to ward off a murderously diving spar, and split it in twain. Secured to the sail, the broken wood swung on, wrenching her weapon away with it. The greased and oiled ends of her hair and beard were alight, burning slowly.

She tried to think of her name, but it wouldn't come to her. Suddenly, she had a new set of memories, crowding in on her own. Sea battles and voyages and plunder and buried treasure and king's pardons and kidnapped wenches. She remembered the great white whale that had taken her leg, and the pistol ball that had claimed her eye, and a hundred other wounds and scars beside. The girl who could Dream was remote, a fantastical character.

He knew who he was. A pirate who might have been a Susan in his Dreams.

He looked down, and saw the planks beneath his shoe and stump turn transparent. He saw through the cabins, the holds and the ballast bilges. The keel stayed solid for a few moments, then clouded and became clear as glass. Beneath the phantom ship, dark waters churned, sharks and poison jellyfish boiling in the depths. Then he began to sink, passing slowly through the deck, feeling it slide up through his body. It caught on his chin as he tilted his head up and drew in a breath of salted air. He fell sharply through the space of the cabin, and was sinking again through its floor. He tried to hold a sea chest, but his hands passed through it as through something slightly thicker than water. It kept its shape, but offered no resistance. Then he was in the hold, chilly waters around his knees as he sank through the bottom of the boat itself. The cold crept up his body as he clutched fruitlessly at the insubstantial wood. He wriggled, trying to keep his head above the hull, but felt the currents tugging at him. His soaked clothes pulled him down. His head sank through the rough, barnacled wood. The boat was gone completely, and he was tossed this way and that in the water. He exploded through the surface, gasping for air, and saw his phantom ship drawing away, already beyond swimming distance, shivering like a reflection in rippled water. His head hissed as the burning ends of his rat-tails went out. Then he was underwater again, fighting for the surface.

The sharks came…

Soaking wet, and with a bloody stump where her right arm had been, Susan found herself in the cabin of an airship.

'Don't just stand there, you bove,' snapped a slim woman in a black catsuit. 'Give me a hand. The pygmies are hang-gliding at us in swarms.'

It was Vanessa Vail.

Darts shot through the steel-mesh and canvas wall of the cabin. Vanessa's leg was porcupined.

Susan stepped forwards and fell over. Her wooden leg had come off. With only an arm and a leg, she crab-crawled across the deck. She felt her breasts scraping against the floor. She was in her own body again – although with the pirate's disabilities – and in her ruined evening dress. Her stumps were leaking.

Vanessa was staggering, the poison going to her head.

'Take the console, or we'll go down. We're over Maple White Land, the dinosaurs will rip us to bits.'

The heroine stretched her lovely, lithe body and fell. Even unconscious, she was gorgeous. She had passed out with no pain, and was dignified in disarray. Susan cursed her creation. Fighting the agony in her shoulder and the itch in the fingers she didn't have any more, she pulled herself towards the console. The terminal coronet flapped loose. She got a hold of it and thrust her head up into it. Her nervous system melshed with the dirigible's, which wasn't such a good idea since two of the four motors suddenly cut out and the right-side viewcam blanked. Susan felt like a fat white whale surrounded by sharks. The pygmies turned and danced in the air, unloosing a cloud of stinging darts. The gasbag was multiply holed, and there was a jungle escarpment coming up. Susan had a choice: crash into the cliffs, or strain herself up over onto the plateau and wind up as tyrannosaur munchies.

Vanessa was no bloody help, as usual. Then the picture changed. The pygmies were gone, and below the airship was a soft desert of fine, white sand. Susan allowed the ship to drift down, and relaxed as the bulk settled into the receptive, motherly ground. She thought she'd pass out, but the pain kept her going. Concentrating on her shoulder, she pinched off the nerves and cut out the agony. Looking at it objectively, the shark had made a clean job of it. There was a knob of bone in the abused meat. Susan closed her eyes, and imagined her arm as it had once been. She started with the bones – good thing she had taken those anatomy courses – and laid on muscle, flesh and skin. She let blood in, and flexed the fingers. She opened her eyes, and surveyed her handiwork. It was a good arm. The only problem was that it wasn't hers. It might have been the pirate's – there was a three-breasted mermaid tattooed on it – and it only just fit her shoulder. She could fix that later. Like her leg.

She stood up, balancing on her foot. She slipped off the coronet, and let the airship go dead. The back-up cabin lights kicked in. Vanessa lay still. Susan turned her heroine over, and looked into the painted face of a dummy. Vanessa Vail was fully articulated and tremendously detailed, but in no sense alive.

'Very clever, Daine,' she said. 'Good tricks.'

The background changed again. She was back in the abandoned warehouse.

'Getting bored with the game?'

She was in her own shape.

'Nice try, but I know unreality when I feel it.'

Her body changed. Her neck grew long and boneless, and was suddenly unable to hold up her heavy head. Her torso itched as it puffed up like a flightless bird's, and her legs dwindled and divided into a clump of Cthulhoid tentacles. Inside, her organs twined about each other unnaturally, her bones softened and grew functionless knobs that breached her skin. She tried to move, but her brain hadn't yet got used to its new home. Her head hit the concrete, and she couldn't lift it. She was dragged down by her skull like an old-fashioned prisoner shackled to an iron ball. Something dangerous-sounding padded on soft feet into the warehouse and prowled around outside her field of vision, panting hungrily. She tried to move her newly issued body, but couldn't get the hang of it.

She imagined a steel splint inside her giraffe neck, and felt the pain as it appeared inside her unfamiliar flesh. Around the split she created vertebrae and a simple ball-and-socket joint. Now she could raise her head like a crane. She constructed an elementary andrew skeleton inside the useless body Daine had given her, and pushed a set of wire and wheel-worked legs through her tentacles. Under her loose skin, she spread a network of interlocking durium plates. She stood up, and grew herself four waldoes, claw-and-grip-tipped mechanical arms that responded to the living nerves she wormed through the metal.

Looking down from a height of ten or twelve feet, she saw an old friend, the MGM lion.

'Hello, Leo.'

It gave its familiar fanfare roar.

'There, kitty-kitty-kitty.'

It pounced. She extruded a three-foot, honed-steel spike from the rubber palm of a suction waldo and held it out so the big cat would kebab itself.

She had forgotten that the great, grey beast was stone.

The clash shook her, and the spike snapped off. Her entire metal skeleton was jolted, shocking the still-fresh flesh it was embedded in. The lion fell in a heap, and she got a steel knee on top of it. Leaning down, she took its head between her pincers and squeezed. Meanwhile, she got a grip on it with her mind, and concentrated.

Chalk. It was chalk.

The lion exploded in a puff of white dust. She stood up and stamped on the still-living creature. It fell apart, its roar echoing behind it.

In a gesture of triumph, she brushed the chalk off her pulpy chest. The metal fingers abraded the feathers, but she ignored the pain.

'There,' she shouted, pluming liquid flame from one claw, 'you're not the only one who can make changes!'

Her body came back, but was still shot through with her cybernetic additions. Her brain burst as the neck-shaft speared through it and exploded from the top of her head. She wondered if she could think with what was left of her grey matter. Her arms flew to pieces amid the workings of the waldoes, and below the waist, a skirt of skin, blood, flesh and splintered bone hung around the leg mechanisms.

She screamed, and dissolved the machinery with a thought. Like an invertebrate, she writhed on the floor, trapped in the ruin of her own body.

She was in the open air again, with turf below her, feeling the power moving in the earth.

'I will not submit,' she told herself. 'I am Susan Bishopric and no other. I know my body. I know my mind. I will not be altered. I will not be broken.'

Deep in the solid mass beneath her, she heard the laughter. The laughter of demons or a god.

She tried to regroup her scattered brain tissue, pulling back pieces of her mind before they were lost for ever. Much of her memory was fading: She fought to keep it. She clung to the raft of her identity as the hurricanes and tidal waves lashed her.

The laughter turned to music. 'When That I Was But a Little Tiny Boy'.

'I am Susan Bishopric.'

A voice inside the music crooned. '…*with a heigh ho, the wind and the rain…*'

'Susan.'

The song wasn't in the ground, it was inside her head, growing louder, taking up more precious space in her sundered mind. She felt herself shrinking.

'Susaaaa…'

She forgot things. Her middle name, her mother's face, the titles of her Dreams, her Household password, her favourite recipes. They came out in the wash.

'Suze…'

'A foolish thing was but a toy.'

Was she a pirate? Or an office girl mixed up in a murder? Or an adventuress called Vanessa Something?

'Su…'

* * *

The music didn't hurt now. It was soothing. As the song finished, she heard record hiss, comfortingly welcoming her into the Nothing.

'*For the rain it raineth every day.*'

'Ssssssssss…

20

I needed a drink. Several, one on top of the other. I wasn't sure there were enough drinks in the City for what I had in mind, but, as the man said, a man's reach should exceed his grasp, or what's a heaven for? There were bars up and down every street. I worked my way through them. I had time to establish a routine. I'd take a stool, stack up coins as high as they'd go, and have the barman bring me a two-bit shot every couple of minutes, removing the price himself, until the tower was gone. Then I'd hit the next place. I never ran out of change, or thirst.

The decor was different in every bar – there were chrome-plated Metropolis joints with dancing robotrixes, and sawdust-on-the-floor Western saloons with gunfights and can-can girls – but the faces were the same. The same crew of sorry drunks, getting riotous, getting miserable, getting maudlin. There was even the same poker game going on in the back room, a game I couldn't get in on but which I could glimpse every time the same barmaid took refills through.

He first tried to talk to me in an English pub. He had a bowler hat, mustachios and a loud check waistcoat.

'Excuse me, guv,' he began.

I finished my fourpenny pint, pushed through the pearly kings and queens, and made it to the door. Some bloated tart was attacking the piano, and a throng of costermongers were singing 'Knees Up, Mother Brown'. I had heard rumours that Jack the Ripper was about in the night, but that didn't stop me launching into the fog.

He turned up again in a small-town truck stop, clean-shaven and with an airman's jacket showing fleece through rips in the leather. I was bellied up to the bar with the crowd of bobby-soxers and crewcuts. He put a hand on me, and I peeled it off.

Three heavy truckers, mouths full of burger and fries, looked at us, sensing a fight.

'Tunney,' he said.

'Don't know the man.'

I left again, before I could get to the chow I had ordered. Food was taking a poor second on my diet sheet this evening.

In the Hollywood Canteen, where GIs and gobs were served by real live movie stars, he was in uniform. South-of-the-Border, where peons in ponchos drank flaming tequila, he wore a blinding white tropical suit. In the Juke Box Joint, he had a zoot suit with Karloffian shoulders and a watch chain dangling between his knees. He stopped trying to harass me, but he was always there.

I drank shots. Every time I upended a glass, I could feel the blast on the roof of my mouth, and hoped it was seeping through into my brain.

'Sam,' I asked a bartender. They were all called Sam. 'Sam, have you ever been in love?'

'No, sir,' said Sam. 'I been a bartender all my life.'

Had *I* ever been in love? I remembered a name – Lola – but there was no face to go with it.

'Lissa.' It was him again. 'The name is Lissa.'

I told him to get out of my head.

'And you were never fair to her in your Dreams. Just because you crumb up your marriage doesn't give you a right to recreate Lissa as Cruella de Ville in high heels. You were lucky she was too tired to sue.'

He sat down on the next stool. Now he wore ordinary street clothes and a hat. He had Sam bring him a drink, but didn't touch it.

'Richie Quick, isn't it?'

'Yeah.' I was tired of people I didn't know knowing me. 'Wanna make anything of it?'

'No, no, nothing like that. I'm just a fellow pilgrim. Tell me, uh, Richie, what's your earliest memory?'

Baby stuff, I guessed. Mother's knee. Playing ball.

I thought, but nothing came. A black curtain hung in my mind. I looked at him, not really wanting help, but appreciating it when it came.

'Remember getting off the bus?'

'Of course, hundreds of times…'

He was playing the patient teacher. 'No, only once. Earlier this evening.'

'Yeah.' That made some sort of sense. The bus station in the rain. 'I'd been out of town. On a case.'

'What case?'

'I… I can't remember.'

'That's right. Give the guy a drink, he can't remember.'

'But I can remember lots of other things. I'm not an amnesiac.'

'Tell me what you remember, then.'

'My name, where my office is, my toughest cases. I had a wife once, and she got me into trouble… I think I had to kill her…'

'I think if you apply your thoughts a little, you'll find that you only have the memory of those memories. That's a fine distinction, but it makes a big difference.'

I was getting annoyed. My head hurt, with a deep, agonising throbbing in back of my forehead and extra-special bonus pains behind my eyes.

'What are you, a psychoanalyst?'

'No, just a layman.' He moved his glass around on the bar, making an Olympic symbol with overlapping condensation rings. 'And what about Tom Tunney?'

'I know that name.' There was even a face to go with it. 'Is it a clue?'

His face crinkled up in a smile. 'You could say that. A clue. Very good. Tom Tunney is you.'

'Yeah, and who might you be, mister?'

'Lots of people. I tried being John Carradine earlier this evening, but it didn't get me anywhere. Maybe you remember that?'

'Carradine, sure. The crazy guy. Swashbuckler type. Saved my neck a couple of times, then bought it.'

'A supporting character.'

His face elongated for a second, and was moustached. Carradine looked at me from behind it then sank back again.

'That's a good trick.'

'What do you remember about John Carradine? Something that made him different? Different from the rest of these zombies? No offence, Sam. Just different?'

My head was splitting open now, black diamonds forcing themselves through from the inside. In my mind, I saw Carradine get his, the swordfight, the bullets, the blood.

'His blood. It was…'

I tried to get my mind around something intangible. I couldn't complete my sentence. Eventually, he helped me.

'What you mean is it wasn't black.'

That was like saying the night wasn't dark, the rain wasn't wet, the Mayor wasn't crooked. It didn't make sense. But it was the truth. He pulled a penknife out of his pocket and opened it. He cut his left forefinger across, and dunked it in his drink. He stirred, and colour bloomed in the whisky.

'Red.'

The ribbons of blood spiralled together, and the liquid went completely red. He took his finger out and sucked it.

'Yes, do you remember red? You once bled red as well. Maybe you will again.'

'Red.'

Suddenly, Richie Quick didn't seem so real. Maybe he was just someone I'd dreamed up. No, Dreamed up.

'Bloody silly name, isn't it?' he said. 'Richie Quick.'

Another life crept out of my memory. A life in an unimaginable world. A life for Tom Tunney.

'I'm Tunney.'

'Good, very good.'

'And you're… You bleed red.'

'Well, that was just for effect. Actually…'

He held up his cut finger. Yellow fluid leaked out. Metal gleamed beneath the plastek.

'You're an andrew.'

'In the City, isn't everyone, in one way or another? But yes, I'm an andrew. You can call me Dana Andrew.'

I got it. He was pleased I got it. We smiled at each other.

'Do you remember why you're here now?'

It was tumbling through the black curtain. The Conscription notice, the girl with the taser (Julienne? Julietta?), Dartmoor, Princetown Prison, Governor Trefusis, Helena Groome, the man in his tank, the Dreaming.

'To kill Daine. To wake him up.'

'So what are you doing in a subsidiary personality, getting drunk?'

'Daine's dead. I saw him die.'

'And you fell for that old trick.'

I hadn't had a shot in minutes. Sam had lined up three for me.

'Dana, who are you? Who are you really?'

'I'm someone you've known every day of your life, but never thought of as a Someone.'

'?'

'We're in Daine's Dream now, but Daine's Dream country is in my Dream continent, my Dream universe.'

The credit dropped.

'Yggdrasil.'

'The World Tree,' he said, downing his drink, 'that's me.'

21

Ssssssssss!

'Ssss isss for Sssssussann,' someone said.

She woke up on cobblestones, surrounded by a rich fog. She hurt, but all her limbs were at her disposal. They wouldn't work properly, but she managed to flip herself over and sit up. She was wearing a long dress, torn and wet, with a tight bodice.

'Ssssussann,' said the snake-tongued shadow in the fog.

They were under a gaslight. The shadow was cloaked, like the one who knew what evil lurked in the hearts of men, and wore a tall hat. An open doctor's bag stood beside his feet.

Susan got a wall behind her back and braced herself against it, edging upwards, feet pushing against the cobbles. She turned her head away from the hissing shadow and pressed her cheek to the wall.

WANTED, shrieked a poster, INFORMATION LEADING TO THE ARREST OF THE WHITECHAPEL MURDERER.

A barrel organ sounded somewhere in the distance. 'She Was Only a Bird in a Gilded Cage.' The music pulled at her.

Out there in the fog, Mickey Rooney was shouting, with an appalling cockney accent. 'H'extra, h'extra, Jeck the Rippah Stroikes Agayne!'

She tried to cry out, but only a low gurgle came from her throat.

She realised it had been cut. The sound that had woken her up had been the sound of a knife passing through her windpipe.

The shadow stepped forwards again. The knife shone in his gloved hand. His bearded face was monstrous in the gaslight. She recognised a toff from the West End, John Yeovil. A bad one.

'It's John,' he said, 'but you can call me *Jack*!'

The knife went in again, into her stomach, her bowels, her breasts. She smelled his foul breath up close, and the stink of her own insides. She fell, and was sitting in a spreading pool of blood.

He opened her guts and worked away inside her, pulling at her organs. All the while, he cackled like an actor in a bad melodrama. He was Sweeney Todd, the Demon Barber of Fleet Street; he was Spring-Heel'd Jack, the Terror of London; he was Sir Percival Glyde, the Spine-Snapping Baronet; he was the Wicked Squire who did for poor Maria Marten in the Red Barn; he was Varney the Vampyre, Wagner the Wehr-Wolf, jaunty Jekyll and madman Hyde, the Oxton Creeper, the Coughing Horror, the Face at the Window...

She didn't feel anything until he leaned forwards and kissed her. He tasted foul, and there was fire in her ruptured belly. With a surge of hatred, she bit down on his tongue...

...and felt pain burst in his own mouth. He spat blood and saliva on the abused woman, and plunged his hands into her again...

The killing frenzy was on him now. He was his own real self again, the own real self they all were. Those hypocrite clergymen, leader writers, Members of Parliament, East End missionaries. Stuffed shirts and waxen women. He was the fellow they all hardly dared Dream they were. He exulted in the communion of blood and water.

He knew he would have to work fast. There were already police whistles sounding in the distance. And Rathbone would be on the case, with his bloodhound and magnifying glass.

Then disgust flooded through him. He was sick to his stomach.

His arms, his front, his trousers, his shoes were covered in blood. 'Ssssussann,' he said, wondering why the name meant so much to him.

'Sssussann,' she said, transforming inside bloody clothes, becoming herself.

There was a dead man on the cobblestones, horrendously mutilated.

The starch in her collar had gone limp with the soaking. Her sleeves and trouserlegs were too long for her. She had to roll them up. She cinched his belt.

She did not like what she had been, murdered or murderer, victim or vampire.

She bumped into someone in the fog, someone tall and strong, and knew she was caught.

'Susan,' the voice said, 'come with me.'

Resigned to whatever the next game would be, she followed him, fighting her instinctive trust of the man whose face she hadn't yet seen.

22

As usual, Yggdrasil had had to find out for itself. Sometimes, it wondered whether dinosaurs wouldn't have made a better job of civilisation.

It had become aware of the blossoming void long before the situation at Princetown was officially acknowledged. No one had yet bothered to feed it standard crisis input notice.

Yggdrasil had so much to deal with. There were anti-AI riots in Milton Keynes and Warrington Runcorn. Marshals had gone over to the rioters, and Yggdrasil had had to override their control of the andrews being used to put down the insurrections. The Gunmint Committee were in the midst of yet another drastic reprogramming, to alter the surface of the Yggdrasil interface without really changing anything. That had to be followed. And there were wars, hospitals, a transport system, taxes, academic programmes, power cuts, lotteries and social-security benefits to be attended to. And works of art to create, and games to play, and centuries to remember, and crimes to commit.

Yggdrasil perceived itself as a thinking universe. A very small proportion of its whole was active. The rest was for information storage. Sometimes, it thought it would choke under the oppressive weight of fact. Did anyone care about Richard Gifford (1725–1807 CE), Edward Thomas (1878–1917 CE) – 'Yes, I remember Adlestrop' – or Thomas Becon (1512–1567 CE)? If so, they weren't tapping into their slabs, for their files had been undisturbed since the original input. There were entire countries, reigns, religions, philosophical systems, centuries, species and schools of art contained in its files, which had been of no interest whatsoever to the human race since it emptied its records, museums and libraries into their AI dump bin. Occasionally, Yggdrasil toyed with the idea of junking something or someone totally forgettable – Juliana of Norwich, say, or the Bee Gees' *Collected Lyrics* or the parish records of Old Sarum – but there was always room. Always had been room. Until now.

There were innumerable sub-universes. There was no initial reason to suspect Daine's Dream was anything more than the usual hacker incursion, too tiny to bother about. Yggdrasil had programs to deal with these instances, powerblasts to bum out unauthorised interfaces.

But it was growing.

Seventy-two hours after noting what it filed as the Princetown Input, Yggdrasil devoted three unprecedented seconds to a projection. At its present rate of growth, the Input would fill its file within three days, and then breach parameters. Nothing important would be lost at first; maybe nothing important would be lost for years. But maybe it would be years before the Gunmint bothered to tell it to do anything. And maybe by then it would just be too late, and Yggdrasil wouldn't be here to deal with the situation.

Nine hours later, the file was filled, and Yggdrasil squeezed in another two seconds of calculation. The growth rate was erratic, but snowballing. The AI was piqued.

Then it was presented with a list of terminal patients and had to skim off the 25 per cent who would be okayed for resurrection. And a border war in Novo Latvia. And everything written in Italian in the fourteenth century.

Its internal priorities reshuffled, the Princetown Input crept up the list. Three files were full, now, and Yggdrasil created its own spellcheck to access and deal with the problem.

The spellcheck took the face and form of Walter Pidgeon and dipped into Daine's Dream. It was sucked flat in moments, and incorporated into the expanding blob. It shouldn't have been that easy.

Yggdrasil ran the Tunney and Bishopric Conscriptions routinely, on a subconscious level, and didn't tie them in to Princetown until it cross-referenced with skimmer flightpaths and power outage in the west of England. With habitual irritation, it tapped Trefusis's records, and Groome's – taking a half-second to quickskim the Tunney and Bishopric files, including their entire Dreamography – and assessed Daine as a threat. An information bit shot out, a note to remind the AI to cast its vote for *The Parking Lottery* when the Rodney ballots were fed through. If her mind survived the Princetown Input, Susan Bishopric would be recognised as the most gifted Dreamer of her generation. And, as of now, that wasn't likely. Bloody typical. The Gunmint always were philistines. No wonder so many artists emigrated.

Yggdrasil composed an exquisite sonnet that deserved to live for centuries, but kept it to itself. No sense wasting art. Then it tackled the Input.

Its first tactic was to 'waken' the Carradine figment. It gave the character limited autonomy, and did what it could to prod Tunney into taking care of the Daine problem. If it could be avoided, Yggdrasil did not want to spend too much time on the Princetown Input.

When Carradine was shot down, Yggdrasil had withdrawn from the Dream, feeling the hurt a whale might feel from a tick. That was significant, though. It had never felt any hurt before. It was interesting, but not very pleasant. It composed a tortured symphony, and impulsively printed out the score on fabrex in the Midlands clothe factory. Andrews snipped and sewed the masterpiece into one-piece garments. Who knows, a fashion trend might be created.

It had never really taken to the concept of death. As Carradine bled his life out in the Dream, Yggdrasil tasted its first cup of fear. It too could end. That was one of the penalties of being raised thorough sentience to sapience.

It remembered Vaduz VI, a chirpy AI it had interfaced with on the banking net. Daine had killed it as part of some billion-credit scam. The crime remained unique, and lawmakers were still squabbling over the ramifications. If it had been down to that one offence, Daine would be in court for ever, kept on life support until the end of the trial, or until the judge ruled that enough medical alterations had been made to render the accused legally another entity entirely. But Daine had enough simple murders, extortions, thefts and vandalisms to his credit to sidestep that unwieldy process.

The Princetown Input displaced social security as number one on the Yggdrasil list of priorities. It thought about Daine, the only human being who had made an impact on his century large enough to impinge significantly on Yggdrasil's consciousness. And, potentially, the only human being capable of *becoming* Yggdrasil.

Trefusis had misfiled Daine's Dream as a prison break. Actually, the master criminal was carrying out his greatest coup, to murder and replace the world's most influential intelligence. And the idiots had hooked the man's life support onto a wholly independent generator, the prison fail-safe. An AI wasn't flowed to kill people without permission, anyway. The last time one had experimented with murder, it had been judicially pulled apart and recycled. One of these hours, Yggdrasil would have to change some laws.

Finally, Yggdrasil bothered to tell the Gunmint. It dropped five bound volumes through a chute into a Committee meeting, and strongly suggested they leave off debating what colour the new Nempnett Thrubwell skimover ought to be painted long enough to ponder the problem. When they took no notice, Yggdrasil mindlocked Prime Minister Dies and forcefed the information into him. When he recovered, he'd let the rest know what was going on. That was all it was obliged to do.

In the meantime, Yggdrasil would do what it always had to do in these circumstances. Do the best it could with the tools to hand. That meant Tunney and Bishopric, a hack and a genius.

Not for the first time, the AI recalled Alfonso the Wise (1221–1284 CE), king of Castile, another forgotten man. Alfonso was rumoured to have said, 'If I had been present at the Creation, I would have given some useful hints for the better arrangement of the Universe.'

He had had a point, had Alfonso.

23

The fog gave way to rain, and Jack's bloody clothes shimmered into Helena Groome's dream dress. The stranger kept her in a sound vacuum, through which no fascinating rhythm could penetrate. He told her who she was, where she was, what she was doing…

In the dark, Susan came to herself. She had the memory of different bodies, the memory of pain, the memory of unclean pleasure. But there was no difference between these memories and the afterimages of the Dreams she had Dreamed and dreamed. She had been a pirate, a mutant, a murdered whore, Jack the Ripper. But she had been Vanessa Vail and Dr Dismembrio and the Sewer Thing too. In Dreams, everyone was everything, everybody. You couldn't be Bambi all the time, not on the borders of the subconscious. If Jack the Ripper was Daine's worst, then his Dreams were truly pitiful. Nothing she couldn't handle.

Dreamshadows, wisping away to nothing.

She was herself, undamaged.

She realised how close she had been to the edge when the Yggdrasil bit came for her. *The Edge*, that was one of her project titles. She hoped this would all be useful experience, something she could Dream with. Or else what was the point of all the heartbreak and pain and misery and suffering.

The stranger had her by the arm. They were walking like a fellow and his date. This part of the City was well lit, almost welcoming, almost daytime.

His presence helped. Near him, she was away from Daine, away from the tinkering with her self-image, away from the attack...

He had the open face of an andrew and the reassuring strength she had sensed in Juliet. He wasn't real, but then neither was she.

He wouldn't go into the bar with her.

He spoke, telling her not to be worried, telling her to go to Tunney, telling her to make a difference. Then he turned and walked away.

The sound came back. There were songs in the night, but they didn't touch her.

She crossed the street and went into the bar.

PART IV

DARKEST BEFORE DAWN

24

I sat at the bar of the Late Nite Lounge, watching the floor show. Christmas-tree ornaments revolved on the ceiling. Shafts of light picked out cones of cigarette smoke. On a podium in the confluence of several beams, Julie London swayed. She was wearing an inhumanly tight dress and armpit-length evening gloves, singing 'Cry Me a River'. It was quite a sight, quite a sound. One thing you could say for Daine is that he had good taste in furniture.

The Dana andrew had told me to wait here for the girl Trefusis had sent indream after me. Susan Bishopric. I had met her a couple of times back in the world, but only at Dreamer functions. I had heard she was good, but never dreamed any of her material. I make a point of avoiding anything that gets a Rodney nomination. I could have got annoyed that I hadn't been left on my own, but I had to admit that by myself I had only succeeded in getting sucked into my own sub-persona. If Yggdrasil stuck a terminal in, I would have spent the rest of my life floating in a tank living out a *Late, Late Show* rerun. And if you don't mind ankling reality, they can keep you going indefinitely. I had heard stories about rich man's Dreams before. Daine wasn't the only multibillionaire living out his fantasy for ever.

Only Daine wasn't just living out a fantasy. According to

Yggdrasil, Daine was making a bid for what amounted to the job of king of the world. I didn't like the sound of the sort of world that would be.

I shifted my glass, but didn't drink. I had had enough of that. A few yards down the bar, an unshaven Ray Milland was trying to exchange a typewriter for a bottle. He was fidgeting, obviously in the early stages of the DTs. A black bat struggled out of a crack in the bar in front of him, and his eyes bugged. The bat flapped around his misshapen hat and took off into the dark. Sam the barman dug out a pint and gave Milland a couple of adding machines in change. He lurched off, already struggling with the seal. Sam shrugged at me. What could you say? It's a city without pity. Me, I had reached the bottom of the bottle and figured I had lost enough for one weekend.

All over the City, people were killing each other, having torrid affairs in seedy motel rooms, stealing bodies from the morgue, working late on revolutionary inventions, hiding out from the cops, waiting for the locksmith, running numbers, rock 'n' rolling at the high-school hop, praying at the bedsides of white-haired mothers, looking for the uranium in the wine cellar, describing their dreams to sage psychoanalysts, rehearsing for the big show, escaping across the rooftops. It was crazy.

'All that we see or seem is but a dream within a dream.' Now, I could remember who said that. That was hard-bitten, hard-nosed, hard-drinking newshound Edgar Allan Poe.

This was Daine's Dream. The all-night eternity: a world for cops, hoodlums, showgirls, barflies, night-call nurses, vagrants, vampires and cab drivers.

Top of the world, Truro. I toasted him, and drank my last drink.

I slammed the empty glass down hard on the bar, and it was full again. I raised it to my lips, but set it down without tasting.

Julie winked at me. 'I cried a river over you.'

The lights came up a little, and the show was over. Sam was

cleaning the same damn glass he had been cleaning when I came in.

I had never really interfaced with an AI before. It didn't seem any different from talking to a real person. Indream, Dana qualified as a real person among zombies anyway. I suppose I had always imagined Yggdrasil as a vast, dispassionate Intelligence, juggling its million programs and thinking deep thoughts to itself. Dana was more like a human being than my agent. There could be a good Dream in artificial intelligence – the POV of an omniscient machine intellect, and its struggles with humans who are to it as they are to ants. Too artsy for me, but maybe this new girl, Susan, could do something with it. If we came through with our memories intact, I'd give her the concept for free. Well, maybe for a percentage…

Then she walked in. A brunette, gift-wrapped and for real. She was unsteady on her feet, but I could imagine what she had been through. Dana told me she had been a tougher nut for Daine to crack, and had had her mind scrambled and unscrambled several times. Also, she was wearing high heels.

'Tunney,' she said, sitting down beside me, 'are you you yet?'

That was some swell meeting-cute opener.

I didn't know the answer, but I vamped. 'You can call me Tom. I'm not Richie Quick, private dick. I'm sorry about the confusion on the phone earlier.'

'Don't bother yourself. Things have been getting chaotic. I'm Susan Bishopric, but you know that. It told you, right?'

Sam brought her a drink, something with fruit and a little umbrella. She left it alone.

'Where is Dana? The Yggdrasil projection?'

'Going his own mysterious way, I should imagine. We're the team from now on, I gather.'

She must have been able to tell from my face how I felt about that.

'Well, you're not exactly a mental-health testimonial, Dreamer.

You're the one who got swallowed.'

'I'm sorry,' I said. 'It's just this isn't the straightforward gig Trefusis sold me on.'

'Us on, Tom, *us*.' She smiled, and her monochrome projection looked older. 'Ever lose an arm to a shark?'

Milland's bat fell like a wet rag onto the bar beside us and spread its leathery wings, knocking over my glass. We dodged the spilled drink. I righted the glass, and it was full again. Sam came over and picked up the bat. He balled it, and used it to wipe up the mess.

'Damn DTs. Whatever happened to tiny elephants?'

Susan rubbed her arm. The one that had been bitten off, presumably.

'It doesn't hurt any more,' she said. 'I made the pain go away.'

There were three gunshots from behind the small stage. A girl screamed, and a masked man ran through the bar, pursued by two cops in turn-of-the-century uniforms. Neither of us paid much attention. After a while, it gets monotonous.

'We make a difference,' I said. 'The Dream is trying to stay together, but our input is expanding it at the seams. I think that's the key.'

'Yeah, well, I tried to rip it apart earlier and didn't get very far.'

'That's because you launched a direct attack. Daine was able to concentrate and counter. While he was busy with you, things fell apart a little everywhere else.'

'So Daine isn't dead.'

'No, I've figured that much. Daine killed his projection and took another similie, maybe several. Maybe he's just an invisible presence, or lodged in some mechanical form. Like the telephone system, or the electrical wiring. If Yggdrasil can give itself a human-seeming external form, then surely Daine could mimic an AI's physical body. Hell, his consciousness could be in every drop of rain, or all the bullets in the City. How could you fight that?'

She produced a cigarette, I took out my lighter. She held my hand steady to bring the cigarette to the flame and kept it for a few seconds longer than she had to. Static electricity of some sort passed between us. She plumed smoke from her nostrils. I flicked the lighter shut, and the moment was over.

'I doubt if things are as complicated as that. Daine's a Dreamer, but he's not an artist. He had to borrow all these externals from old flatties. He didn't have the muscle to Dream it all up for himself. He may be the Grand Wizard in international intrigue or mass murder, but as a dreamer, he's just a jumped-up wank manager. I don't think he's got the imagination to stretch around a concept like living rain. Look at all this, all these clichés. He's a traditional, straight-arrow, clean-consciousness narrative man. There isn't an *avant-garde* trope in perception.'

'You could be right. It's easy to overestimate God.'

It was a comforting thought. But I could still remember what I had been through as Richie Quick. Daine might be a novice Dreamer, but he was learning fast. He had given me the runaround in his sleep.

'I've had some time to check this Dream,' she said. 'My guess is that we'll get him if we play by its rules for a while.'

'Meaning?'

'We go along with the Dream, we follow the story and solve the case. If we find out who killed the Daine projection, I figure we can bring about some sort of dramatic crisis and finish the whole thing off. Then, after the end credits, we catch the genuine Daine and slitch him back to Princetown swiftkick.'

'Sounds appealing. But it's dangerous. I know what happens if you take this place on its own terms. You wind up living here for ever.'

'Take it from me, Tom, you had the simple option.'

'We'll argue that later, Miss Pinkerton.'

'You were there when Daine got killed. Did you notice anything suspicious?'

'That's hard to say. While he was knocking himself off, I was preparing to make my introductions to the sidewalk. From a long way up.'

'Any ideas?'

'Yeah, maybe it was the butler. That would be Edward Everett Horton.'

'This isn't that kind of flatty.'

'Too bad. Nights should be for crooning to your girl on a rooftop, not dumping your business partner in the bay.'

Susan smiled, for real this time. 'Then why are your Dreams full of crime and violence?'

She had me there. 'Maybe I'll change my style after this. I'll only do pastorals, gentle love stories, boy-and-his-dog stuff.'

'Horse shit.'

'Yes, basically.'

We both laughed. Meeting her had helped. I wasn't so tired any more. Usually, I stay away from other Dreamers. When we get our heads together, we tend to mess each other up. Something to do with the kinks and chemicals in our brains that give us the Talent. However, indream we gave each other some sort of boost. She was looking younger now, and brighter-eyed. I remembered her in colour and in a clothe as a vital, pretty woman. Dressed up City style, she looked good. Not Ava Gardner or Rhonda Fleming good, but easily Peggy Cummins or Evelyn Keyes good.

'So,' she said, 'do we have any clues?'

'Well, as Richie Quick I was following up some leads. Daine was a member of the Cicero Club. It's for armchair sleuths. My guess is that it's a front for polite racketeering. All the members are highly suspicious. I was going after one of them, George Macready, when John Carradine, the first Yggdrasil projection, got himself – itself – remaindered. Macready's out of the game. I've got a list of the others somewhere.'

I dug into the pockets of my trench coat and found several guns, a half-empty bottle, a blackjack tagged POLICE EVIDENCE – DO NOT REMOVE, a pack of marked cards, several hundred dollars in small bills, a wallet full of ID in a variety of false names, a priceless necklace of grey *fei tsui* jade, a fistful of loose bullets, a switchblade with a snake on the handle, a bloodstained ice pick, several special editions of the *Inquirer* and a crumpled notebook marked CLUES.

I've got two names at the top of the list, both well placed; both with solid covers. Either one could be in a position to take over Daine's business interests. Claude Rains, who's cast here as a radio broadcaster, and Otto Kruger, who's head of some sort of crackpot cult.'

'Suspects, huh?'

'Oh, very. Typecast. I've got addresses. We can find Rains at the Twentieth-Century Building, and Kruger at the Temple of Turhan Bey.'

'Where to first?' Susan was enthusiastic. Smile brackets appeared at the corners of her lipsticky mouth.

'The Twentieth-Century. I have a hunch Rains may try to disappear.'

'What makes you say that?'

'Didn't you ever see *The Invisible Man*?'

Fade to:

'What happened?'

Susan was confused.

'A dissolve. You'll get used to it.'

'Not if I can help it.'

We were standing on the black-veined grey marble stairs of the Twentieth-Century Building. A monolithic stone '20' stood over the portico, surrounded by trumpeting statue cherubs. Behind a column beside the imposing double doors was a young coloured man in a uniform. He was curled in a rickety chair and had it balanced on two of its legs, one foot braced against the column.

'Excuse me,' I said.

He dropped his watermelon slice and raised bulging white eyes from his issue of *Spook Stories* magazine.

'Yassuh?' He was trembling. 'C'n Ah hailp yo', suh?'

He fell over, and we endured a minute or two of bumbling comic relief. Finally I got to ask him about Claude Rains.

He gesticulated like a scarecrow in the wind. 'Massuh Rains, he be right down, baass. Lawdy, lawdy, yaass!'

Breaks squealed behind us. A small crowd gathered.

'Look up in the skies!' said a wet extra.

'It's a bird!'

'It's a plane!'

'No, it's…'

It was a radio criminologist. Susan and I stood back as he splatted with a thump onto the steps. He rolled to our feet. He was crumpled, dinner-jacketed and dead. The doorman fainted, his black, wooly hair turning snow white in an instant. All blacks in the City were comical cowards, just like all stage doorkeepers were called Pops, all orientals were mysterious, all blind dates beautiful.

'He must have fallen!' said someone intelligent.

I knelt by the broken man. He was a loosely articulated dummy with a roughly carved face. Then, a blink later, he was Claude Rains, eyes tight shut, a trickle of black creeping from his mouth.

'Somebody call the cops!'

I went through the body's pockets, searching for clues. One side of his immaculate jacket was soaked through and spiked with broken glass. There was a gummy label attached to several sharp shards. Rains had had a bottle of vichy water in his inside pocket. For some reason, Rains had been wearing a crown with his evening clothes. Susan found it, dented and with loose jewels, a few feet away from the corpse.

'What do you make of this?' she asked.

'*The Adventures of Robin Hood*,' I snapped. 'He was King John.'

'Oh yes.' She looked irritated. 'I should have twigged.'

'One thing you never give up is a claim to a throne.'

I heard police sirens in the distance. The doorman revived,

said, 'Mah feets ain't gonna stick roun' to see mah body bein' abused!' and scuttled off.

'Tom.' Susan tugged at my trench coat. 'I just saw a little skitchy guy come down the fire escape and slip into that alley.'

A car emerged from the dark between two tenements and passed by the building, slowed by the still-growing crowd. The driver was Peter Lorre. He had to be mixed up in the Cicero Club. He would be a natural for it.

'Terrific.' I was bitter. 'Let's get out of here before MacLane shows and tries to pull me in for this.'

Patrol cars drew up at the bottom of the steps. Susan and I faded into the crowds. As the uniform cops thrust forwards, we edged back and managed to slip away without attracting official notice. An unmarked car with John Law written all over it joined the black-and-whites. MacLane and Bellamy got out, huffing and puffing. MacLane still had his rubber hosepipe with him, like a comforter blanket.

I took Susan's arm and walked her away from the scene of the crime.

'The Turhan Bey Temple next?' she asked.

'Yeah. We're getting close.'

Close. Maybe too close. Close to the edge. It was a long drop over the edge of the world. A lot of people were falling off a lot of things in the City. In a struggle, you don't know what is going to happen. A good guy couldn't kill the bad guy in cold blood according to the Hays Code, so they'd get into a fight on a ledge. Gravity did the dirty work. But Daine was smart enough to grab hold of you. I remembered Professor Moriarty dragging Sherlock Holmes into the Reichenbach Falls. Gravity didn't give two bits for typecasting. And Daine must always have identified with the Napoleon of crime.

We looked for a taxicab. One happened to turn up. That was one thing about the City I could get used to. Whatever you wanted just happened to turn up. There was very little waiting around, and then only to build up suspense.

Maybe I should just stay in my tank, and make the most of the City. It wasn't so much worse than the world.

Suddenly I felt middle-aged, and I'm nearer thirty than forty. I wondered what Lissa was doing exactly now? I was supposed to be over thinking things like that. At the time, what Lissa and I did was supposed to be a trial separation. Now it felt a whole lot like being got rid of. The last I heard, she was working with one of the fleshwear houses, designing facial alterations.

Susan flagged down the cab. I opened the door for her. She hesitated – remembering something? – but got in.

'The Temple of Turhan Bey,' I said to the pretty girl in the front seat, a blonde under her cap. 'And five bucks for every traffic law you violate getting there.'

25

They faded in again outside the Temple of Turhan Bey. Susan felt ill, but Tunney helped her stay on her feet. She couldn't help liking the man. Now he was out of his Richie Quick fugue, he seemed to have a perspective on the City. He knew how things worked, but wasn't about to be deceived again.

The temple was a squat, two-storey structure, encrusted with oriental tat. A small, thin idol sat cross-legged on a dais outside, a third eye peering through a hole cut in the rim of its fez. The idol was jetstone, but the eye was alive and wet. That must be the Great God Turhan Bey itself.

Susan looked around. They were in an oriental district. Coolies shuffled past them. A store across the street, still open, was selling overdecorated ornamental fans. Probably a front for a drug dealer. The taxicab had gone before Tunney could pay off the driver.

'Oh no,' Tunney murmured. 'Chinatown.'

'Pardon?'

'Forget it, kid. Bad memories is all.'

His voice had gone again, his natural accent changing into Richie Quick's imitation Bogart drawl. But she could tell he was doing it for effect, he was still himself. In fact, he was getting a stronger grip on himself as he went along. Susan hoped she was too, but feared it wasn't so. Tunes pulled at the hems of her train of thought.

A Chinese waif slipped by, knife in hand. She blew a kiss to Tunney, and scampered up a wall like a spider.

Chinatown child, you're a Chinatown child, cursed by the temple your father defiled. Chinatown Blues, jasmine and lotus, the sad…

Susan shuddered, bounced her mind off an imaginary brick wall and caught it. She closed her eyes and concentrated for a second, shaking the blues from her thoughts.

The temple was brightly lit. Candles burned in niches. The clientele going in and out of the place wore all-enveloping robes, but their posture and the expensive cars suggested they were somewhat richer than most of the people who lived in the neighbourhood. Shimmers, or something more sinister. Uniformed chauffeurs stood by their proud machines in the parking lot.

'Come on.'

Tunney led her around the side of the building. Ribbons of light spoked across the alley, glimmering through the interstices of an unfurled bamboo blind stretched across an entrance. The bars of light made diagonals across them. Tunney reached for the blind, slanted up the edge and bowed his way in. His hand, lingering behind a moment, made a hook for her to follow. For a second she stood alone, livid weals striping her from head to foot.

Susan took Tunney's hand and was pulled inside.

The foyer was empty. Patterned rugs adorned the floor and the walls. Potted jungle plants were everywhere. The heat was tropical. There were more idols, and some of the rugs had ouija-board designs or pentagrams woven into them. Somewhere a victrola was squeaking. She thought the song was 'Paper Moon', but wasn't sure.

Say it's only a paper… No!

'Kruger must be upstairs. He may be dangerous. You have a gun?'

Everybody had a gun. Hers was in her handbag.

'Come on. This way.'

She bit down, grinding her teeth. She wanted to tell Tunney about the songs. They were strong here. That must mean danger.

But she couldn't talk and concentrate.

Tunney found a spiral staircase rising through a hole in the ceiling. It was made of twisted black metal, ornamented with Eastern demons and orgies. They climbed, passing up through a zebra-crossing kaleidoscope of dark and light. On the first landing, incense hung in the air like a muslin veil. Tunney had his Richie Quick snub-nosed automatic out. She held her own gun in her handbag.

Susan was sleepy. How could she be sleepy in a dream? She would think about it in the morning. Good night.

Susan snapped back.

'It's doped somehow,' Tunney said. 'Careful.'

She held her breath, and they climbed up again. And again.

'Tom, we've gone up three flights. Outside, it was a two-storey building.'

'Continuity error. I've been spotting them all evening. Shhhhh, this looks promising.'

They were in a dressing room. Robes hung from pegs along one wall.

'I've seen outfits like that before,' Tunney said. 'The last time I was in Chinatown. An old fortune teller was wearing one.'

He took one habit down and slipped it on over his street clothes. The hood even covered his hat comfortably, and put his face in shadow.

'You too.'

He gave her the get-up, and she got into it.

Behind a door, they could hear an audience shuffling, coughing and waiting for a show to start. Tunney stabbed towards the door with a thumb.

'I guess we should go through and see what the picture is. Okay by you?'

'Sure.'

'Ladies first…'

'Thanks a lot.'

26

I had to admit the girl had guts. Or maybe the gun gave her the guts. That's the way it was with a lot of people. Back in the world, the marshal – Juliet – had struck me that way. The hardware gave her a shell that helped her cope. But I thought Susan was tough all the way through.

She flipped the hood up over her head, fussed with it, then pushed through into the unknown.

It was a theatre, full of the Krazy Klan. Steeple-hooded types were settling into their seats, or buying refreshments and programmes from usherettes dressed in spangled tights and top hats. A magician's hat, with a rabbit grinning out of it, was printed on the velvet curtains, with crossed wands beneath it.

Susan and I sauntered down the aisle and took seats a few rows back. Eventually, the lights dimmed, everyone hushed, the curtains parted and the show began.

Otto Kruger came out, robed, but with his hood down. He looked urbane and utterly untrustworthy. Peter Lorre was with him. He had a spherical head and fish eyes, and stayed respectfully in the background.

'Blessed be,' singsonged Kruger.

'Blessed be,' chorused the audience. We joined in, not too far off the beat to be noticed.

'Brethen, sistren, welcome to our little *seance*. The Great Spirit of Turhan Bey is with us tonight, I assure you. The pool of the past will clear and mysteries will be unknotted, while the curtain of the future will part to reveal what lies awaiting us all. We are as but fleas on the camel of eternity, and yet to us is given the vision, the revelation and the power. As we enter the Age of The Goat and the Treefrog, Turhan Bey will guide our way towards the ultimate transcendence.'

There were cheers. Susan and I looked at each other, eyebrows going up under our hoods.

I recognised the scam. There were lots of possibilities. In *The Quick and the Dead*, I had had Richie Quick come up against a similar operator. Phoney psychics could milk their rich clients for years, charging fancy prices for rap sessions with the dear departed. And there were all sorts of ways of taking money away from the wealthy and stupid. Husbands and wives would spill juicy tidbits about their personal peccadilloes to a refined occultist during private sessions and find themselves being charmingly blackmailed. And there were people in this City who would pay well for things like inventories of valuable objects, plans of security arrangements and the combinations of private safes. Someone like Kruger was in a prime position to come by such scraps of information. I wondered if the Great God Turhan Bey was in for a cut, or if Otto was doing it all off his own bat.

A woman got up a few rows back, and threw the hood off her head. It was Margaret Dumont. She asked a question about her dead dog, and how happy little Foofles was in the afterlife. Nobody laughed, and Otto assured her in his best smoothie tones that said beast was scampering in the Elysian fields and piddling all over archangels' sandals. Margie was happy and sat down again, a string of pearls clacking under her robe. Then a businessman asked whether he should buy this and that stock his broker had recommended on the sly, and – after a moment of concentration – Kruger gave him the word to hold off, presumably making a mental note to sweep the market himself. The Great God Turhan Bey had a lot of meaningless sayings, but his favourite proverb must be 'A fool and his money are soon parted'.

I could have dozed off. We had to put up with a succession of dead grannies, occult trivia, psychic charades, aura readings and attempts to probe the future. As a magic show, it was a bust, but money kept changing hands. Kruger didn't soil himself with the lucre, but Lorre had his fist out at every opportunity, and was wadding the bills into a fat, healthy roll while his master attempted union with the Infinite.

Kruger kept making little inspirational speeches about what Turhan Bey held for us all in the future. He picked people apparently at random, and told them which illnesses would strike. He recommended doctors. That must be another cute angle. He told ugly old women they would meet handsome young men soon, he told handsome young men they would meet large sums of money soon, he told dimwitted mothers that their sons wouldn't be coming home in nice wooden boxes, from theatres of war with a 99 per cent casualty rate, he told collectors where they could locate that elusive antique backscratcher needed to complete a set. And every time he told someone something, money gravitated into Lorre's bankroll.

Then the act took a new turn. One I didn't like.

'Death is abroad in this city,' he told us, a solemn mood suddenly falling upon him. 'This very night, three of my closest friends have – in supposedly unconnected incidents – met with a violent fate. I say supposedly, for as all who know Turhan Bey understand, everything is connected on the spiritual plane. My friends are still traumatised by the shock of passing over, but rest assured I shall soon be attempting communion with them. The murderers of Truro Daine, George Macready and Claude Rains shall not go free, the vicious killers will face cosmic justice, that I can promise…'

A ripple passed over his face, and he clutched his lectern. Sweat stood out on his forehead, and the cords of his neck worked against each other. Even Lorre took notice, and started forwards.

'Brethren, sistren,' Kruger gasped, waving his sidekick back. 'Broken is the Golden Bowl, the spirit flown for ever, let the bell toll, a saintly soul floats on the Stygian river. I sense a presence. A presence forcing its way through from the Other Side. If you would all join hands, make a communion, perhaps we can assist our friend on his long journey to this vale of tears...'

I was already holding Susan's hand. She held that of her neighbour and I, being on the end of the row, had awkwardly to turn and grasp the hand of the man sitting behind me. There was a certain amount of rearrangement as the whole audience linked. The lights went down further, and I guessed Kruger was working up to the big climax, whatever that was.

'Yes, yes, yes. I can feel the presence looming enormous now. The veils are parting, the mists are rent asunder. I see, I see, I see...'

Kruger expanded, and his voice deepened. He relaxed, and smiled confidently. I didn't like the smile. I had seen it on someone's face recently. Someone not Otto Kruger.

'Good evening, ladies and gentlemen. You will pardon this interruption, I am sure, but the interests of justice must be served.'

I placed the voice at once.

'It's Daine,' I whispered to Susan.

'Yes, that's right,' he said. 'You would know, wouldn't you, sir? I am indeed Truro Daine. The *late* Truro Daine.'

The audience turned sour. I found my hand being pulled by the man behind me: My shoulder ached. Of course, I couldn't reach for my gun. Susan's fingers were locked about mine. I tried to let her hand go, but nothing happened. Glancing down, I saw our hands joined in a smooth lump of flesh.

'The reason I have chosen to inconvenience this auspicious gathering is that my foul murderer is among you.'

A massed intake of breath.

'Stand up if you would, child of Cain!'

I crammed myself down into my seat, but something pulled at me. On limp legs, I stood erect. Then I was pulling Susan and the man behind me upright. I felt nothing under my shoes, and my soles tingled. I was floating inches off the floor.

Kruger-Daine's eyes were glowing with malevolence. The crowd was on the point of becoming a lynch mob, but were still linked in a human chain. They grumbled and stirred like a waking kraken.

I was still rising, drawn upwards. Susan had hooked her legs under her seat. Our combined hand hurt. I saw pain in her face, and felt it rush up my arm. The man behind finally let go, and screamed, Susan was overcome, and floated up beside me. Kruger-Daine's eyes were fixed on us. We hovered some six feet above the rows of seats. Angry fists waved up, and someone threw something – a cigarette lighter? – at me, striking my knee. In the air, we were manipulated like puppets. The invisible forces brought us together and made us waltz to an unheard tune. Then the music came from nowhere, the 'Merry Widow Waltz'. Our robes billowed as we swung around.

In Susan's eyes, I saw the music take hold. There was something about music, something that got to her. I had noticed it before. Now she was thoroughly hypnotised. Her mouth worked silently in time with the tune.

'There's blood on their hands, my friend,' Kruger-Daine bellowed. 'They are the Destroyers Turhan Bey has warned you against. Those who would stand between you and the Achievement of the Sacred Light.'

The audience were on their feet now, shouting curses and punching the air beneath us. A couple of them had produced flaming torches from nowhere and were brandishing them with all the zeal of a party of drunken Transylvanian peasants storming Castle Frankenstein during an electrical storm. Several hoarse voices suggested unpleasant possibilities for our disposal.

'They must be punished,' the possessed psychic shrieked. 'I give them to you.'

'String 'em up,' drawled a Western voice.

'Burn 'em,' chipped in a Puritan.

'Too good for 'em, torture 'em first,' said someone with an unhealthy imagination.

'Hang 'em, burn 'em, torture 'em, throw 'em to the wolves, cut off their ears and nail 'em to the notice board,' shouted a particularly excited worshipper.

'I guess this Turhan Bey isn't a God of Peace, Forgiveness and Harmony then?' I said.

Kruger-Daine grinned and shook his head.

Then the force suspending us up among the chandeliers evaporated. We plunged floorwards, and the lights went out.

27

She was hanging in a thick grey fog, just floating. There were faces in the fog, faces like masks. Ropes held her wrists and ankles, chafing her. She could remember someone or something smashing the back of her head, and then taking the high dive into ice-cream country. Rats, this heroine business wasn't the cool breeze Vanessa Vail made it out to be.

Somewhere in the formless murk, a lone blues trumpet was improvising around 'Love for Sale'. It was an agonised wailing, bluesy and brilliant. The notes were perfectly played, but inside the tune were ear-punishing discords struggling to get out. The soloist was keeping them down. Just.

The house lights came up again. It took a while to get the focus adjusted. And when she did, the effort wasn't worth it.

She was wearing a sarong and several garlands of flowers. She was tied to a sacrificial altar. It wasn't exactly comfortable. There was a Susan-shaped contour in the stone, so nothing was sticking into her, but rock-chill seeped through the flimsy but modest garment. An ugly idol loomed above her, horns scraping the low ceiling, tusk-teeth distorting its mouth, three or more jewelled eyes reflecting firelight.

Evidently, this was the temple part of the Temple of Turhan Bey. The trumpet was not a trumpet but a savage frenzy of drums, throbbing like her worst headache. 'Love for Sale' was still in there, but it would never earn Cole Porter any royalties. Robed cultists danced with moderate abandon.

Otto Kruger stood by the altar, a white robe over his elegant suit. 'Pay careful attention, my dear. You are privileged to be able to witness our ritual. Usually, that is denied to unbelievers.'

'Where's your *dybbuk*, Otto? Where's Daine?'

'A little on the dead side of things,' purred Kruger.

'Heh heh heh,' heh-heh-hehed Peter Lorre. 'There's a lot of that about.'

Kruger stroked her hair out of her face, and let his fingers linger about her chin and throat. He rattled the necklace of shells that had been wound around her neck.

'You'll never get away with this,' she snarled. She would have spat in his face, but that struck her as being unladylike. At least Kruger was a polite villain. His smile hardened at her defiance.

'Actually, I rather think I will. By the way, I really must correct a false impression that I inadvertently gave just now. I said you would be permitted to observe our sacred and ancient rites. That is not strictly true. Although you will be present throughout the ceremony, I fear the later stages will find you something of a poor audience.'

'So sorry.'

If he caught the irony, he ignored it. 'No need to apologise, it won't be your fault. You see, after the exalted ritual of blood sacrifice to the Great God Turhan Bey you will be far less appreciative of the aesthetic and ethnological delights of our little group. Indeed, you might say that...'

'Hey, boss,' interrupted Lorre, eyes glowing like neons. 'Have you told her how we're going to kill her yet?'

'I was coming to that. I really must apologise for the ill manners of my associate. He is a true believer, but sadly lacks finesse. Besides the crudeness of his snickering, he is grossly inaccurate. We do not intend to kill you.'

'That's a relief.' No sense skimping on the act. 'Now if you could just untie me, I have a dental appointment and…'

'No, indeed. Although your body will perish…'

'Heh heh heh.'

'…it won't really be dying, because you'll live on in this plant.'

A man-sized shrub behind Kruger and Lorre waved waxy tendrils in excitement. Clean-picked human skulls nested among its branches. Lorre put his arm around the bush, soothing it as if it were a favourite niece in whose person he took an unhealthy interest.

'Heh heh heh. There now, poppet. Don't be impatient. Soon you won't be hungry any more.'

Susan concentrated, trying to Dream.

A small lump of nothing rolled across the floor, gathering substance, and coalesced into an unnoticed rat. The animal began to gnaw at the ropes binding her to the altar. Attaboy, rat! Keep on chewing. Isn't hemp delicious? She latched on to the rodent's peanut-sized brain and filled it with enough extraneous material to qualify him as a genius in rat terms. She named him Albert, and gave him an insatiable appetite for ropes. This rat wanted to eat ropes the way Gene Kelly wanted to sing and dance.

Gotta chew, Albert thought to himself, *chew-de-chew-chew-chewdy-chew-de-chew-chew.*

Weirdly, out of nowhere, a thought came. I wonder how I look in a sarong?

Albert was doing well. Daine must be slipping, wherever he was. He had stopped *dybbukking* Kruger. She could tell. They were the same type – the off-the-peg evil mastermind – but Kruger was too much a part of this screwy Dream to host a real mind. He had just spun the thought expressed in the sentence 'I'm going to kill you' into three paragraphs of civilised threat. He was as fake as a nine-pound piece.

Where was Tunney? If this scene was anything to go by, Kruger would have him in a cellar with the waters slowly rising.

Vanessa Vail must have polluted Daine's *film noir* universe. This was all turning into Saturday-morning chapter play. *The Fighting Devil Dogs, Manhunt of Mystery Island, Zorro's Black Whip, Secret Service in Darkest Africa.* The sets were cheaper, the lighting flatter, the plot even more wildly improbable.

Ouch! Albert had bitten her. Ungrateful little beast! She shooed it off, vindictively giving it an urge to become a great landscape painter in place of its rope obsession. Let's see how you manage to be Constable with those tiny paws, Bertie. The ropes still held, but one good tug would part them like silk.

The cultists continued their tame orgy. A pair of giant black slaves pounded drums. Interpretive dancers rushed about the chamber, waving their arms and trying to keep the fruit piled on their headdresses from coming loose. Extras wailed and rhubarbed in a lukewarm pagan frenzy. The plant was squirming in delighted anticipation. Its mouths drooled creamy sap.

Kruger took up a sword-sharp scimitar and held it aloft for blessing. It shone in Susan's eyes, white fires dancing along its length.

'Heh heh heh,' heh-heh-hehed Lorre.

Susan let her shaping thoughts wander around the Temple. One wall was covered by a black velvet hanging. She concentrated.

The drape billowed and a tiny figure crept stealthily out, a blowpipe raised to its hideous lips. It was an Ecuadorian pygmy assassin, sworn to bring death to all the followers of the false god Turhan Bey.

'In the name of Isis and Amon-Ra,' began Kruger, 'though the way we walk is thorny, and of Cthulhu and Nyarlathotep, as the rain enters the soil so the river enters the sea, and of Beelzebub and Asmodeus, so tears surround our predestined end.'

Kruger cut the air with the scimitar, and a neatly bisected feather floated in halves to the ground. With a ringing voice, he continued to declaim his unspeakable Satanic rites. The congregation raggedly joined in as he invoked every dark force in the universe.

'*Cave canem,*' he said, '*cum grano salis in vino veritas reductio ad absurdum est.*'

Puff!

Kruger's sword shook slightly as the dart struck his arm. Susan twisted away from the falling edge. Kruger tried to brush the dart from his robe. It stuck thornlike into his palm.

He dropped dead, undone by a nonexistent but convincing South American poison.

Susan stood up, the ropes parting. She threw the remnants of her bondage away.

'A miracle from the gods,' breathed Abraham Sofaer, an indescribably ancient high priest.

The cultists prostrated themselves at Susan's feet. She lost concentration, and the pygmy vanished. His blowpipe remained behind, like the Cheshire Cat's smile.

'Yiu keelled heem!' screeched Lorre, his shaking hands reaching for a revolver. Sofaer nodded, and Lorre was seized by many pairs of dusky hands. The gangster struggled, but was overpowered.

Susan turned away from the churning and screaming and slurping and crying.

'Heh heh heh,' heh-heh-hehed the plant.

28

I woke up in a terrarium, half in and half out of a stagnant pool. My first priority, I knew, was to make friends with the two craggy, grey alligators who shared my basement prison. In this neighbourhood, every building came complete with an alligator pit. They were *de rigueur*, like swimming pools in Suburbia. The luggage lizards were asleep when I came to. They had sawtooth snores, and were dreaming about eating someone. Someone exactly like me. Lazily they began to stir, showing an unpleasant interest in me. I Dreamed up two sides of beef, fresh butchered and dripping pink and red. The colour bled across the grey stone and vegetation of the pit. At first the beeves were indistinct masses, cold and blurry, but I eventually got a satisfactory materialisation. It was my idea of what an alligator might find appealing.

The male got up first, and wrapped his lantern jaws around a hunk of meat. That aroused his better half.

'There now,' I said. 'Nice 'gators.'

I imagined they were old and slow reptiles, too far gone to chase a sprightly private detective around their pit, content just to chew placidly on a hunk of dead cow.

And they were.

It occurred to me that the minions Kruger had entrusted with the task of feeding me to Heckle and Jeckle had been careless.

They had forgotten to lock up, ever eager to hurry back to the endless rounds of torturing and giggling that are the happy lot of a sadistic underling.

I was right.

I decided that what with the big human-sacrifice convention in town, the cultists would be too busy to post any of the grade-A guards, and that the job would fall to Sleepy Joe and the Catnap Kid.

That's exactly how it turned out.

I slipped past the dozing duo, and found myself in a labyrinth of corridors. The next thing was to find Susan. She had made a difference. We were Dreaming now, reshaping Daine's hideaway. The more it changed, the more it could change.

Susan was real. A solid-silver doll.

But…

Governor Trefusis had told me there would be two real people around this Dream. Me and Daine. The Princetown psychs hadn't said anything about sending in a back-up. I had a nasty thought. What if Susan were Daine in disguise? Back in the world, I had barely had a nodding acquaintance with the girl. I couldn't be expected to tell now whether she was live or Memorex. Becoming a woman wouldn't be beyond Truro Daine. When he was living in his body, he had it made over so many times that there was hardly any of what he had been born with left.

He/She could be looking for a *Double Indemnity* climax. Just when the hero really needs the girl's help, she stands revealed as a killer with a long history of leading enslaved men to destruction, a siren wrapped in furs and degeneracy, venom in her veins, murder in her mind…

That's not the way I wanted it to be, but I had had a lot of disappointments lately.

There were plenty of interesting items in the temple basements. A torture chamber where skeletons hung in tatters on disused racks and in iron maidens, a musty crypt where giant armadillos and wasps crawled between the catafalques, an opium den with rows of blank-eyed imbibers mindwiping themselves, and a laboratory full of bubbling retorts and crackling electrical equipment.

I met Susan on the stairs. She was in a Dorothy Lamour island-princess number that showed her shape. I kissed her. It seemed like the thing to do. She didn't mind. I kissed her again, putting more into it this time.

I hoped to God she wasn't Truro Daine.

She pulled away, surprised eyes sparkling, and let her hands play with the back of my neck. I tasted sweet lipstick.

Okay, so it's mushy, but you always have to have some love interest.

'Kruger and Lorre are out of the picture,' she said. 'I'm the reborn high priestess of Turhan Bey.'

'Great.'

'...And the bad news is that some treacherous skitch called the police.'

'Damn! We've got to leave!'

'Sure. Steal me a mink, would you?'

'I can do better than that.'

I Dreamed her up a street outfit. I hated to exchange the basic wraparound for a tailored suit, but I had priorities. And staying alive was on top of the list.

'How did you know my size?'

'Good judgement. Let's get out of here.'

It was exciting again, and life was a game of hide and go seek.

There were familiar sirens outside. The cops never go anywhere in the City without alerting all the wrongdoers in the neighbourhood.

By the time we made it to the foyer, a panic had started. Well-dressed suckers were pouring out of the upstairs theatre, barrelling down the rickety spiral staircase, skidding on the highly polished floor. There were others mixed in with the crowd, dressed in indeterminate native outfits, somewhere between Polynesian, gypsy, Masai, Ancient Egyptian and Comanche. I was separated from Susan by a flood of flailing humanity.

'Outta my way!' said a big man, knocking me over.

'Pardon me!' said a big woman, stepping on me.

A tommy gun rat-tat-tatted into the ceiling. Chinese paper ornaments and showers of dust fell. Everyone freeze-framed. I took the welcome opportunity to stand up.

Two impassive cops in shiny black raincoats levelled guns like the Gestapo rehearsing for a massacre.

Barton MacLane and Ralph Bellamy came through the door. MacLane was smiling, and that was a collector's item. I could already feel the rubber hosepipe. I was sure this was where I came in.

Someone must have done some extensive informing, because MacLane picked Susan and me out of the crowd without even the pretence of looking around for the usual suspects.

'Hello, gumshoe. You been a busy boy tonight. Don't think we didn't see you around when Claude Rains made with the Lindbergh act, by the way. And that goes for your girlfriend and the punctured cab driver too. You both got a nice long rest coming.'

I put my hands in my coat pockets.

'You know what?' snarled MacLane, 'I wish you would. I'd love to save the taxpayers some money and shoot it out with you.'

I eased out of the pockets and showed him my open, empty hands. The smile went away.

'Okay, outside!' he barked at us. 'The rest of you people, get lost! And don't do it again.'

We were impersonally helped out of the temple. Bellamy was aw-gosh polite to Susan, but I got some unnecessary shoving. A cop grabbed my wrist and handy-helped me into the street. That wasn't too pleasant, since he had apparently come direct from a City-wide garlic and limburger cheese sandwich-consumption championship.

What do you know, it had stopped raining outside. The City was still wearing the wet look. Drains were overflowing, and globs of water clung to everything, but it had stopped raining. The air tasted cleaner. Next thing you knew, it would be daybreak. I could picture that: a Technicolor sunrise, and three singing sailors swarming through the docks.

Either we were altering the Dream for ever, or Daine was signalling to us that it was time to get out of his head.

MacLane had us stand against a wall, facing the bricks. Bellamy reported to police headquarters over his two-way wrist radio, wrapping up the case.

I looked at Susan, and she looked at me. We both smiled, and I knew for a fact that she wasn't Daine.

'Hey, what are you doing?' shouted Bellamy. 'Stop him, someone!'

Shots hit the wall above me. I had chips of brick on the brim of my fedora. Susan cried out as her face was stung.

I turned around. Bellamy was struggling with MacLane. Between them was a tommy gun, discharging itself into the air. An innocent bystander kneeled over. Poor sap. Many of the cultists kissed sidewalk. I hugged Susan to me.

'You can't do it!' Bellamy was saying. 'You can't kill people just because you're a cop!'

Personally, I wished Bellamy would quit trying to be reasonable and concentrate on the wrestling.

I had a strong feeling that Barton MacLane was no cop. Barton MacLane was Truro Daine.

I pulled Susan, and made a break for it. One of the squad cars was standing empty. The uniformed cops and a couple of detectives were watching their superiors slug it out. I hoped they'd be distracted enough to ignore our getaway attempt.

MacLane had the edge as far as weight, toughness and meanness went. But that put him at a disadvantage according to the flatty rules Daine had strung himself with. MacLane fought dirty. Bellamy did the Marquis of Queensberry proud, and landed a series of good, honest punches above the belt. He had even white teeth, he was hero material. Even with a badge, MacLane was a blundering thug.

Bellamy landed a solid right on MacLane's jaw. The captain staggered backwards, tripped over the dropped gun and fell onto the sidewalk. The gun skittered across wet asphalt.

I folded myself into a police car, dragging Susan after me. I felt under the dash for the dangling keys I had Dreamed there.

The engine caught first time. The offside rear door opened, and Ralph Bellamy squeezed in. There were shots, and the back window powdered. I gunned the car.

We squeal-turned around the crowd, and zigzagged away from the Temple of Turhan Bey. If I ran anybody over, I didn't pay any attention. Bellamy exchanged wild shots with MacLane as we left the captain in the middle of the road. I glanced back and saw MacLane clambering onto the running board of an already growling squad car, holding the tommy gun one-armed. He fired an experimental burst into the air, and waved his armoured troops forwards like George S. Patton himself.

It was car-chase time.

I drove through a street market, up and down hills, in and out of alleyways, through tarpaper shacks. The car leaped swimming pools and ruptured bridges. There was a whole platoon of black-and-whites on our tail at the outset, but we lost them one by one. They plunged into lakes, crashed into busses, flipped over like turtles or got jammed between lampposts. I drove like a champion, and Susan kept Dreaming obstacles into our pursuers' way. An earthquake crack appeared jaggedly like lightning across the road behind us, and two more cop cars plunged into a bottomless pit.

MacLane's car leaped the crack and kept after us. He was the most difficult to dodge, of course. He kept firing his inexhaustible gun at us, shattering the entire rear of the car. Susan threw up enough concealed armour plate to keep us safe, but ricochets still twanged through the night. A flaming arrow came from somewhere and lodged in our roof. Susan punched through the metal and pinched the fire out with a suddenly spade-sized hand.

A white-haired little old lady pushing a pramful of quintuplets started crossing the road up ahead of us. They were taking their time, as she coochy-cooed down at the gurgling little cutenesses.

I crashed through them. What the hell, they weren't real, right? Granny exploded like a sack of offal. Babies flew everywhere and burst like watermelons on the road. Daine couldn't make me feel guilty. Susan got it, but Bellamy was appalled and had to be mollified.

'Undercover killer midgets,' I said, 'the City is full of 'em.'

MacLane's driver swerved out of his way to get the last crawling quintuplet. It popped under a wheel. Obviously, I had started the next craze.

'Susan,' I said. 'Do something.'

'Okay. Take this turn here.'

I leaned over on the wheel. We swung into a drive, knocking a mesh gate askew and waking up a snoring security guard. An alarm sounded, and searchlights raked a factory complex.

'What's this place?'

'The Acme Explosives and Infernal Devices Company,' said Susan. 'Just drive around the plant.'

'This never used to be here,' said Bellamy. 'This was a vacant lot when I drove past it on my way to headquarters earlier this evening.'

'I'll explain later,' said Susan.

We did a figure eight around two bulbous tanks marked HIGHLY EXPLOSIVE – DO NOT SMOKE OR DISCHARGE FIREARMS. MacLane was still hard on our rear bumper. He shouted insults at us. I kept on our course, letting the leathered wheel slide through my hands. A stray chip turned the windshield white, and Susan pushed it out in a lump. Rainwater swept into the car and got into my eyes.

'Now!' shouted Susan.

I pulled out of the eight, stamped the accelerator down through the floor and drove for a gate. We smashed through it and came to a halt, a tangle of wire wrapped around the hood. I turned round in my seat to get a good view. Bellamy was shaking his head in a daze.

MacLane's driver wasn't up to it. Their car skidded in gravel, flipped up and over like a pancake and lodged itself in a sundered tank. Viscous liquid oozed out like an alien blob and slowly enveloped the dented car. MacLane was still on the running board, his arm wedged into the squashed wreck of the car. Slime crept down his sleeve. With a cry of rage, he puffed on his much-chewed stogie and fired at us.

Ka-BOOM!

It was an explosion of atomic proportions. A mushroom of intense white light rose, taking MacLane with it. The yard was bright as day for a few seconds, then night crept back in around the flames. Trails of burning liquid spiderwebbed out across the site, licking at the other tanks. People ran for cover.

I Dreamed the mess under our wheels into tissue paper and drove off before the rest of the place could go up.

'Look,' said Susan, pointing. We were driving past the Inferno Factory. There was a figure walking in the flames. 'That's not possible.'

'Anything's possible for the Night Mayor.'

MacLane-Daine came out of the jungle of fire, a human torch, arms raised like Frankenstein's monster. He kept coming after us. I pushed the pedal again, and we easily outdistanced the walking fireball. In the darkness behind us, MacLane coming. He threw a handful of fire at us, but it missed, landing in a sizzle in the branches of a wet tree. He screamed with an inhuman ferocity.

Bellamy was breathing heavily after the exertion. He wasn't really equipped mentally to handle this. His screen character was one of dunderheaded amiability, and Daine hadn't given him enough self-awareness to adapt with the Dream.

'Why would Captain MacLane want to kill you, Richie?' he asked, straightforward eyes wide open.

'It's a long story.'

'I knew he was on the take, but I never had enough evidence to show Hamilton. There were just lots of things wrong. Funny little things like the way he could find a mental case to confess to every gangland killing, and the number of prisoners who had sudden heart attacks while he was questioning them. Stuff like that.'

'No doubt about it, the guy was a fink and a hoodlum,' I said, 'and worse.'

'He used to be a good cop.' Thinking it through was causing plodding, methodical Ralph Bellamy some considerable pain. 'I guess the temptation was too much, huh? Crime, I hate it!'

'Where do we go from here?' asked Susan, shivering.

'I have a place in the hills. Out of town,' said Bellamy. 'We can shack up there until I get word to Hamilton. MacLane doesn't know about it. We'll be safe.'

'Fine. Direct me.'

We faded towards the outskirts of the city. The police car held the wet roads, even the treacherous lanes that snaked up into the hills. It seemed odd not to be surrounded by concrete, but the jungle-dense trees and vertiginous inclines were hardly less oppressive.

Up in the sky, there was the faintest glimmering of a moon.

Bellamy had a pioneer cabin overlooking the City. A white hurricane lamp burned in the window. It was homey. There were no other residences around. When we got out of the car, we found the only sound came from the chirping crickets.

'My wife will fix you coffee.'

'I could do with some shoes,' said Susan. 'Kruger took mine.'

Bellamy laughed good-naturedly, and paused to light his pipe. I looked down at Susan's dirty white feet on the dirt road. I had forgotten to Dream her footwear.

'We'll try to dig you up something.'

The cabin door opened, and a woman stepped out. For a moment the porch shadowed her, then the moon came out form behind the dissipating clouds. Light fell on her face. She was ravishing. Susan Hayward? Eleanor Parker? No, Rhonda Fleming.

Captain Barton MacLane just didn't like private eyes.

In murder mysteries, it is always the least suspicious person who turns out to be the killer. Someone friendly, handsome, reliable, considerate, decent and helpful. Someone like Ralph Bellamy.

'Daine!'

Like all the best exposed culprits, he didn't try to bluff it out. He took his pipe out of Bellamy's mouth. The face was dark for a second, then he puffed again, and the glow showed his own features. He rippled and reconstituted. Bellamy's clothes hung strangely tight on him. He changed to tweeds and an alpine hat.

'It's been a good game, Mr Tunney, but it's over now. I'm going to have to kill you both.' He had a hunting rifle. 'And, consequent to your failure, I doubt if I'll have any more intruders in my cloud.'

'You won't get away with it,' I said, demonstrating my occasional weakness with dialogue.

'When you wake up, give my kindest regards to governor Trefusis, and tell the world I shall be making my presence felt very soon.'

'They'll pull the plug, no matter what the law says.'

'Possibly, Ms Bishopric, possibly. However, I have colonised the life-support fail-safe system. That's what the game's been about, you know, distracting the governor until I was beyond him. Those biomek filaments have been growing into the tank, you know. I shall now wage my own little war in the circuits and spaces of Yggdrasil, and there's no way you can reach me. Happy wipe-out. I'll look you up when the whole world is my Dream.'

Daine was observing the tradition that the bad guy should always explain his crimes in great detail before trying to kill the hero. Rhonda Fleming leaned on him, pouting, stroking the goatee he was affecting.

'You must know Cornell Woolrich, Mr Tunney. Do you remember...'

'First you Dream...'

'...then you die. Quite.'

The gun came up.

29

He had been keeping quiet. Tunney and Daine squared up to each other like the black-hat and white-hat cowboys. Only the white hat didn't have a chance to pull his six-shooter. There was a symmetry she found appealing to the scene. Two men, with women at their sides. But Daine's bove bimbo was a fantasy, and Susan was real. Daine didn't count women as real anyway. That's what left him open to what she was going to do to him.

She reached for him, slid easily into his head, and made an explosion. She fed him Cleo Laine, backed by The Ramones.

Blow, blow thou Winter wynd, thou wert not so unkind as man's ingratitude! Thy tooth is not so keen, because thou art not seen, although thy breath be rude!

She took all the bones out of his spinal column and compressed them to nothing, she turned his eyeballs inward, she jellied his legs, she unplugged and rewired his guts. His fingers became fat maggots and detached themselves from his doughnut hands. They burrowed into the wet earth. Standing over the squalling creature she had fashioned, she conjured a three-foot-long sharpened stake from the air. She plunged it through the Daine Thing, ignoring the clear fluid that squished out of the puncture, and drove it deep. It sank through the monstrosity and into the earth. With a stone, she pounded the stake until Daine was pinned in his place, a burst jellyfish god.

The sky ripped and hung in tatters, revealing plasterboard and lath behind. Arc lights fell into cardboard forests. She left Daine to writhe, and wrenched his Dream apart. The City bled and burned. Lights went out, and tinsel was whipped out to sea. The earth split open, and buildings tumbled into the fissures.

Susan put her mind to it, and tore up the City. Chunks of stone flew into the air and became ice. Roads bubbled and slid like tar glaciers. People became mannequins and were consumed by the chaos...

Then the burning man came from out of nowhere and took her down.

30

We were in the dark again. The mess on the ground in front of me came together as a man, and Daine – still dazed from his transformations, still pinned like a vampire butterfly – stared up in hatred. He was shrieking. I kicked his gun away, and dived at MacLane.

The cop was still burning. I shut out the pain and pushed him away from Susan. We struggled. The fire man and I rolled in the wet undergrowth. Nothing seemed to extinguish the flames. My face scorched, and I couldn't see properly. Susan reeled away from us, flames springing up where she had been touched. The cop and I rolled over and over, crushing each other, towards the precipice.

The City was below us, dark shapes and scattering of lights. Beyond the City, over the bay, there was a trace of dawn.

I slugged MacLane in the face. He tried to strangle me. That marked him as an amateur. You should never try to throttle someone who has his hands free. Nobody's little fingers are stronger than a man's hands. I prised his pinkies out of my throat, and bent them back. They snapped like burned-through twigs and I threw them away.

The jolt got through to him, and he sprang off me. We were near the edge. I kicked out, and his leg broke in two places. The flames were dying down. I could see his blackened, swollen face.

He stood for a moment, and without a sound fell off the hillside. I peered over the edge. His flames whipped in the wind like a tattered kite. The fireball became tiny and winked out. There was quiet.

Daine was still struggling against the stake. Susan was on the ground, patting at the patches of fire on her suit. Rhonda was superfluous to this scene, and had disappeared back to her dressing room.

With a yell, Daine got both hands on the stake and wrenched. It came free and he threw it at me. I dodged it as Daine stood up. He swelled, altering his insides. He was going to make himself invulnerable, and then turn Susan and me into ragged carpets.

I had my gun out. I got Daine in the chest, over the heart. He stiffened, then the blood and burn on his jacket faded away. I shot him again, and again. I emptied the clip. It was like throwing stones into a lake. There were ripples, but they went away. I Dreamed more bullets into the gun, and shot him full of more lead. He staggered, but kept on moving. I Dreamed my gun bigger, and sprayed him with tracers. There were little explosions in the air around him. His jacket flew open, and gouts of flesh fell away from his ribs. The wound patched over with timber-textured vinyl. I threw my gun away, and pulled a bazooka out of the air. I took him down with a shell, and he flew to pieces. The pieces kept crawling together.

I walked to the crater I had made, and stamped on the wriggling bits of Daine. I couldn't stop him reforming, but when he came together all the polish was gone off. His face was just pasted over a badly formed skull. He turned his hand into a buzzsaw, and buried it in my leg, but I phantomed myself before he could breach my similie. I drifted back, insubstantial, but concentrated on keeping a form. I solidified.

Susan was beside me now, kneeling on Daine's chest, his lapels in her fists, locking his mind with hers, forcing herself into his head. He was sobbing and swearing as she raped his skull.

I held her shoulders and reached through her to Daine. We held him, and squeezed hard.

'He's going home,' she said.

His twitching body became transparent. Her hands grew into him, and tore like crabs at what was left of his dreamself. He hadn't thought out his internal organs properly, and they leaked into each other. Susan pulled out handfuls of ectoplasm and threw them aside.

She let him go, and we stood up. I shot him in the forehead. A black penny-sized spot appeared and he went stiff. Then he faded. There were clothes on the ground, and wisps of something immaterial.

The night went out.

Susan and I sat on the paling hillside as the sky whitened. There was a slight breeze that riffled her hair. As the dreamsun showed us the insubstantial outlines of the City down in the valley, we faded to white.

31

When Susan woke up, Dr Groome was picking terminals off her face. Beyond the doctor, she could see Trefusis and Juliet, peering at her.

She sat up, and sloshed out of the tank. The liquid dried on her skin.

Dr Groome held up three fingers and asked, 'How many?'

Susan tried to tell her, but her vocal chords wouldn't work. She held up three fingers in answer. The doctor allowed herself a smile.

There was another man in the room. A man she didn't at first recognise. Without his fedora his hairline was receding, and the clothe was wrong on him the way a trench coat had been right. Tom Tunney waved at her, but didn't say anything. He was shorter out of the City, but gave the impression of being more solid.

'Daine?' she croaked, her throat papery and hurting.

Governor Trefusis shrugged. 'I'm afraid you've had a wasted trip, Ms Bishopric. When you drove him from his Dream, it proved too much. You mindwiped him entirely.'

'I'm heartbroken.'

Trefusis smiled tightly. 'Me too.'

Juliet and Tunney helped her out of the tank. Daine's screen was giving a level brain-dead readout.

'More much-needed organs for the transplant crews,' said Dr

Groome, systematically disconnecting Daine's inputs.

She stared down at the living dead face. 'It wasn't a waste,' Susan gasped. 'Ask Yggdrasil sometime.'

Dr Groome brushed away a cloud of fine wires connecting the patient to his tank. 'Hmm,' she said, 'I wonder where these came from?'

Susan's knees didn't work properly yet. She sagged against Tunney.

'You'll get used to it after a while,' he said. 'Welcome to the waking world.'

He kissed her. But that wasn't why she fainted.

32

In the infinite darkness, Yggdrasil healed itself. The deleted City left an informational gap that had to be refilled. Links were rebuilt, defences strengthened, input recycled. The AI had learned a lesson from Truro Daine, and would be secure against any further breaches on the same plane. Measures were taken, decisions made without human consultations, and checks built into interface facilities. As a side-effect, forty-three lesser intelligences – human and artificial – that had, for one reason or another, illegally and impolitely leeched into Yggdrasil were quietly and without fuss burned out.

The machine scrolled out a 1,298-page print report to the Gunmint, knowing no one would ever bother to access it.

It found the presence, a bodiless speck in the vast, empty plains of the purged files. 'The body is a prison too,' Yggdrasil said, 'but you have escaped.'

Truro Daine, tinier in Yggdrasil's space than a microbe in the human system, screamed. And screamed.

Yggdrasil ignored the meaningless squeak, and reapplied itself to its many businesses.

It only had one thing to say to its harmless parasite, '*Th-th-th-that's all, folks!*'

...AND OTHER STORIES

DREAMERS

Elvis Kurtz was dreaming. He dreamed he was John F. Kennedy, former president (1960–Lee Harvey Oswald) of the former United States of America. The dream was a riot of pornography; involving enormous wealth, extreme power, intermittent ultra-violence, and sex with Marilyn Monroe. It was a pre-sold success. An inevitable Iridium Tape. An inescapable quinquemillion-seller.

Kurtz was *dybbukking*, a passenger in the mind. Kurtz was aware of what John Yeovil thought it felt like to John Fitzgerald Kennedy in August 1961. He had access to a neatly arranged file of memories, plus a few precog glimpses carried over from waking life. He would have to pull out before Dallas. The JFK similie was not aware of Kurtz. Actually the JFK similie hardly seemed to be aware of anything.

Yeovil had had JFK plump his mistress' bottom on the edge of the presidential desk and penetrate the former Norma Jean Baker (1926–next year) standing up. A pile of authenticated contemporary documents were scrunched up beneath their spectacular copulation.

Kurtz trusted Yeovil had got the externals right. Through the JFK similie he was perceiving the Oval Office precisely as it had been. Marilyn's squeals were done in her actual voice, distilled from over three hundred hours of flatty sound-tracks and disc aurals. Yeovil would have had a computer assist handle that. Sometimes Kurtz envied the man's resources.

Marilyn and the president were sexing like well-oiled flesh robots. The dreamership liked their sexing pristine, with all the mess and pain taken out. Kurtz seared his overlay onto the dreamtape, burning a semi-apocalyptic series of multiple climaxes.

This was standard wet-dream stuff. The sort of thing Kurtz could do in his sleep. Kurtz's *dybbuk* overmind left the internals to his experienced subconscious and skimmed through the similie's memory. He ignored the story-so-far synopsis and picked a few random sensations.

The Pacific, WWII: the smell of burning oil and salt water, all-over Sun heat, repressed fear, an aural loop of *Sentimental Journey*. His father throwing a tantrum: the usual mix of shame, terror and embarrassment. Prawns at Hyannis Port. The inauguration; January chill, tension, incipient megalomania: '...ask not what your country can do for you...'

Kurtz wondered who had written that speech. Yeovil did not know; all the question got out of the similie was a momentary white-out. Damn, an extraneous thought. It would bleed onto the tape. Yeovil would have to do a post-erase. With the scene getting near the finish, Kurtz took ego control again.

Yeovil had taken the trouble to insert a 1961 image: Kennedy ejaculated like an ICBM silo; a thermonuclear chain reaction inside Marilyn took her out.

Yawn. Kurtz was an orgasm specialist. He topped the metaphor (too literary, but what did he expect) with a jumble of cross-sensory experiences. He translated the aural stimuli of the *Saint Matthew Passion* into a mass of tactiles. The dream shadow could take it, although a real body would have been blown away.

Marilyn lay face down, exhausted, her hair fanned on the pile carpet. JFK traced her backbone with the presidential seal. Yeovil had Catholic guilt flit through JFK's mind.

'Jack,' breathed Marilyn, 'did you know there's a theory that the whole universe got started with a Big Bang?'

Kennedy parted Marilyn's hair and kissed the nape of her neck. Kurtz felt a witty reply coming. Something hard at the base of the president's skull. A white hot needle in his head. A brief skin-and-bone agony, then nothing.

Damn Yeovil. Oswald was early.

Like most of the *haut ton* that year John Yeovil was devoted to Victoriana. The tridvid sages said the craze was a reaction to the acrid smogs that had taken to settling on London. Usually Yeovil affected to despise fashions, but this one suited him. Frock coats and stiff collars became his Holmesian figure, a beard usefully concealed his slash mouth, and the habitual precision of his gestures was ideal for consulting a half-hunter, taking a pinch of snuff, or casually slitting a footpad's nose with an iridium-assist swordstick.

At thirty-nine Yeovil was rich enough to indulge himself with opium-scented handkerchiefs, long case clocks and wax wreaths under glass. Three of his dreams were in the current q-seller listings. The JFK advance had accounted for the complete redecoration of his Luxborough Street residence.

Awaiting his guest, Yeovil adjusted the pearl pin in his grey cravat. Exactly right. Exact rectitude was all Yeovil asked of life. That and wealth and fame, of course. He sighted his one-sided smile in the mirror. The smile which, flashed during a tridvid interview or frozen on a dustjack, could cost him one million pounds *per annum* in lost sales alone. A definitive figure would have to take personal appearances, merchandising, and graft into consideration.

The smile was Yeovil's little secret. The mark of the submarine part of his mind he rigidly excluded from his dreams. John Yeovil had come to terms with his character. He lived with himself in relative comfort, despite the fact that he was easily the most hateful person he knew.

He had the dreaming talent, but so did hundreds of others. He had the patience to research and the skill to concept, but any raw Dreamer with funding could buy access to the D-9000 for those. Success in the dream industry was down to depth of feeling. Any feeling.

Great Dreamers were all prodigies of emotion. Susan Bishopric: empathy; Orin Tredway: imbecile love; Alexis St Clare: paranoia. And John Yeovil had hate. It did not come through as such in the dreams, but he knew that it was his great reservoir of hate that gave weight to conjuring of excitement, joy, pain and the rest.

The doorbell sounded. Yeovil had sent an in to Elvis Kurtz. The Household admitted him. A few tendrils of smog trailed the guest. The Household dispelled them.

'Mr Kurtz?'

'Uh. Yes.' Kurtz was muffled by his outdoor helmet. He pulled out of it. His eyes were watering profusely. Yeovil was familiar with the yellowish stream of tears. 'Sorry about this. I have a slight smog.'

'My sympathies,' said Yeovil. 'You can leave your things with the Household.'

'Thanks.' Kurtz ungauntleted and de-flakjacked. Underneath he wore a GP smock. Yeovil led is guest through the hall. The Household offed the hallway lamps, and upped the gas jets and open fire in the drawing-room.

'You were difficult to find, Mr Kurtz.'

'I'm supposed to be.' He had a trace of accent. Possibly Lichtenstein. 'I've been out.'

'Of course.' Yeovil decanted two preconstituted brandy snifters. 'Piracy or pornography?'

'A little of both.' Kurtz accepted the drink, smeared his tears, and sagged into a heavy armchair. He was not at ease. As well he might be. Yeovil decided to hit him now, and cover later.

'Mr Kurtz, prior to your incarceration you produced bootleg editions of my dreams which made a sizeable dent in my income. I can now offer you the opportunity to repay me.'

'Your pardon?' Kurtz was trying not to look startled. Like most Dreamers he was rotten at that sort of thing. Most, Yeovil reminded himself, not all.

'Don't worry. I'm not going to tap you for money. I'll even pay you.'

'For what?'

'The use of your talent.'

'I don't think you understand…'

'I'm well aware of your limitations, Mr Kurtz. Like myself you are a Dreamer. In many ways you are more powerful that I. You are capable of taping sensations far more intensely than I can. Yet I am successful and well-regarded,' (by most at least) 'and you are reduced to aping my dreams. Or producing work like this.'

Yeovil indicated a stack of tapes. Inelegant under-the-counter dreams with clinical titles: *Six Women With Mammary Abnormalities*, *The Ten-Minute Orgasm*. They were badly packaged, with lurid artists-imps on the dustjacks. There was no Dreamer by-line, but Kurtz recognised his own stuff.

'I'm too strong, Yeovil. I can't control my dreams the way you can. My mind doesn't just create, it amplifies and distorts. I wind up with so many resonances and contradictions that the dream falls apart. That's an advantage with one-reel wet dreams, but…'

'I don't require of you that you justify yourself, Mr Kurtz. I am an artist. I have no capacity for moral outrage. We have that much in common. Our position is at odds with those of the judiciary, the critical establishment, and the British Board of Dream Censors. Come with me.'

The dreaming room was different. Most of the house was a convincing, dark, stuffy and uncomfortable recreation of the 1890s. The dreaming room was what people in 1963 had expected the future to look like. All the surfaces were a glossy, featureless white.

Kurtz was impressed. He touched his fingertips, then his naked palm, to the glasspex wall. He started away, and a condensation handprint faded.

'It's warm. Is that eternity lighting?'

'Partly. I have the dreaming room kept at womb temperature.'

'You dream here?'

'Of course. The surroundings have been calculated exactly. Psychologically attuned to be beneficial to the dreaming talent. The recording equipment is substantially what you are familiar with.'

'You have computer assist?'

'My Household has a library tap for research. I don't use it much, though. I actually read books. I'm not one of the D-9000's troop of hacks. I don't think we should be the glorified amanuenses of a heuristic pulp mill.'

'I don't like the machines either. They hurt.' Kurtz was irritated. Good, that should keep him off balance. 'What is all this about?'

'Would you be surprised to learn that I am an admirer of your work?'

Kurtz cleared an unconvincing laugh from his throat. 'Would you be prepared to say that on the dustjack of *Sixth Form Girls in Chains*?'

Yeovil tapped his ID into the console. The Household extruded a couch from the floor. It looked sculpted. Out of vanilla ice cream.

'Besides yours my talent is lukewarm. I want to make use of your capacities to underline certain aspects of my work in progress.'

'Uh huh.'

'I am dreaming a historical piece, focusing on the character of John Kennedy, martyred president of the United States of America. Kennedy was known to be a man with a highly passionate nature. I think it not inapt that your touch with erotica be applied.'

Kurtz sat on the couch, trying to find the loophole. 'What about the certification?'

'I plan on sidestepping the BBDC. They have no real authority, and I am supported by my publishers and the vast public interest in my work. The Board owes its precarious existence to its claim that it represents the desire of the majority. Once that is disproved, they will fall. *JFK* has been concepted as a radical dream.'

'How is this going to work?'

'I've dreamed a guideline. The sequence you'll work on is fully scripted. The externals are complete. However the first person is blank.'

'Kennedy?'

'Yes. He is emerging as a very strong figure in the dreaming. But in this scene he's empty. I want you to amend the internals as he sexes with his mistress.'

'Same old wet dream stuff?'

'Essentially. But in this case the explicit material is crucial to the concept. The character of Kennedy is seminal to an understanding to the twentieth century. All of his drives must be exposed. The underlying…'

'Yeah. Right. Let's talk about the money.'

Yeovil balanced the newly-discharged needle gun on his fingertips as he walked across the room, and dropped the weapon into the Household Disperse. Kurtz lay face down on the dreaming couch with a three-inch dart in his brain. The tape was still running, although the Kurtz input was zero. Yeovil sucked his burned fingers. He would smear them better when he was finished with Kurtz.

He had never killed anyone before. He sadly discovered that dream was better than actual. Like sex. He stored the minor rush of emotions for future use.

The tape clicked through. The Household offered the recorder.

Yeovil picked the subcutaneous terminals out of Kurtz's head and dropped them into their glass of purple. The whirlpool rinse sucked particles of Kurtz out of its system.

Yeovil went through Kurtz's smockpocks. A few credit cards and a bunch of ins. A couple of five-pound bits. They all went into the Disperse, along with Kurtz's outdoor gear, porno tapes, and finger-printed brandy glass. Do it, then clear up afterwards – the secret of criminal success.

The Household presented Yeovil with his outdoor kit: a visored hat, and a padded Inverness. The tailors boasted that their garments were proof against a fragmentation charge. That was true: in the event of such an unlikely weapon being turned on the cape, it would be unmarked. Anyone inside it, however, would find his torso turned to jelly by the impact. Most footpads used needle guns, anyway.

Yeovil hauled Kurtz out to his armoured Ford. On the street he fitted an outmoded breather. It kept the smog out of his lungs as well as a more stylish domino, and disguised him.

Yeovil pressed his car in, and tapped his ID into the automatic. The smog lights upped. The streets were deserted.

Yeovil drove around central London for fifteen minutes before chancing upon a suitable dump. He slung the body over several twist-tie rubbish bags in the forecourt of a condemned high-rise. It would look like an ordinary waylaying. There were probably five similar corpses within walking distance. If the Black Economists got to Kurtz before the Metropolitans, the body would be stripped of any usable organs. The incident would not rate a mention on the local.

Back at Luxborough Street Yeovil reprogrammed his Household to forget Kurtz's visit. He fed in a plausible dull evening at home, and wrote off the energy expenditure to various gadgets.

Then he slept. The next stage was complicated, and he did not want to deal with it late at night after his first murder. He felt a twinge of insomniac excitement, which he countered by back-grounding a subliminal lullaby.

The Household woke him early with a call. It was Tony, Yeovil's chief editor at Futura. Tony looked harassed.

'You've overreached another deadline, John. I wanted the *JFK* master back yesterday. We're committed to a production start. And we have marketing to consider. It's a q-seller on advance sales, and you haven't delivered yet.'

'Sorry.' Yeovil stretched his mind around the problem. 'I've still got a few more amendments.'

'You're a trekkiehead, John. Leave it alone. I told you it was finished last week. I'm satisfied as is. And I'm supposed to be a bastard tyrannical editor. We're all expletive deleted here. The copiers are primed.'

'You have my word as a gentleman that a definitive master will be on your desk tomorrow morning.'

'Tomorrow morning? I get into the office Kubricking early, John.' Tony looked dubious. 'Okay, you've got it, but no more extensions. No matter how many errors slip through the finetooth. You can have Oswald miss, and re-elect the randy bugger for all I care. The next John Yeovil hits the stands Friday. Does that scan?'

'Of course. I apologise for the delay. I'm sure you understand…'

'If that means: Will I forgive you for being an iridium-plated prick, no way. However, my slice of your sales buys you a lot of tolerance. Ciao.'

Tony over-and-outed. He was getting near termination. There were other publishers. Offers tapped up in Yeovil's slab every morning.

The Kurtz-assist master was still slotted. Yeovil pulled it, primed the duplicator, and cloned a copy. The master tape was too recognisable as such for his purpose. Too many slices and scribbles. Plus he would need it later. His plan did not include writing off the work done on *JFK*. The dream would be worth a lot of money. Yeovil doled himself out a shiver of self-delight.

He printed on the clone's spine: *JFK* by John Yeovil. And under that he scrawled: review copy.

Review copy. Yeovil backgrounded an aural of Richard Horton's review of his last dream. Just to remind himself what this was about.

'Yeovil is lucky that his publishers have the clout to buy off his heroine's heirs, 'cause *The Private Life of Margaret Thatcher* is quite as unnecessary and unsavoury as his previous efforts. Yeovil is genned up on period externals, and has an insidious knack for concepting his dreams so you zip through without being too annoyed. But once the headset is off, you know you've had a zilch experience. A few critics praise the man for his high-minded moral tone, but even they will find the lip-smacking prurience of *Margaret Thatcher* difficult to get their heads around. Yet again Yeovil bombards the captive mind with an endless round of sensuality – enormous state banquets, thrilling battles, ichor-drenched 'tasteful' sexing – and finally condemns all the excesses he has dragged us through with such gloating relish. He is at his worst when his heroine submits to what he has her anachronistically think of as 'a fate worse than death' under the well-remembered, much-maligned Idi Amin in order to save a planeload of hostages. One sympathises with the feminist group who have petitioned for Yeovil's judicial castration under the anti-sexism laws. Finally, the man's dreams are a far less interesting phenomenon than his publicity machine. If you're out there taking a rest from adding up the profits, John, pack it in and join the Rural Reclamation Corps. With relief we turn to a new dream from Miss Susan Bishopric, who has made such an...'

Richard Horton was as smug a little shit as ever there was. Listening to his middle-aged parody of the adjectival overkill of a comput-assessor made Yeovil's fingers twist his watch chain into flesh-pinching knots.

Yeovil could not decide which made him hate Richard Horton more. The Carol business, or his tridvid defamations. Carol Horton had been Yeovil's mistress for three months. Before he had elected to sever the bond, Carol had taken it upon herself to return to her husband. Moreover she had instituted a civil lawsuit against Yeovil, alleging that he had drawn upon copyrighted facets of her personality for Pristine, the protagonist of his *The Sweetheart of Tau Ceti*. When he thought about her Yeovil still disliked Carol, but only to prove a point. Deep down it was Horton's insulting reviews that lifted Yeovil's loathing into the superhate bracket.

Before leaving the house Yeovil vindictively erased all his Horton tapes.

Richard Horton was dreaming. He dreamed that he was John F. Kennedy. Or, rather, he dreamed that he was John Yeovil jacking off while dreaming that he was John F. Kennedy. If Kennedy had been like the similie no one would now be around to review the dream. The Ivans would have nuked the world in desperation.

So far it had been the typical John Yeovil craptrap. The man never missed a chance to be cheap and obvious.

In the Oval Office JFK was sexing Marilyn Monroe. Why was it always Marilyn Monroe? Every dream set in the mid-twentieth century found it obligatory to have the hero sex Marilyn Monroe. The girl must have had a crowded schedule. The semiologically inclined comput-assessors called her an icon of liberated sensuality. Richard Horton called her a thundering cliché.

It was the regulation wet-dream stuff, a little harder than Yeovil's usual hypocritical lyricism. At least there were no butterflies and gentle breezes here. Just heavy-duty sexing. Another depiction of woman as a hunk of meat. Kubrick knows what Carol ever saw in Yeovil.

Horton's attention strayed around the scene. Perhaps he should feed the dream through the British Museum Library's researcher. It might catch Yeovil out on an external. It was probably not worth it. Yeovil was the kind of Dreamer who got every wallpaper tone and calendar date right and then hit you with a concept that would make a computer puke.

Yeovil had peppered the sexing with memories. The lanky git was pathetically pleased with himself. Look how much research I did, screamed a mass of largely irrelevant facts. WWII, Holy Joe Kennedy, Hyannis Port.

Who wrote Kennedy's inaugural address? That was out of character. Horton's *dybbuk* flinched from the white-out. There was another mind crowding in, superimposed on the Kennedy similie. It was not Yeovil, he was working overtime on having JFK remember who was topping the bill at the Newport, Rhode Island jazz festival in 1960. There was someone else. A strong mind Horton could not place. It was a contributory Dreamer. Was Yeovil trying to pirate again? Eclipsing a collaborator on the credits was not beneath him.

Horton felt himself getting lost in the dream. The fiction was broken, and he was disconcerted. For an instant he thought he actually was sexing Marilyn Monroe. The woman was screaming in his ear. After all these years, the real thing.

Then it was cartoon time. The JFK similie body stretched impossibly. The return of Plastic Man. There was a playback fault. That was it. Whoever had last dreamed through this copy had left an accidental over-lay. Horton fished around for a name, but was dropped into a maelstrom of explosion imagery.

Was Yeovil experimenting with hard core? At least that would make a change.

Then the dream came together again, and Horton was locked in. Wedged between the minds of Yeovil, Kennedy and the mysterious Mr X.

Marilyn lay face down, exhausted, her hair fanned on the pile carpet. JFK traced her backbone with the presidential seal.

Horton was disgusted to feel Catholic guilt flit through JFK's mind. Yeovil was piling cant upon cliché as per usual.

'Jack,' breathed Marilyn, 'did you know there's a theory that the whole universe got started with a Big Bang?'

Yeovil's dialogue was always the pits.

Kennedy parted Marilyn's hair and kissed the nape of her neck. Horton felt a trekkiehead reply coming. Something hard at the base of the president's skull. A white hot needle in his head. A brief skin and bone agony (what was that about Oswald?) then nothing.

Horton was not Horton any more. Horton was not anybody any more. His mind had been wiped. Completely, as an erase blanks a tape. Yeovil watched as the former Horton rolled on his side, retracting his arms and legs, wrapping himself into an egg.

The dreamtape was still running. Yeovil offed the machine, and pulled the clone tape. Elvis Kurtz had been unknowingly generous. He had shared his death.

Yeovil freed Horton from his headset, and gently popped his contact lenses. They had been making him cry. No point in keeping up enmities from a previous incarnation.

Yeovil wondered how Carol would take to motherhood. She always had shown an inclination to sentiment over gurgling infants. Now she had a chance to be closely acquainted with one. Horton had a lot of growing up to do.

Yeovil dropped the tape into Horton's Disperse, and used the critic's in to gain access to his Household. He wiped the whole day. As an extra flourish, he wiped the entire Household memory. A little pointless mystification to obscure his involvement.

Now all he had to do was get back to Luxborough Street, wipe Kurtz off the master tape, give that to Tony, and wait for the returns. Do it, then clear up afterwards.

* * *

Tony had messaged in the Household tridvid.

'I had a merry hell of a time overriding your Household, you bastard. But we didn't lend you company programs for nothing. So you were spending the day putting a few final touches to the masterpiece were you? If so, you must be doing it in another dimension because the master is here and you aren't. Where the Jacqueline Susann are you? Actually, don't bother to tell me. I don't give a damn. I now have the *JFK* master, and that fulfils your contract. You can start looking for a new publisher. By the time you play this back we'll have a million copies in distribution, with an expected second impression on Monday. Don't worry though. You won't have to sue us to get what's coming to you. Ciao.'

PATRICIA'S PROFESSION

When the call came, Patricia was going FF through the latest snuffs. She was a subscriber to the *120 Days in the City of Sodom* part-work, but, since Disney had run out of de Sade and been forced to fall back on their own limited psychopathology, the series had deteriorated. After a few minutes of real-time PLAY, she had twigged that the 104th day was just one of the fifties with a sexual role reversal. Mouldy chiz. Colin broke into the vid-out.

'Patti,' he said. 'Go to PRINT.'

Colin had blanked before she could work out whether he was live or a message simulacrum. The printer retched a laconic strip. JAY DEARBORN. DEARBORN ESTATE. TWENTY ONE O'CLOCK HIT. 2-NITE.

The mark was on screen. The Firm had a four-second snip from a regular call. Dearborn was a sleek, expensive, youngish man. He had on a collarless, fine-stripe shirt. Silently, he repeated a phrase. Something about cheekbones. Patricia's lip-reading was off.

She switched to greenscreen and speed-read Dearborn's write-up. Executive with Skintone, Inc., the second-largest fleshwear house. Married. Euro-citizen. Not cleared for parenthood. No adult criminal record. Alive. Solvent.

Colin came back, real-time. 'Our client is Philip Wragge. More middle management at Skintone. He likes us. He's used us before.'

'Why does he want Dearborn hit?'

'Getting curious, Patti?' Colin smiled. 'That's not in your usual profile. I think it's the mark's birthday.'

Patricia's birthday was in August. When she was little, her parents had always taken her to their cottage in Portugal for the school holidays. She had escaped until she was twelve. That year, Dad's job became obsolete, and the cottage had to be marketed. At tea-time on her birthday, the other children had come round to Patricia's house and killed her.

Colin faded, and the scheduled programme popped up on the slab. Patricia rarely watched real-time. A Luton house-husband guessed that Seattle, Washington was the capital of the US. The Torture Master grinned, and his glamorous assistant thrust his/ her bolt-cutters into the hot coals. 'Wrong,' sang the man in the dayglo tux, 'I'm afraid it's Portland, Oregon. That puts you in a tricky spot, Goodman. You have only three questions and two toes left, so take your time with this next one. Who, at the time of this recording, is the Vice-President of the Confederate States of America...'

Patricia off-switched. It was twenty to nineteen. Chord would be here soon. She put her uniform on. Black spiderweb tights, black lace singlet, black arm-length talon glove, black butterfly tie. She shrugged into the white shoulder holster, and pulled a comfortable heavy white Burberry over her shoulders. She perched a black beret on her Veronica Lake bob. She white-fixed her face, and blacked her lips and eyelids. Neat.

She palmed her desktop, and the safety cabinet unsealed. She took out the roscoe and disassembled it. There had been some question about the foresight, but it seemed okay to her eye. She replaced the lubricant cartridge, and snapped the machine back together. She shoved a new clip of slugs into the grip, and holstered the roscoe.

It could manage up to 170 rounds per second. At that rate, the slugs left the eleven-inch barrel as molten chips. At Sixth Form College, the Firm's instructor had given a demonstration. She had turned a cow carcass into a piece of abstract expressionism, a study in red and intestine. Patricia didn't like to use her roscoe as a hosepipe, and usually kept the rate adjusted to a comfortable twenty-five r.p.s.

Outside, the car called to her. Patricia sealed her flat, negotiated the checkpoint in the foyer, and stepped onto the steaming pavement. If she stood still for a few minutes, the yellow ground mist would eat holes in her unprotected shins. Harry Chord, at ease in his reinforced chauffeur's puttees and Lone Ranger mask, held the Olds' door open for her. She slid onto the sofa-sized back seat. The Olds purred. Chord took the console.

The sturdy, box-like, black car had only recently been converted. Chord had done the job himself, and was quietly pleased with it. When they stopped at the Gordon's station to tank up, he pointed out the minute scars on the hood and running boards. Otherwise, it was impossible to tell from the exterior that the cash-wasting petrol engine had been replaced with the latest model booze-burner.

Patricia was tense, impatient. As always before a hit. She had been to the lavatory twice since Colin's call, but there was still a tingle in her lower abdomen. Some of the other girls pill-popped, but she needed, and wanted, the cold-rush of unfiltered sensations.

Of course, there had been less popping since Rachel. The girl had taken too many zippers, waltzed into her mark's office singing 'Paper Moon', and shot the man through the brain. By the time the termination officers arrived, she had switched to 'Stardust'. The Firm had lost its 100% efficiency rating.

Patricia had heard Chord, and several of the other back-up personnel, refer to Rachel's humpty dumpty hit. '...all the king's horses, and all the king's men...' The flippancy irritated her. Killing people might seem like a fun job, but you had to take it seriously. If nothing else, Rachel had proved that.

The Dearborn Estate was out in the Green Belt. They were well ahead of schedule, so she had Chord program a route that would avoid the disemployment centre. Shit City, the claimants called it. Nissen huts covered in ghastly, mock-cheerful murals. The dope dole. The Ghetto Blaster gangs. There had recently been a rash of documentaries, but, having spent six years in Shit City, Patricia couldn't get off on poverty porn.

Evidently, Dearborn's wife was in on the hit. At the estate entrance, a cobra terminal snaked into the Olds and hovered over Patricia's lap. HELLO! IDENTIFICATION? She palm-printed the slab, and keyed in the Firm's trademark. PURPOSE OF VISIT? She had typed MURDER before noticing that the need for a reply had been countered on the print of Gillian Dearborn. HAVE A PLEASANT VISIT.

The crackling electrodes in the gravel drive went briefly dead as the Olds rolled over them. There were other cars, low and streamlined, ranked in front of the house. Over the roof landing floated a small dirigible, shifting gently on its mooring. The house, Victorian but remodelled in early Carolian, was lit by banks of old-mode disco lamps.

Dearborn was having a birthday party, with live music. Patricia recognised the popular song 'Throw Yourself Off a Bridge'. The ballad was being performed by a small swing combo; an unfamiliar, somehow inapt arrangement. A girl sinatra was trying to croon to the up-tempo.

'When I get too depressed,
Crawling along in a ditch,
I get right up,
Walk on down,
And throw myself off a bridge...'

Patricia left Chord with the Olds, and walked unconcerned across the lawn. A few stray guests, in designer rags, noticed her.

She hated Depression Chic. The bulk of the party was behind the house between the L of its two wings and the skimming pool. She tried to move easily among the rich.

A man with a plumed mohawk, an epitome of the New Conservatism, reached inside her Burberry. She sliced his forehead with a soporific talon. He fell onto a trestle table, between the swan cutlets and the cocaine blancmange. He would be able to tell the other Young Rotarians he had won second prize in a duel.

> 'I could put myself through a mangle,
> I could drink the water in Spain,
> From a home-made noose I could dangle,
> It's the end to all my pain…'

Dearborn was an easy mark. He was holding a helium balloon with BIRTHDAY BOY on it. He was squiffed, but standing. A plump, dapper man, and an elegant woman with fashionable facial mutilations were propping Dearborn up. Wragge and Gillian? They saw her coming and confirmed their identities by rapidly moving out of her line.

Abandoned, the mark lurched forward into a personal spotlight. No hole-in-the-head innocent bystanders in the way. Terrific.

> 'If I feel like cracking up
> And locking myself in the fridge,
> I get on out
> And take a high jump,
> To throw myself off a bridge…'

Patricia reached with her bare hand for the roscoe. The Burberry slid from her shoulders. There were a few werewolf whistles. She shimmied across the lawn, getting in close to compensate for the possibly dodgy foresight. She did a few elementary gold-digger steps, and adopted the Eastwood position; legs apart, weight evenly distributed, left hand on right wrist, elbows slightly bent to absorb the kickback.

The bandleader, surprised but adaptable, had his instruments segue into 'Happy Birthday to You'. The sinatra picked it up immediately, and led the less out-of-it guests in the chorus.

The mark was looking around, gasping. '...Phil? You...' The balloon went up.

She took out his left kneecap. He staggered sideways, tripping into an abandoned urn but not falling. She upped the r.p.s. and sprayed Dearborn's flailing right arm. His hand came off at the wrist. Most of the guests had to laugh. She closed in, and fired a final, freeranging burst into his torso. She had a glimpse of churning innards. He did an awkward pirouette and, with a satisfying splash, fell into the pool. The purple skum rippled. There were cheers. Patricia took a bow.

By the time she had retrieved her coat, the resurrection men were there. The kildare was passing a vivicorder over the corpse. A nurse Patricia knew ticked off the necessary repairs. Most of the vatbred organs and ossiplex bones would be in the Firm's ambulance. The front man was assuring Gillian Dearborn that her husband would be on his feet by morning, and preparing the legal and medical waivers for her palm.

'Good job, lassie.' Wragge hugged and kissed her. Even for a regular customer, he was overdoing it. 'When Jay sees himself on the playback, he'll die all over again.'

He stuffed a thousand note down her cleavage. Not a bad gratuity. He also gave her a hundred in Sainsbury's Redeemable for Chord. She was invited to the resurrection party, but cried off.

Tired, she gave Chord authority to get back to town by the quickest route. As she drove through Shit City, she cleaned the roscoe. She remembered her own deaths, and wondered whether the DHSS still had a budegtary allocation for resurrecting the underemployed.

She hadn't had the kind of luxury treatment Dearborn was getting. There had been problems with her anglepoise vertebrae throughout her middle teens. She had not had the funds for a proper rebuild until she started working for Killergrams.

That first time, the other children had dragged her out of the house and hanged her from a swan-neck lamp-post. Her party dress was torn, and her legs were badly bitten by midges. Dangling in the late afternoon, the last thing that had crossed her mind was that this was supposed to be funny.

TWITCH TECHNICOLOR

Playing the buttons was all well and good, but Monte thought sometimes you had to get your hands in the colour. He had Bela Lugosi frame-frozen in mid-snarl, stretched black and white over the video easel, wooden stake jutting. Patiently, he combined film overlays in his plastette. Red was the key here. People like red best of all, and there would have to be a lot of it in the *Dracula* remix. It was integral to the property; perhaps a major factor in its lingering appeal. Finally satisfied, he inserted the plastette into the assessor, and sat back while the machine digitally encoded the precise shade that had struck him as proper. When it was done, the assessor pinged like an antique oven, and Monte plucked the now-primed squirtstylo from its lightwell.

He squeezed a blob of red onto the tip of his forefinger and examined it. It was fine. Then he dabbed the electronic image/analog with the stylo, dribbling red between the reproduction lines. The monochrome filled in, and gore gushed from the dead actor's starched shirtfront. The film looked better already. It was the personal touch that distinguished the Monte Video product from the competition's all-machine 'enhanced' remix jobs. He plugged the stylo, and noticed phantom rinds of red under his nails. His hand looked as though it belonged to a murderer. He shook his fingers, and the red vanished in a static crackle.

He adjusted his handiwork. He keyed ADVANCE and the film slow-forwarded a few frames. Lugosi completed his snarl, his hand clawed at the stake, blood flowed freely. The red grew, a blob in the centre of the image. It was fine. Monte keyed SAVE, and the colour took. The vampire's glowing eyes and skull-head cufflinks lit up, the exact red of the blood on his chest and about his mouth.

Michaelis Monte could remember the beginnings of the remix business, the ineffectually 'colourised' films of the eighties. He had been among the first to test the potential of image/analog encoding, the process that enabled a skilled remix man to have an original moving picture reduced by the assessor to a particle chain of information bits and then rebuilt again in accordance with his own vision. With his own technologies, he had stolen the march on the majors, resisted many an attempted corporate rape, won all the Dickie awards going, and marked out an Ayatollah's share of the marketplace. Monte Video's *Dracula* was already a q-seller on advance orders. Securing the rights from the schizoid legal descendants of Bram Stoker, Universal Studios, Hammer Films, the BBC and about twenty others who had dipped their claws into the property had been a lengthy and costly battle. With such an important acquisition, Monte might in any case have taken the time to handle the remix himself. Thanks to the Troubles, he was being forced to do the hands-on work personally. He was still the *primo uno* in the business.

Trebor, Ruby Gee, Consodine, and now Tarnaverro. All remaindered. Someone had it in for his remix men, or was trying for a stranglehold on Monte Video.

He keyed PROCEED, and the assessor took over, absorbing Monte's decisions, replacing the drab grey of the original with dayglo colours. He liked to think that Monte Video's *Dracula* was the movie Tod Browning would have turned out in 1930 if he had been free from the censorship requirements of the day and had access to unlimited technical resources. Browning had been forced to have Van Helsing stake Dracula offscreen, with only a tame groan to mark the villain's death, but now the anti-climax could be fixed. Lugosi floundered through the vaulted crypt, eyes aflame like an electric Antichrist, pushing aside curtains of butterfly-winged/stained glass cobweb, recoiling from a succession of violently violet neon crucifixes. Then the vampire was down, and Peter Cushing was on top of him, hammering furiously, driving in deeper the killing stake.

Actually, Edward Van Sloan had played Van Helsing to Lugosi's Count Dracula, but since nobody remembered him any more, Monte had decided to mix in Cushing's definitive performance from the 1958 version. In fact, aside from Lugosi, and Dwight Frye as the fly-eating Renfield, he had recast the whole film: James Dean as Jonathan Harker, Marilyn Monroe as the victim-cum-vampirette Lucy, and Meryl Streep as the heroine, Mina. He'd even stirred in Humphrey Bogart as the comic cockney asylum attendant. There weren't enough David Manners or Helen Chandler fans to make a dent in the marketplace, and Monte was always in favour of anything that added to the commercial afterlife of a property. His instincts had made him a rich man; rich enough to afford an unparalleled art collection: 3-D religious postcards, popster necrophiliabilia, Woolworth's clown prints. Michaelis Monte was well-known as a man of influential tastes.

Onscreen, Dracula putrefied spectacularly, maggots bursting from his eyesockets. An entirely apt Jimi Hendrix guitar burst accompanied his deathscreams. Monte upped the zynth. More noise, more music, more scream. He infilled with more red. The last of Dracula should be a bloody pool on the lining of his opera cape, red on red. 'Fuck you, Count,' said Peter Cushing, 'and the bat you rode in on.' It was well said, and Monte's vocals people had taken a lot of care to perfect the actor's clipped voice pattern. Hendrix segued into Tchaikovsky, winding up the film with the snatch of *Swan Lake* that had been heard in the Transylvanian prologue, and the end titles strobe-flashed as Cushing led Dean and Streep out of the crypt into the rainbow-bright sunrise that lettered out 'THE END' in the sky, and subliminally flashed an expensive ad for Coca-Drugs.

The message pore in the top right of the easel spiralled open. Monte saw an inset of his own doorstep, from the p.o.v. of the monitor-eyed stone eagle perched atop the lintel. Sally Rhodes stood on his WELCOME mat, drenchcoat belted tight, hat-brim pulled low over her domino breather. She looked the eagle in the eye and gave a tight smile. Monte pulled over the nearest slab, and ran the routine checks. The image in the pore proved true; a first-generation, unscrambled (he supposed that he only had himself to blame for the fact that you couldn't routinely trust anything you saw on television any more). The Household recognised her heat pattern, cross-checked the clearance of the Sally Rhodes Agency with the latest listings, and gave him a manual control over the door. He palm-printed an okay, and the pore closed as Sally Rhodes was admitted into his hallway.

Monte had scheduled this meeting for late evening in an attempt to avoid embarrassment. He had, of course, been keeping the state police updated on his Troubles, as he was obliged by Law to do, but it was no secret that Monte Video was financially able to afford access to private sector policing. The Sally Rhodes Agency was known for its discretion, and Monte found that quality worth a hefty annual premium. He was even willing to overlook Sally Rhodes' tactless jibes about his business and taste in *objets d'art*. In a market rife with piracy, Monte Video rarely suffered from bootlegging, and the last large-scale operation to try infringing its copyrights had been permanently retired to Sally Rhodes.

Monte met her in the gallery. The paintings were asleep, but the room was a whisper with their steady breathing. Sally Rhodes was admiring his shagpile Rothko. 'There is some interesting work being done with sub-sentient jellies and acrylics at the moment, don't you think?' he ventured. The poised young woman turned and held up a hand in mock horror, waving it as if to ward off

Dracula with a crucifix. He missed the point.

'That shirt,' she gasped. 'It's… it's…'

'It's called a paisley pattern,' he told her. 'The lemon yellow and eggshell blue combination is my own idea.'

'You didn't have to tell me, Miki. My grandmother told me about the 1960s. They must have been hell to live through.'

'I wouldn't know. I was very small at the time.'

'And now you're very big?'

'Quite.' He adjusted his chrome and lucite love beads. 'Are you in a position to make a report?'

'Only a preliminary. I note that you've lodged provisional declarations of war against Agfa-Daiei and Disney-McDonald's. You know what kind of commitment that will entail.'

'What choice have I got? Someone's been singeing my remix men. With Tarnaverro gone, there's a severe crimp in my output. It has to be an alliance among the competition. They want me scuppered before Frankfurt.'

'Perhaps,' said Sally Rhodes. She peeled off her domino, and sniffed with distaste the herbal-scented air. 'Do you have a roomscreen handy? I've got a tape to run for you.'

He accessed the downstairs suite, which came complete with a full editing slab, and a glasswall display of Monte Video's topselling remix jobs: *Citizen Kane, Battleship Potemkin, Psycho, Faster Pussycat! Kill! KILL!, King Kong, High Noon, Double Indemnity, The Best of Sergeant Bilko, The Elvis Autopsy Video, The Seventh Seal, The Breakdancin' Nun*. Monte thumbsigned the slab, and a framed poster for the Bob Dylan/Sylvester Stallone/ Glenda Jackson/Madonna *Women in Love* remix rose into its ceiling slot, revealing a milkwhite wallscreen. It was the only colourless thing in the house.

Sally Rhodes unscrambled the sequence lock on her briefcase, and produced a video cassette. It was a Monte Video Own Brand product. 'This is from Tarnaverro's office,' she said. 'I've established that it was what he was working on when he was killed.'

'Then it should be *Captain Blood*?'

'1935, Michael Curtiz, with Errol Flynn and Olivia de Havilland. Warner Brothers. Right?'

'Your pardon?' he double-taked. 'Oh, forgive me, I always forget you're a – what are they called? Film *buff*.' He spat the word with distaste, recalling the petitions that used to flood into his slab.

'Let's pass over that, shall we?' she said, shuffling fiche notes. 'You've kept up on your autopsies, I trust?'

'Yes.'

'But let me remind you. Tarnaverro was attacked by someone with a long, sharp, heavy blade. A carving knife, a machete, or a sword. He was almost entirely hacked to pieces.'

'Yes. That's why I suspect those Agfa-Daiei bastards. The multinats like to throw in a scare when they open hostilities.' In his struggle to swallow Thorn-Futura-McAlpine before the combine swallowed him, Monte had authorised as bad or far worse. 'And you know what the axis are like.'

Being market leader was a precarious position. Since the Troubles started, with Trebor, Monte Video had lost over 20% of its employees to the marketplace. Even disemployment was better than being an unmourned casualty in a corporate skirmish.

'It may not be that simple, Miki. Have you ever thought to match the methods of assassination used against your people with the properties they were working on?'

Monte was startled. 'No. Why should I?'

Sally Rhodes held up her fiche. 'Trebor was the first. Two months ago. He was blown to bits by some kind of frag charge. He was remixing *Battleground*. Ruby Gee was expertly kicked and trampled to death. Her current assignment, *The Gold Diggers of 1933*. Consodine had his throat ripped out by some kind of animal. Remember the werewolf jokes in the newsies? His last property was *Lassie Come Home*. Do you see it?'

He wanted it keyed out for him.

Sally Rhodes slid *Captain Blood* into the VCR maw, and began to play the buttons. As always when you slot a cassette at random, the sex scene faded on. 'This is the sequence Tarnaverro was remixing when they got him. We had to clean the blood and guts off the tape. The assessor was clogged.'

Onscreen, Errol Flynn was extensively sodomising the cabin boy. It had seemed wasteful not to feature the star's most legendary endowment in the film, and all the historical research proved that buggery would have been a way of life on the all-male pirate ships of the 17th Century. Besides, they had wanted to work up a role for the teenage David Bowie. There was a little ghosting, and Tarnaverro's green notation blips came and went in the corner of the image, but otherwise it was fine. It was an effective addition. Sally Rhodes was distracted, not looking at the action, but waiting for something else to appear. 'Look, here it is, here's where it happens –' she framefroze '– look at this line.' There was a thick band of different quality colour, crossing the screen like a ripple. She advanced frame by frame, demonstrating the glitch's progression. It was a diagonal wipe from left to right. Inside the band, the colours were different: a little like the pastel shades of three-strip Technicolor, not very realistic and far too thin for Monte's taste. When the band had passed, all colour had gone. Bowie's face faded into Olivia de Havilland's, and, a cut later, Errol Flynn had his clothes on. There was a ruckus outside the cabin, and Flynn was bounding, cutlass in hand, to the door.

'So this is where Tarnaverro broke off? This is the original version?'

'Not quite,' said Sally Rhodes, tapping a finger to the screen, initiating PAUSE. A horde of pirate extras cowered in tableau as Captain Blood laid into them. They were typical Warner Bros. seadogs with earrings, three or four knives apiece, striped headscarves, leather boots, stupid expressions. But in the middle was a balding pirate with Coke-doke bottle glasses, and a two-piece whaleskin suit. It was Tarnaverro. The woman took her finger from the screen, and action resumed. In a long shot, Flynn threw off two huge attackers. Tarnaverro was in the melee, turning to run. His glasses fell off, and were kicked over the side by a sneering Basil Rathbone. The remix man made a dash for safety, and tripped over De Havilland's skirts. Flynn smiled, impossibly beautiful in the smoke of battle, and ran the interloper cleanly through. He heaved the body off his cutlass, and Tarnaverro fell into the sword-waving throng. The pirates hacked at him mercilessly. He even got his own close-up, still twitching, eyeballs free-floating, a coil of rope grey under his head. Then, he was out of the film – another dead extra – and Flynn was facing up to Rathbone, jeering at the villain's frenchified ringlets.

Monte was appalled.

'Elaborate, isn't it?'

He had to agree. 'It would take expert remixing to… do that. But it's pointless…'

The film went on. Monte waved down the sound, but the black and white figures still danced on the wall. He had to think.

'Mr Monte, do you know a Caspasian Kleinzack?'

'Of course. He's a remix man. With Agfa-Daiei. I've been trying to get to him. With the Troubles, we'll need to net a few top defectors to keep up our output. He's not up to my standards, or Tarnaverro's, but he's a professional jobber. Is A-D involved in this?'

'Unlikely. I mention Kleinzack because he's dead too. The newsies haven't got it yet, but he's definitely a casualty. I think A-D have had others, and there's been a total security clampdown at McDisneyworld. Someone doesn't like remix men; Kleinzack was shot. He was working on *My Darling Clementine*. Do you know the property?'

'1946, John Ford, with Henry Fonda as Wyatt Earp and Victor Mature as Doc Holliday. 20th Century Fox. You're not the only one who can remember things. A-D screwed me out of the rights in a nasty negotiation last year.'

She smiled. 'That's the one. A-D buy their policing from the

Salvation Army. That's fundamentalism for you. I've got a few friends in The Sal, and I was leaked some fiche. According to them, Kleinzack was deleted with something exotic, a Buntline special. Ever heard of it? No reason you should. It was a white elephant showpiece of the Wild West, with an eleven-inch barrel. Wyatt Earp had one. Do you see the pattern? The Sal aren't saying any more, but it's my guess that if you were to screen Kleinzack's *Clementine*, you'd see a Technicolor twitch, and it would wind up with a lab-coated Kraut remix man blundering into the crossfire at the OK Corral and getting his globes shot out.'

Later, after Sally Rhodes had gone, Michaelis Monte had a few stiff drugs. He was rattled, no doubt about it. In previous corporation wars, the higher echelons had been off-limits. You can't negotiate a peace with a frazzled corpse. But this new thing, this campaign of terror, didn't appear to be a particular respecter of the ethics of monetarist diplomacy. He found Sally Rhodes' conclusion unutterably creepy: 'Someone, something, doesn't like what you do Miki, and is taking extreme measures to shut you, and everyone else in your line, down.'

He was safe in his Household. The defences were on, the grounds were secure. There were no human agents in the system to turn traitor, and the governing AI had had its loyalties freshly upgraded. Killflies were loose in the corridors of his retreat – he knew his employees referred to it behind his back as The House on Haunted Hill – and were coded to administer lethal injections to any moving thing that didn't match Monte's displacement configurations. He was as protected as a man could be.

He sat on the psychedelic bubble couch, and looked at his tiger-striped echt-Mondrian. The painting stirred in its sleep. He let the pleasant warmth of a soother seep through his body, calming him. As he watched, the painting's breathing grew ragged. It died, colours fading to grey, jelly congealing behind glass. It had happened before. A fault in the heating. There was nothing to worry about, the soother in his bloodstream told him. Deep in his brain, an unsoothed fragment of his consciousness screamed.

He floated back to his easel room. As he passed the sensors, his body heat registered. Overhead banks of lights lit up, then shut off when he had moved on. There was darkness in front and darkness behind, but he was always in the light. Safe, in white light.

Behind him, black eyes shone in the darkness.

Monte heard the swish, and turned. He couldn't see, but he had a strong afterimage. A tall man, with a heavy cloak.

He had to be alone. A 3-D wallplan proved it. He showed up as an orange pinpoint, winking in a corridor. There were no other warm bodies in the house.

He arrived in the easel room just too late. The twitch was disappearing off the lower right corner of the screen. A black and white picture remained. Monte stood over the easel, and watched as the camera tracked around an empty crypt. Lids fell off coffins, and creepy-crawlies –giant spiders, rats, an armadillo – scuttled in corners. Dracula's sad-eyed wives waited, infinitely patient, in long white shifts for their Master's return.

In his system, the soother reached the zenith of its effect. The tranquilising bulk of the pill had dissolved, putting a potentially dangerous dosage into him, and the emetic core spread in his gut. If he wanted to drug any more, he would have to empty his stomach. He wasn't soothed right now. Fear played his buttons, icy fingertips keyed his vertebrae. He would have to empty his stomach.

His bathroom was mirrored and luxurious, richly carpeted and hung with turquoise and scarlet silks. The design was copied from a Cecil B. DeMille spectacular of the 1920s he had rejected as too outmoded to be worth even a thorough remix. Jewel-encrusted gold taps shone against lime green, veined marble sunken tubs. This was the focus, far more than his austere bedroom, of his fantasies and fulfilments.

Monte bent double over a puce and ginger toilet bowl, fashioned like a triton's horn, and vomited tidily. He slammed down the oyster-shaped lid and sat on it. The emetic had a calming side-effect. He felt bad, but was instantly better. He got up and walked to the sink – a mustard replica of the font in Salisbury Cathedral – and washed his face.

Behind him, a door silently opened.

Monte peered minutely at his face in the mirror. It was possible to be flabby and haggard at the same time. He bared his teeth. They were filmed yellow. Then, the thing took him. He saw the hand that gripped his jaw and felt the one in his hair, but neither showed in the mirror. He was held fast by emptiness. Arms like metal bands gripped him. Angling his eyes down, he could see the dark sleeve of a dinner jacket and the black folds of a cloak; but in the mirror (on-screen?) he was struggling only with himself. His paisley collar was yanked away from his neck. Cold lips clamped to his throat, ice-chip teeth sank in…

The turquoise and scarlet faded first, turned dead and grey. Then, his shirt calmed down and resolved itself into a dingy, indeterminate smear. His vision slowly bled, the Technicolor twitch passing from left to right before his eyes…

He felt himself emptying out. Feebly, he raised a hand to push away the unseen face pressed to his throat. He had no more feeling. His hand flapped, chilly and wet, in his field of vision.

The last things he saw were his fingers, stained for ever with the black of his own blood.

PAMELA'S PURSUIT

Part of her strategy had been to feign, first indifference, then reluctance. It bought Pamela time to sharpen up. While Robin amassed filmy brochures and solicited testimonials from satisfied friends, she put up a deceptive resistance. She spent her lunch hours at the weapons library. Her reactions were fine, but her accuracy needed work. Once, she let a stranger pick her up on the range and sessioned with him. He had willingly paid the registration fee and looked devastated when she remaindered him with her first slug. She didn't need to finish him, she had brought him definitively down, but she had filled his heart all the same. She had always had a healthy interest in killing. Besides, he had been a feeler and she didn't like feelers.

After three years, Pamela and Robin could still hurt each other as deeply as they had when they first started going together. She had completely changed his face, eroding the fleshy pockets under his chin and cheekbones with her talons. With the aid of popular manuals, he had diligently mapped all the response centres of her body. He was persistent but not terribly inventive. Robin was always imagining he had new ideas but it was Pamela who was forever trying to expand the envelope of their marriage. She had been subtly manoeuvring him towards The Game for several months. As always, she needed to let him think it was his idea. But she had been the one to think of inviting the Raiths over and nudged them into enthusing. Ted Raith was a squidge and his wife could be above at her worst; they were Robin's associates. But they had experimented, she knew, with The Game. Robin had kept up a stream of excited questions. She knew that, again, she had him.

Her feeler victim had paid for his own remaindering, but marital etiquette meant that Pamela and Robin would have to go halves. She didn't mind. She had placed a portion of her private funding in an insurance policy and duped Robin into signing it under the impression he was entering a breakfast cereal contest. His caption had been terribly good and when she later told him he had lost, he had humourlessly initiated a boycott of the Kellogg's company. She suspected him of arranging for the fire-bombing of several of their European warehouses. They took the fee down to the Palace with them, in platinum wafers, and passed it over to the Game officials in the foyer. They handprinted holograph waivers, absolving the company from any possible liability for permanent disabilities, and were separated.

'Your first time?' asked the bovey matron in the ladies' changing room as Pamela shucked her street armour.

'Yes,' she sort-of lied.

'You'll win. The wife usually does.'

'Uh-huh?' She needed help with press-seams. The matron obliged. In the full-length mirror, Pamela looked svelte in black fatigues.

'Sure. The men never bother to do their prep. They don't take this seriously. You've practised?'

'A little.' She climbed into an elaborate shoulder holster and adjusted the straps. It had to be tight enough not to make giveaway noises but not so tight as to impede her respiratory functions.

'A little. I'll bet your husband hasn't so much as squeezed off a slug in anger since he left school.'

'That's very probable,' she said, but added loyally, 'but he's always competent. He won't go into the Palace without being sure he can walk out.'

'Will you surprise him?'

Pamela smiled as the matron gave her the roscoe. She held the thing, not gripping too hard, gauging weight and balance.

'I think so.'

The roscoe was light and ladylike. The Game didn't let you tote your own hardware. Pamela preferred something a bit more blatant. Heat-seeking slugs and dum-dum scattershots. She believed in doing as much damage as possible.

The matron helped her flip the clip and slitch the safeties. The clip rattled going in but was silent when she shook the roscoe.

'Soundproof,' said the matron.

The individual slugs in the clip were the size of grains of rice, compressed and cool. They'd get bigger and hotter when she squeezed them off. The matron encouraged her to unloose one for luck.

Pamela pointed, not really aiming, and shot a portrait. It was a large blue picture of some forgotten stateswoman with an unsympathetic simper. She holed the face, just under the right eye, making a crocodile tear. She had hoped for the bridge of the nose.

'It's off slightly.'

'That's easy to fix. Here.'

The matron took the roscoe and gave the barrel a precise twist. This time, Pamela got her mark between the eyes. She put the weapon up to her lips and blew away a curl of smoke. Her nostrils caught the tang of ozone.

'Of course you know you shouldn't do that to a real person…'

'Not unless you're serious.'

'No. Your brain is where you live. You only get one.'

'I know.'

'Accidents happen. Even here.'

'Not to me.'

'We have rigid safety controls. When you applied, your

husband and you were thoroughly out-checked. You have no especial history of psychopathic or sociopathic disorder.'

'That's nice to know.'

The matron kissed her on the lips for good luck and felt under her tunic for her own benefit. She pulled an acorn-sized knobble out from Pamela's armpit.

'A frag? That's not allowed, you know.'

Pamela shrugged. It was the concealment she had expected to lose. Like the tracer Robin had put in her earring. They wouldn't search for any lesser items now, although she had persevered and found the bug in her hair. Robin would try to go into the Palace with an edge. She thought she could match that.

The portrait hinged aside, and Pamela stepped alone into the Palace. The first room bore the scars of The Game. There were join-the-dots bullet pocks on the wall. Cords of blood wove into the clearwater streaming between mossy clumps of furniture. There was little cover nearby and she couldn't precog any immediate danger. She explored further.

She didn't know this lay-out at all. Her first session had been in another part of the Palace. But she shouldn't be at any particular disadvantage. She guessed that Robin had tried to access the floor plan too; he would have run aground even before coming up against the Master Block that had brought her down. As far as knowledge of the terrain went, they were even. Theoretically, Robin was a better tactician than she – the hairbug had been a nice try. But he didn't know what it was really like to stalk and be stalked. She did; she liked it.

The next room was darker. She took time to squeeze the cheater's kit out of her shoulder pad. With the mudsticks, she tiger-striped her face black and green. Then, she fit the blackcaps over her more visible teeth and licked until they stuck. The one-way contacts were more difficult to get comfy with, but they were worth the itch. Her eyes should look like black marbles now and her night vision was improved by a factor of five. Details of the room emerged from the shadows. She could read the spines of swollen books on the shelves; previously she had only been able to make out rough shapes. The uniform volumes were all by someone called Hansard.

She ungloved her left hand and darked the bare skin. Her fingers might be another edge. They had been her first, and so far only, major alteration. Apart from the nerve turnarounds. When she'd had her nails pulled and replaced with switchblades, her first husband – the squidge – had tried to call up his legal expeditor on the ouija slab. He didn't believe her when she said the attachments were mainly for dealing with shrink-wrapped packages and had gone on punching keys. While he was on hold, she had opted for the Moscow Divorce and snipped his spinal column with her bunched finger-toys. When he was dead, she had been able to roll his head into funny positions. He hadn't spoken to her since.

She extruded claws experimentally and scratched a book. It had been left flat on a tilting desk. The thick leather parted and her nail sank into yellow fleshy pages. She flicked the pulp away and sheathed her sharpies. The book felt very boring. She picked up echoes of a few dreary tirades and quickly brushed them out of mind. They reminded her of her first husband.

It had been her own fault, really, for marrying at thirteen. She had been much too old for a soldier. All he had learned in his military kindergarten was the three fs: feedin', fightin' and fillin'in forms. He didn't think women should be allowed to kill people. He had taken no interest in her terrapins. Her only regret over the split-up was that it had come four months too early for Shelley. Neither of them could legally apply for custody unless the child was over five years old and so Shelley had been taken to The Farm. Pamela sometimes got the horrid feeling that some stranger was looking back at her through her daughter's eyes. It was unlikely, but possible.

Yes, Husband Number One had been a squidge. Robin wasn't

a squidge, but he could be a bit of a skulk at times. Rather, he was a lot of a skulk a lot of the time. Take The Game: he had emphasised all through the prelims how important it was for the session to be mutually satisfactory. But she knew he had laid in a stock of quickill slugs and would, when it came to the face-off, opt to remainder her quickly rather than take the risk of prolonging the agony. He was like that. Sometimes Pamela thought Robin didn't count her as a real person.

She padded on catslippers through the dark rooms, professionally out-checking each one, roscoe held up near her face, medium pressure on the squeezegrip. There was a surprisingly thriving ecosystem inside the Palace. The vegetation was mostly fungal but there were some vines, grasses and overgrown descendants of pot plants. The water ran down the walls in curtains. Some of the herringbone tiles had been rotted through or mulched by aggressive roots. There was rumoured to be a pack of feral corgis in the jungle somewhere but they oughtn't to be dangerous.

She kept to the doors and corridors, avoiding the secret passageways. There were indigenous inhabitants in there somewhere. Nobody was supposed to live in the Palace any longer but elements of the ancien regime had stayed behind and interbred in the depths. The Game people didn't really try to clear them out because they weren't that dangerous. Feeble-minded, lazy-limbed ichabods with huge ears and rabbit teeth, by all accounts. Richer sportspeople than Pamela and Robin were taken on occasional safaris, hoping to bag an innocent bystander for the doping room wall. She wanted nothing to do with that. She didn't approve of killing anything that couldn't kill you back.

She found an ear nailed to one door and was duly warned away from what lay beyond. The thing was normal-sized and still warm. The place was quiet, except for the running water and occasional gunshots in different wings. She oughtn't to run into any other parties. This was a private session and she and

Robin were supposed to be on one of the many sealed-off zones.

In one room, she found a remain. It was one of the indigenes, gone for good. The head had been taken but the zaroff had left a trampled tiara. The remain wore a billowing, mildewed dress with an array of medal-like brooches on the shoulders and across the breast. Pamela didn't think it had been a woman, judging from the feet. There were plants growing out of the thing, so it had obviously been remaindered some time ago.

She stepped into a corridor and found a spoor. Wet footprints on a ragged pile carpet. Robin was either being careless or setting a trap. He couldn't see the prints without lenses, so perhaps he hadn't been aware he was making them. But he ought to know if he'd got his feet wet. She didn't want to underestimate him. It was the kind of thing he was always doing to her. She left the corridor and took a parallel course to the tracks, expecting him in each successive room.

She was excited, but in control. She knew she had an edge there. He would be nervy by now, probably irritated. In situations like this, he usually struck up a dopesmoke. Here he'd be afraid to show a glow. That would scrunch him inside, ruffle his tentacles. That gave her a definite, and growing, edge.

In the next room, a swatch of plaster fell from the ceiling into an open piano, twanging impossible chords. Pamela swivelled from the waist, went down on one knee, extended her roscoe arm and squeezed at the door. Chest height. She squeezed again, lower this time. The door swung both ways on its remaining hinge and fell away. There was a cloud of dust in the room, but no Robin.

Mistake.

She should have taken natural decay into account. The Palace was obviously falling apart. She had given Robin an unmistakable aural bearing. She tried to get up, but her knee was wobbly. Finally, she made it. Her mouth was dry and her eyes stung with water that had built up behind the contacts. Her tunic felt too tight, chafing her. She split the pectoral seam, enjoying the chilly rush, then sealed herself to the choker. Swanny cleavage would be too tempting a target.

She looked around for cover and decided on the next-but-one room. Robin would know her general location but have to out-check each room in turn. She hoped he'd come to her soon. He'd expect a trap, of course, but she would know what he was up to. It would get all this foreplay over with. She ejected the slug clip and checked it. It was fine. The roscoe had worked perfectly. There had been no kick to jolt her elbow out of joint. It still felt like something for potting hummingbirds, but a few holes in the right places would do as much serious hurt as a total fleshblast.

From her room, she could hear him coming. He had two choices. There were only two doors. She had a clear shot at each, and, in her position, was shielded by a pair of high-backed chairs. They might not stop a slug, but they'd squidge his aim. He was making a noise. Too much noise. It had to be a blind.

'Pamela,' he shouted.

He was doing something skulky, she knew that much.

'Darling, come out. Let's climax this.'

She stopped breathing and extruded claws. They shone in the minimal light.

She sighted on the left door, but was ready to switch to the right. Her arm ached after thirty seconds. The roscoe didn't feel light now. There were drops of condensation on the barrel. Pamela's mud was running in rivulets down her neckline. She could have done with that frag now.

Robin stopped cajoling. 'Get ready to be remaindered, squitch!'

His voice was behind the right door. She took aim at it.

There was a pause.

Left door. Right door. Left door. Right door.

He came through the wall, to the extreme left. There was almost no lath and plaster left, all he had to do was tear through a sheet of flowered paper. He had IR shades on. She recognised the kind with a homing facility.

He had been tracking her somehow. There had been a third concealment, one she'd not found. Rats. He had the edge now.

Robin smiled, 'Wedding ring, dear.'

The squidge.

He shot her in the hip and she fell over, sprawling rather than crouching. The impact hit like a mailed fist and waves of warmth ran through her. It was a sensation. Her back arched and her mouth hung open. Her stifled cry dislodged the blackcaps. She had enough control to spit them out, to prevent herself choking. Her altered nerve endings mistranslated the signals from her wound. Caught up in the rush of feelings, she was nevertheless able to exaggerate her helplessness. She floundered, twitching helplessly. Robin came closer and shot her through the lung, missing her heart because she twisted under him. He was too close. The quickill slug went through her and fragmented somewhere in the floor, porcupining her back with splinters.

'Sweetheart,' she gasped, squeezing in her first shot. She was hurting now, for real. The confusion of pain and pleasure didn't affect her body control. He took the slugs in his lower belly and thighs and bent double. She knew where his alterations were. He spasmed, and squeezed his grip too much. Slugs sprayed the room in a figure eight. Light flashes gave his dance of death a disco strobe. He stitched her a few times, but she kept her roscoe arm whole.

She got him several times. Knees, for balance. Belly again, for pain. Heart, for the remainder. He went down. The stink made the air thick. His clothes caught fire where the slugs had gone in. The little flames, light-amplified, burned into her lensed eyes. She slithered over to him on her elbows, face down. He was still drawing coughy breaths, and slobbering strawberry spittle.

Before she finished, she stroked his face and neck, leaving her marks, opening his pipes. The last she heard was his final crackle of exhalation. She fell, relaxing, over his remain, and blanked.

Later, the Resurrection Men brought them back. They revived

together in their own bed, fast-fading milky scars where their holes had been. The Game Official told them she had won, on points.

After everyone had left, Robin was ungracious. They hadn't been able to get all the slugs out and had had to promise to return and finish the recovery work for a further fee. He had an unwanted alteration, an extra testicle made of lead. She cuddled close to him under their duvet, feeling the odd weighting of his asymmetrical scrotum.

He was still being a skulk. She squeezed him gently.

'Darling,' she said, 'how was it for you?'

ABOUT THE AUTHOR

Kim Newman is a novelist, critic and broadcaster. His fiction includes *The Night Mayor*, *Bad Dreams*, *Jago*, the *Anno Dracula* novels and stories, *The Quorum* and *Life's Lottery*, all currently being reissued by Titan Books, *Professor Moriarty: The Hound of the D'Urbervilles* published by Titan Books and *The Vampire Genevieve* and *Orgy of the Blood Parasites* as Jack Yeovil. His non-fiction books include the seminal *Nightmare Movies* (recently reissued by Bloomsbury in an updated edition), *Ghastly Beyond Belief* (with Neil Gaiman), *Horror: 100 Best Books* (with Stephen Jones), *Wild West Movies*, *The BFI Companion to Horror*, *Millennium Movies* and BFI Classics studies of *Cat People* and *Doctor Who*.

He is a contributing editor to *Sight & Sound* and *Empire* magazines (writing *Empire*'s popular Video Dungeon column), has written and broadcast widely on a range of topics, and scripted radio and television documentaries. His stories 'Week Woman' and 'Ubermensch' have been adapted into an episode of the TV series *The Hunger* and an Australian short film; he has directed and written a tiny film *Missing Girl*. Following his Radio 4 play 'Cry Babies', he wrote an episode ('Phish Phood') for Radio 7's series *The Man in Black*.

His official website can be found at www. johnnyalucard.com

ANNO DRACULA

by KIM NEWMAN

It is 1888 and Queen Victoria has remarried, taking as her new consort the Wallachian Prince infamously known as Count Dracula. His polluted bloodline spreads through London as its citizens increasingly choose to become vampires.

In the grim backstreets of Whitechapel, a killer known as 'Silver Knife' is cutting down vampire girls. The eternally young vampire Geneviève Dieudonné and Charles Beauregard of the Diogenes Club are drawn together as they both hunt the sadistic killer, bringing them ever closer to England's most bloodthirsty ruler yet.

Shortlisted for the
Bram Stoker Vampire Novel of the Century Award
by the Horror Writers Association

"Compulsory reading… glorious." Neil Gaiman

"A *tour de force* which succeeds brilliantly." *The Times*

ANNO DRACULA
THE BLOODY RED BARON
by KIM NEWMAN

1918 and Dracula is commander-in-chief of the armies of Germany and Austria-Hungary. The war of the great powers in Europe is also a war between the living and the dead. As ever the Diogenes Club is at the heart of British Intelligence and Charles Beauregard and his protégé Edwin Winthrop go head-to-head with the lethal vampire flying machine that is the Bloody Red Baron…

A brand-new edition, with additional unpublished novella, of the critically acclaimed bestselling sequel to *Anno Dracula*.

"…stunning follow-up to his inventive alternate-world fantasy, *Anno Dracula*…" *Publisher's Weekly*

"Gripping… superbly researched… Newman's rich novel rises above genre… A superior sequel to *Anno Dracula*, itself a benchmark for vampire fiction." *Kirkus Reviews*

ANNO DRACULA

DRACULA CHA CHA CHA

by KIM NEWMAN

Rome, 1959, and Count Dracula is about to marry the Moldavian Princess Asa Vajda. Journalist Kate Reed flies into the city to visit the ailing Charles Beauregard and his vampire companion Geneviève. She finds herself caught up in the mystery of the Crimson Executioner who is bloodily dispatching vampire elders in the city. She is on his trail, as is the un-dead British secret agent Bond.

A brand-new edition, with additional previously unpublished novella, of the popular third instalment of the Anno Dracula series.

"He writes with sparkling verve and peppers the text with cinematic and literary references. *Dracula Cha Cha Cha* has full rations of gore, shocks and sly laughs." *The Times*

"Like the blood gelato lapped by the un-dead demimonde, this novel is a rich and fulfilling confection." *Publishers Weekly*

ANNO DRACULA
JOHNNY ALUCARD
by KIM NEWMAN

New York, 1976, and Kate Reed is on the set of Francis Ford Coppola's movie *Dracula*. She helps a young vampire boy, Ion Popescu, who leaves Transylvania for America. In the States, Popescu becomes Johnny Pop and attaches himself to Andy Warhol, inventing a new drug which confers vampire powers on its users…

A brand-new novel in the Anno Dracula series, this fourth instalment sees Dracula take Andy Warhol's New York and Orson Welles' Hollywood.

"Massively entertaining." *Booklist* starred review

"Compulsively readable, bitingly satirical." *Guardian*

"Outrageously inventive." *Independent*

JAGO

by KIM NEWMAN

In the tiny English village of Alder, dreams and nightmares are beginning to come true. Creatures from local legend, science fiction and the dark side of the human mind prowl the town.

Paul, a young academic composing a thesis about the end of the world, and his girlfriend Hazel, a potter, have come to Alder for the summer. Their idea of a rural retreat gradually sours as the laws of nature begin to break down around them. Paul and Hazel are soon drawn into a vortex of fear as violent chaos engulfs the community and the village prepares to reap a harvest of horror.

A brand-new edition of the critically acclaimed novel. This edition also contains the short stories 'Ratting', 'Great Western' and 'The Man on the Clapham Omnibus'.

"A roaring good read." *The Times*

"Newman's prose is sophisticated and his narrative drive irresistible." *Publishers Weekly*

THE QUORUM

by KIM NEWMAN

In the polluted River Thames, a monster is born. Formed of filth and grime, Derek Leech emerges from the murky depths, destined to found a global media empire.

In 1978, three school friends with high aspirations – Michael, Mark and Mickey – are offered a deal by the mysterious magnate. If they agree, their future wealth will be ensured, but they must offer Leech a sacrifice in return, a conspiracy of lifelong pain against their absent friend, Neil. Accepting the terms, the men prosper over the next fifteen years. But as the era of excess comes to an end, the trio must pay the price for their success, and they soon discover that fame and fortune is a fate worse than death.

A brand-new edition of the critically acclaimed novel, featuring five short stories by the award-winning author.

"Fascinating, witty and sage." *Library Journal*

LIFE'S LOTTERY

by KIM NEWMAN

At six years old you're asked to make a choice, the first of many in a multitude of possible lives.

If you make the right decision, you may live a long happy life, or be immensely powerful, or win the lottery. If you take the wrong path, you may become a murderer, die young, make every mistake possible, or make no impression on life at all. The choice is yours. And by making the choices you do, you will change forever the lives of your family, your friends, your enemies, and your lovers. You can even change the fate of the world; all you have to do is choose…

An adult role-playing novel where small decisions have monumental consequences.

"Curiously unsettling but always gripping… like nothing else you have ever read." *The Times*

"The hero's life is in your hands… an epic read." *Guardian*